"Don't Be Afraid. We're Alone. There Are Servants, but I Gave Them the Night Off."

Arm around her, he led her a couple of steps, turning up a gas lamp. "I told them to put some champagne on ice. Let's see if we can find it."

. . . He found the wine in the library. He deftly uncorked, poured, came to her, handed her a stemmed glass. . . . She was trembling again. Raising the glass was a major undertaking.

He saw and misunderstood completely, reaching out to take her shaking hand, steadying the liquid in the glass. His sense of honor surfaced.

"Do you want me to take you home, Stevie?"

She looked at him, all eyes. "No."

. . . He pursed his lips. "Then what's wrong?"

She looked at him, swallowing hard. . . . As though speaking to the rim of the glass, she said, "I don't know what you're going to do."

His voice was husky. "Nothing you don't want me to do."

vogue. Everyone will recognize it as a Chambeau and envy you for wearing it."

Dear Reader:

We trust you will enjoy this Richard Gallen romance. We plan to bring you more of the best in both contemporary and historical romantic fiction with four exciting new titles each month.

We'd like your help.

We value your suggestions and opinions. They will help us to publish the kind of romances you want to read. Please send us your comments, or just let us know which Richard Gallen romances you have especially enjoyed. Write to the address below. We're looking forward to hearing from you!

Happy reading!

The Editors of
Richard Gallen Books
8-10 West 36th St.
New York, N.Y. 10018

A Heritage of Passion

ELIZABETH BRIGHT

PUBLISHED BY RICHARD GALLEN BOOKS
Distributed by POCKET BOOKS

Books by Elizabeth Bright

Reap the Wild Harvest
Passion's Heirs
A Lasting Splendor
Desire's Legacy
A Heritage of Passion

A RICHARD GALLEN BOOKS *Original* publication

Distributed by
POCKET BOOKS, a Simon & Schuster division of
GULF & WESTERN CORPORATION
1230 Avenue of the Americas, New York, N.Y. 10020

ISBN: 0-671-44687-8

First Pocket Books printing July, 1982

10 9 8 7 6 5 4 3 2 1

RICHARD GALLEN and colophon are trademarks of Simon & Schuster and Richard Gallen & Co., Inc.

Printed in the U.S.A.

Part I

New York

One

The mirror in the attic was old, cracked and badly in need of resilvering. Yet the image, however faded and distorted, made Stephanie Summers gasp. Never had she seen such a gown!

With the servants off for the afternoon and her great-grandmother napping, it had seemed to Stephanie a good time to explore the attic. As she'd opened a trunk and smelled the sachets hidden within, she had surrendered to excitement, fascination and no small amount of awe. At once she knew what the trunk contained: the special and memorable gowns worn by three generations of beautiful women—Stephanie's mother, grandmother and great-grandmother. It was a family history in fabric and stitch.

Each garment was neatly pressed and folded, obviously put away with loving care. A tag was pinned to every one, identifying who had worn it and when. As she unfolded each gown and held it up against herself, viewing the result in the mirror, Stephanie felt suffused with romance. Such extraordinary gowns! So alluring.

So glamorous. And what memories they must hold. In delight Stephanie came to a gown of rich blue satin. She lifted it from the trunk and read the tag: *Worn by Glenna Morgan at the Inaugural Ball for President Zachary Taylor, March 1849. Also worn by Moira Morgan, May 1850.* Imagine! It was now June 1889. This gown was forty years old.

Stephanie had not intended to try on any of the dresses, but as she held the blue ball gown against herself, looking in the mirror at the shining material, she just had to put it on. Quickly she stripped off her white blouse and stepped out of her gray skirt. Then, as she reached for the blue gown, she realized she could not wear her chemise with it. She hesitated, glanced around the attic, then realized how silly she was. There was no one here.

This girl in the attic was surely an anomaly. Born to a wealthy and prominent Maryland family, she had been afforded every privilege: the exclusive Clarendon School for Girls in Philadelphia, a "grand tour" of Europe with her mother when she was sixteen. She had been doted on by three generations of relatives, as well as prominent politicians and businessmen in Washington and New York, where she lived when she was not at Aurial, the family estate in Maryland. She had a sheen of sophistication. She possessed most of the social graces and her manners were impeccable. As many noted, her aplomb among adults was unusual in a girl of eighteen years and two months.

Yet beneath the veneer of sophistication was a girl who was shy, rather withdrawn and wholly lacking in confidence. Perhaps overprotected by her family, she had simply spent too much time around adults. At school her classmates liked her, but felt she was hard to get to know. In truth, Stephanie Summers spent an inordinate amount of time daydreaming. She was a voracious reader of romantic novels and managed to identify with virtually every heroine in them. She seemed at times possessed of a second consciousness, which her friends at school found disconcerting. This quality, when added to her poise, wholly unnerved the young men her own age who attended dancing classes or other social events at the Clarendon School.

All this Stephanie knew about herself and accepted as her nature. But of late she had become aware she was changing. She felt she was somehow budding. It was as though all her life she had been a seed, lying dormant in fallow ground, and was suddenly awakening, ready to burst forth and blossom. For weeks she had felt a strange irritation, a nervous expectancy. Even now, as she reached behind her back to fasten the blue satin gown, Stephanie sensed her time in life was near. She anticipated it with both eagerness and anxiety.

Moments later she was gasping at herself in the mirror, for the gown, worn off the shoulder, was cut so low that her breasts, pushed up by whalebone, a deep valley between, were almost entirely revealed. Her great-grandmother and grandmother had worn this? She couldn't believe it!

The image in the mirror had a profound effect on Stephanie Summers. All her life she had heard tales about the Morgan-Kingston women, their beauty, great loves, the adventures that had tested their courage and molded their character. Glenna Morgan, Stephanie's great-grandmother, was a living legend—slave, harem girl, first European woman to cross the Sahara to Timbuktu, held captive by a jungle tribe. Moira Morgan Kingston Hodges, Stephanie's grandmother, had gone West with the Forty-niners, survived an Indian attack and a ghastly winter in the Rockies, then run a dance hall in San Francisco. And Stephanie's mother, Danielle Kingston Summers, had been train-wrecked out West and held captive in a mountain cabin. Even her Aunt Miriam, wife of Morgan Kingston, had needed to be rescued from harm. All were great beauties. Controversy, gossip and innuendo swirled about them until fact was immersed in fiction.

Now, looking in the mirror, wearing this daring gown, Stephanie Summers felt this heritage of beauty and courage in a way she never had before. She squared her shoulders and stood tall, for, more than a thousand tales, this remarkable garment gave her a sense of these women, their beauty, daring and, yes, the absolutely devastating effect they must have had on others. How women must have envied them! And men? She smiled.

Suddenly the image changed, and it was not her beloved GlennaMa or Grandmother Moira wearing this gown, but herself, Stephanie Summers. Those were her breasts rising above the fabric, her snowy shoulders exposed. It was she who possessed such allure, she who embodied womanliness. For the first time in the eighteen years she had lived, Stephanie Summers sensed the family heritage was passing to her. Was she worthy of it?

Another person would have had difficulty understanding Stephanie's doubts, for heredity had molded her into a remarkable beauty. Her hair was surely unusual, for she had inherited both Moira's flame-colored tresses and her father's yellow hair, seemingly as alternating strands, falling in long, thick, lustrous waves. Depending on the light, her hair was either red, blonde or reddish-gold, and sometimes it was all three at the same time. From Moira, Stephanie had also inherited a luscious, sensuous mouth, the lips well turned out, extremely smooth without a line or wrinkle, a depression in the center of the lower one. From Danielle and Glenna before her, Stephanie had received extremely fair skin, snowy, almost without a hint of color, and so thin it seemed to possess an inner luminescence, particularly when she was excited, as she was now. From these two, especially Danielle, Stephanie's heritage was a fine bone structure that gave her delicacy, daintiness, an aura of fragility. She could wear this lascivious gown and still look demure.

What made her so truly stunning, though, were her eyes. No one in the family could "claim" them, and it was the subject of much discussion where they came from. Beneath dark brows and double eyelashes— Danielle's, to be sure—Stephanie's eyes were a deep marine blue, lightened by facets of pale, almost silvery tints. Her eyes seemed at times all irises, gemlike, as though fashioned by a master jeweler. It was these eyes that now stared at her own image in disbelief and wonder. GlennaMa, Moira, even her own mother were now predecessors. The mantle had fallen onto her shoulders. Men would now. . . . She blushed, then smiled. Men would think her very silly, dressing up in old clothes from a trunk!

But wasn't it fun? And what else was there to do? She stepped out of the inaugural gown and tried on another. For the next hour or so—she lost track of time—Stephanie explored the trunk, admiring the garments, trying on some. She almost squealed when she found the wedding gowns of Glenna and Moira, but knew she shouldn't wear them. Finally she finished that trunk and opened a smaller one. At once her eyes misted over, for these were her mother's things. And there, on top, was Danielle's wedding gown of Flemish lace. Stephanie held it up, barely able to restrain tears.

Stephanie had once overheard two men discussing Danielle Summers at a party. They called her the most beautiful woman in the world. With all her heart Stephanie believed that. Her mother had classic Irish coloring, hair like polished onyx, sapphire eyes, the fairest, snowiest complexion. Everyone said she looked like Glenna had when she was young. Danielle was now thirty-seven, and the years had simply enhanced her beauty, for there was maturity, courage and, yes, suffering in her face. Her mother was unhappy, sometimes desperately so, and that was why Stephanie could seldom think of her without wanting to cry.

Stephanie had tried innumerable times to understand

why her mother had divorced her father, Walter Summers. Walt had been the great love of Danielle's life, twice coming to her rescue. And he worshiped her. Yet they had divorced. Why? The answers were never satisfactory to Stephanie. Something about racial attitudes and slavery at Seasons, the Summers' plantation near Charleston, South Carolina. But none of it seemed worth the misery resulting from the divorce. Neither had remarried. Oh, Danielle almost had. She was set to marry Benjamin Fairchild, grandson of Glenna's last husband, when he was killed in a train wreck. Stephanie knew several other men had proposed to her mother. She had almost and almost, yet in the end always refused them. Why? Stephanie knew only that her mother was unhappy. And Danielle's melancholy only deepened her natural reserve and reticence—and made her more beautiful.

Danielle's sadness did not keep her from being a good mother. Both Stephanie and her brother Andrew, now seventeen, adored Danielle, for she offered them unstinting love, patience and understanding. If she were gone more than they might like—she was in London at the moment—the love and attention of Moira and Glenna, Miriam, Morgan and their children at Aurial more than made up for her absences. Nor were they denied their father. He visited frequently, at least he had until recent years when he sold Seasons and moved to a ranch out West. But he still sent gifts and wrote often. Andrew, utterly thrilled at the prospect, had gone to Colorado to spend the summer with Walt.

No, Stephanie did not feel her parents' divorce had marred her life. If only she could understand her mother's unhappiness and do something to end it. Oh, how she wanted that. Perhaps this trunk held some clue. Delving further, she found a stunning gown of slinky black satin. She read the label. Pierre Chambeau. Oh, yes, the Frenchman who made many of her mother's gowns. He was famous for his bold, innovative fashions. Stephanie held the black gown up to herself and sensed how it must look—long sleeves, formfitting, with a deep triangle cut out of the bodice. Yes, and her mother's fair skin would be heightened in contrast to the black. And much of her bosom would be revealed. Danielle Summers had the most glorious figure of anyone Stephanie knew. She would be so lovely in this. Stephanie was going to try the gown on, then saw it was ripped down the sideseam. How very strange. Mother was always so careful.

Stephanie laid aside the black satin, for her attention was captured by another garment, this one of filmy blue silk. She read the tag: *Worn by Danielle Kingston to a masked ball, London, April 1870.* That was nineteen years ago. She calculated. Her mother would have been eighteen, just her own age. Stephanie had to try it on.

In moments Stephanie was again gasping at her image in the mirror. Never had she seen anything so gorgeous. She knew enough about fashions to recognize it as a *Directoire* gown, the famous Empire style of Napoleon's day. The gown of sheer blue chiffon over a silk satinet slip was snugged high under the bosom, then fell in soft folds to the floor. In dismay Stephanie saw she was virtually naked above. The bodice, held up by tiny, puffed sleeves, barely covered her aureolae. Her mother wore this? In public? To a ball? It wasn't possible. Stephanie felt so shocked she almost couldn't breathe.

"Stevie! Are you up there?"

It was Glenna's voice. Stephanie had forgotten all about her. "Yes, GlennaMa. I'm up here."

"What are you doing in the attic?"

Chagrined, Stephanie ran to the stairs and descended. GlennaMa had awakened, probably rung for her. She should have been there to help her. "I'm sorry, GlennaMa. I'm so thoughtless."

"I was just wondering where—" Suddenly she stared

at her great-granddaughter. Her mouth came open, then was covered by her fingertips. Tears welled in her eyes.

Stephanie saw the reaction and misunderstood. "I'm sorry. I shouldn't be in these things, I know, but . . . but I—"

Glenna recovered. "It's all right. No harm done." She tried to swallow the lump in her throat. "It's—it's just—oh, my dear, do you know whose gown that is?"

"Yes, mother's." Stephanie glanced down at the tag. "She wore it—"

"I remember exactly when she wore it." There was delight in GlennaMa's voice.

"I'm sorry. I couldn't resist putting it on."

"Of course you couldn't. And you look just divine in it."

Stephanie seemed not to have heard. "There are so many beautiful things. I had to try some on."

"I'm so glad you did. Do they fit?"

"Most, I think."

Glenna smiled, the same warm, genuine smile that had blessed her through the years. "If you'll help me, Stevie, I believe I can make it up those stairs. I want to see you wear those gowns. It'll be like reliving history."

Glenna O'Reilly Morgan MacDoul Fairchild, which was her full name now that she was thrice a widow—although she was usually known as Glenna Morgan, after her first husband—gave old age a mixed review. At seventy-eight she was grateful to be alive and able to get around as much as she did. She still had her mental faculties, and the wrinkles and loosening skin hadn't been too unkind. Actually she was still beautiful in old age, with silver hair, reasonably good teeth and exceptionally brilliant blue eyes. But she had a lot of pain. Rheumatism had gnarled her hands, then settled in her lower back and knees. She could walk with a cane, but only at a price of great discomfort. Nevertheless, she accepted it, and moved around as much as she could. If she once took to her bed for more than a few hours, she knew she would probably never get out of it.

The trek up the steep stairs took longer than Glenna would have liked, but at last she sat in an old straight-backed chair, exclaiming over her great-granddaughter. "Oh, Stevie, you have no idea what a pleasure it is to see you in that gown."

"But, GlennaMa, I'm practically naked." Stephanie raised her hands, holding them in front of her breasts. She needn't have. There was no doubt what she meant.

Glenna laughed. "I do believe that's what your mother said the first time she saw herself in it."

"She didn't actually wear it *out*—in *public*."

"Oh, yes, and she was as lovely as you."

"She couldn't have." Stephanie gripped the top of the bodice. "Why, the edges of my nipples are showing."

Glenna's laugh was generous. "The dress was made for your mother, dear. Your bustline is a little higher and, I think, yes, you are a trifle larger than your mother. Come here and I'll show you." When Stephanie stood before her, Glenna reached up, made adjustments in the bodice, then pulled the puffed sleeves up. "See, isn't that better?"

Stephanie didn't think it at all better. "How could mother wear this, GlennaMa?"

Again Glenna laughed. "With difficulty, I'll tell you. She was so shy and nervous, so embarrassed."

"But why did she wear it?"

"Because I made her. We were all going to this masked ball, quite the social event. Moira was Queen Elizabeth I. I was—oh, I can't remember, but I wore white. Your Uncle Morgan was Napoleon, and Danielle was to be his Josephine. This was the style then, the chemise dress, designed by Napoleon himself. Of course it was always white in his day, but I thought the blue matched her eyes. She was so lovely."

Stephanie looked down at herself, still disbelieving.

"You made mother wear this when . . . when she didn't want to?"

"Oh, yes. Your mother was so terribly shy, withdrawn, much too sheltered, in my opinion. I felt it was time she . . . well, came out into the world." Glenna's smile faded. "Of course, I was upset, we all were, when she was abducted."

"Abducted!"

Glenna hesitated. Could it be true that this child didn't know the story about her parents and how they had met? Clearly Danielle was being much too protective of her daughter's innocence. Ridiculous. Stephanie was now a young woman, a most attractive one, and about to enter the world. She should know about such things.

"Oh, yes. A masked man, dressed as a pirate, drugged her and took her away from the party, kept her that night and the whole next day."

"But what did he do?" There was shock in Stephanie's voice.

The question might have flustered another woman, but Glenna Morgan was unflappable. "I believe he fell hopelessly in love with her." Her laugh flooded over her. "Don't look so worried, my dear. It was your father. Didn't you know that?"

There had been so many stories, three generations of them. "I'm not sure. Tell me."

Glenna told the famous tale. Walter Summers had seen Danielle, fallen instantly in love, had had to have her. But he was a fugitive Confederate spy and couldn't come forward to court her. He took her from the masked ball, then followed her to America and twice rescued her from grave danger before his true identity became known.

Glenna carefully censored the story, omitting any hint of Danielle's exotic ravishment by the "pirate" in his garret hideaway. But she sensed this child standing before her in the historic gown was filling in the missing pieces. Indeed, Glenna could see the questions forming in Stephanie's eyes. To forestall them she smiled and spoke. "My dear, do you mind trying on some of these other gowns? It brings me such pleasure to see them worn again. Turn around. I'll help you out of this one." Not without gratitude Glenna saw her great-granddaughter hesitate, then obey.

As the dress came off over Stephanie's head and she stood naked except for her pantaloons, Glenna had to physically restrain herself from gasping. Stephanie had been a child when Glenna had last seen her naked, and she was now stunned by the girl's figure. Glenna had always thought Danielle had the best figure she had ever seen, but Danielle's daughter exceeded her. Stephanie had the same snowy skin, the same fragile bones, but her waist was tinier. And her hips? Why they could be a boy's, they were so small. And her breasts? Magnificent, almost gaudy, with deep pink buds, the color of oleander. Glenna wanted to exclaim her admiration. Instead she said, quite matter-of-factly, "You have a nice figure, Stevie."

Stephanie's attention was on the gown she was to don next. Now she looked up. "Do I, GlennaMa?"

"Oh, yes, my dear. You are just lovely. I do believe your waist is even tinier than your mother's. What size are you?"

"I'm not sure, GlennaMa."

"We'll just have to see, won't we? There, in that basket, I think there may be a tape measure."

When Stephanie produced it and the tape was spread around her waist, Glenna exclaimed, "Good heavens! Twenty and a half. Your mother was twenty-two, as I remember." Quickly Glenna wound the tape around Stephanie's slender hips—thirty-three—and her bosom —thirty-seven. With effort she concealed her awe and said, "Now what dress are you going to wear, Stevie?"

Stephanie went to the trunk. "Remember this?" She was grinning as she held up the inaugural gown.

"Oh, yes, yes, please put it on." Glenna could hardly speak, and when the gown graced her great-granddaughter, tears of memory and emotion coursed down her cheeks. "Oh, my darling, I know I'm silly to cry, but I can't help it. It's like seeing myself young again."

"Did you really wear this, GlennaMa? It's . . . awfully *revealing*."

"Well, I wasn't as large as you, but—" She smiled. "Yes, I was quite the sensation."

"But why, GlennaMa? Why did you want to be?"

"Oh, I felt then, and still do, that a woman should be a woman. She should stand tall, take pride in herself, in her womanliness." Glenna laughed. "Besides, Daniel, your great-grandfather Morgan, wanted me to wear gowns like that. He was in the Senate and a noted abolitionist. He said that very gown would earn him twenty speaking engagements."

Stephanie laughed, too. "If you went along, I'll bet." She looked down at her breasts, now suddenly not so threatening. She felt pride in herself and overwhelming admiration for Glenna Morgan. "Why did grandmother wear it?"

"That's quite another story." Glenna hesitated. The memories were painful. "I wore that gown in March, I believe. Daniel was killed on Thanksgiving Day that year." She sucked in her breath. It was so hard, even after all this time. "I loved him so. I thought my life had ended." She forced a smile. "Of course it hadn't. None of us knows what life brings or what we can bear." A deep sigh escaped her. "I went into deep mourning. I neglected Moira terribly. She was eighteen, your age. She loved her father, too, grieved for him. But life went on. She had to live it." Glenna shook her head. "She was smarter than me in that." Another sigh. "Anyway, she wanted to go to this party at the Kingstons'. It was down the road, not part of Aurial then. Bradford 'King' Kingston was to be there, your grandfather's brother, the handsomest man, quite a rake really. Moira wanted to impress him. She snitched that dress from my closet and wore it to the party. That's the story."

"But it isn't, GlennaMa. There has to be more."

There was. Moira, always impulsive, had thrown herself at King, and been as putty in his hands—the hands of a very experienced man. Glenna was not about to tell the story. "I'm sure there was, but I was in mourning. I only heard of it . . . later."

The historical fashion show continued, with Stephanie donning several gowns. Glenna had a good cry when she saw her own wedding dress on her great-granddaughter. Stephanie held up a white blouse, sheer, frilly with ruffles. "This was Grandmother Moira's?"

"Yes. Daniel gave it to her. Try it on."

But, putting her arms into the sleeves, Stephanie said, "I'll need a chemise with this."

Glenna's laughter bubbled out of her. "I don't know why. Moira didn't wear one." She realized her mistake at once.

"Grandmother? She didn't!"

Glenna's laugh was now more nervous, forced. "Don't you breathe a word of it. But, yes, she wore that. Oh, I wasn't there, but Jessie told me. She was madly in love with King Kingston. She wanted to impress him. I'm sure she did."

"Grandmother?"

"Moira was wild when she was your age, impetuous. I'm sure she'd kill me for telling you now."

There were other gowns. Finally the black satin was held up. "Mother's?"

"Yes. I never saw her in it, but I understand she was breathtaking. Try it on."

"It's ripped. I can't."

"So it is. Too bad. Pierre Chambeau created it, you know. He's a genius at dressing women."

Stephanie had only one question. "How did it get ripped?"

Glenna sighed. "After your mother met the pirate, your father, she felt—well, she loved him but believed she would never see him again. Then she met a man named Hamilton Garth. He was terribly rich, handsome I suppose, but he was cruel, ruthless, not at all the sort for Danielle." She looked at Stephanie in great discomfort. "She—she lived with him. He gave her—this gown."

"He tore it from her?"

Glenna's sigh was prolonged, deep. "He was impulsive, I'm sure."

Stephanie stared at the torn garment, imagining her mother wearing it, having it ripped from her. All the images profoundly affected her.

Glenna saw the change in mood and moved to avert it. "Why don't you put on the Josephine costume, Stevie? I'd like to see you in it again."

Aroused from her reverie, Stephanie said, "I've already had it on."

Glenna smiled. "Perhaps with a few adjustments you could wear it. I know, we'll hold a masked ball. It'll be perfect—again."

Stephanie was suddenly thrilled at the thought, but she said, "Oh, I could never, GlennaMa."

"Listen to me, child. I detest false modesty. Your mother was shy, genuinely so. You are not. You have been to innumerable balls at your grandmother's in Washington, Aurial, here. You have been admired all your life. You even went to Europe with your mother. You speak fluent French. You're accomplished. You know you're beautiful. Don't pretend you're not."

Stephanie's smile was wry. "Thank you, GlennaMa."

She donned the *Directoire* gown again, letting Glenna fasten the back. "I believe the blue satin slippers are in the trunk there somewhere." They were found and put on, Stephanie feeling her elevation in the heels. "Your hair isn't right." Stephanie wore it naturally, long, flowing down her back. "See if you can find some ribbon in the basket, blue preferably." In a moment a piece was produced. "Can you kneel, darling? I can't reach so high." Stephanie knelt and felt the ribbon encircling her hair, pulling it upward. Glenna smiled. "Now go look at yourself in the mirror."

Stephanie did, and she liked what she saw. Glenna had pulled her hair up high at the back of her head. "Is this the way it was worn?"

"Something like that. Actually the fall should be in curls. We'll do that when we have the party."

Stephanie turned to her. "Oh, GlennaMa, could we?"

"I don't see why not." Glenna grinned. "Who will you have as your Napoleon?"

"Oh, I don't know."

"Come now, Stevie. A stunning girl like you. There must be someone?"

Stephanie pursed her lips. "No, GlennaMa, really, there is no one."

From long experience Glenna read her expression. "Must we have secrets, Stevie? Who is the young man in your life?"

And Stephanie saw the warm smile on her beloved GlennaMa's face. "There really isn't, but—"

"But what?" Glenna laughed. "Or should I say, but who?"

Stephanie hesitated. It was her secret. She had kept it for years, telling no one, not even her mother. For as long as she could remember, Stephanie Summers had loved Thomas Hodges. He was family, but no blood kin. He and Miriam Hodges Kingston, Morgan's wife, were the children of Lawrence Hodges's first marriage, before he wed Moira. Technically Thomas was Stephanie's step-uncle. But she never thought of him that way; at least not for a long time she hadn't.

Among her earliest memories was cuddling into Thomas's teenage lap to be read to. It was he, not her father, who had taught her to ride. From Thomas, too, she learned to swim, play croquet and tennis. She was five when her parents separated and she went to live at Aurial. Thomas, even more than her Uncle Morgan, had helped compensate for the loss of her father. Thomas, then seventeen, had spent endless time with her, playing games, roughhousing or just quietly talking to her. She had grown up adoring him, certain of the special affection between them. Most of all, she liked the way he treated her, not as a child, but as a friend. She had cried when Thomas had gone off to law school and she didn't see him so often.

It seemed to Stephanie that she remained a skinny stick forever, then her maidenhood burst upon her, seemingly overnight. If at first bewildered, she was nonetheless thrilled by her metamorphosis. The summer she was fifteen, Thomas Hodges spent several weeks at Aurial before going off to a new job in Chicago. He was the same friend and confidant to her. Yet there was a difference in the way he looked at her. She saw admiration in his eyes, delight, something else. And he seemed more restrained in touching her. She had to take his hand when they went on walks. Or was the change in her? Or was she imagining the whole thing?

They went horseback riding, then decided to walk the mounts a bit. When Thomas helped her down, she lost her balance and fell against him, sliding down his body. He held her a moment, his hands at her waist.

"You're becoming very beautiful, Stevie. Such hair you have, and eyes."

She smiled her pleasure, then at once knew he was going to kiss her. She felt the tightening of his hands, saw the forward movement of his head before she closed her eyed, expectant, breathless. But the kiss never happened. She opened her eyes, saw his face, so serious. He seemed to be waging an inner struggle.

"I'd best wait, Stevie."

"Wait for what?" She was surprised at the huskiness in her voice.

He smiled. "Just wait."

"How long, Thomas?"

He nodded, as though in resignation. "Much too long, I think."

She had not seen him in three years. He had gone to Chicago. On his visits home she was always somewhere else, maddeningly so, in school, in New York, in Europe with her mother. But she had not forgotten. A thousand times she had relived that moment, imagining the kiss, what it would be like, what each of them would say and do afterward. Thomas Hodges, greatly magnified in her mind, literally became the man of her dreams, the handsomest, most wonderful person. Boys her own age were just that—boys.

Now, under the gentle prodding of her great-grandmother, Stephanie decided to test the reaction to her secret passion. "It's terrible, GlennaMa—and don't you tell a soul—but as long as I can remember, I've had a crush on Thomas Hodges. It's awful, I know, his being family and all."

Glenna grinned. "I don't see anything terrible about it. Thomas is a fine young man—and has become quite handsome. Besides, the family thing was settled when Miriam married Morgan."

Glenna's reaction thrilled her; still, Stephanie protested. "But he's too old for me, GlennaMa. It's just a girlish crush."

"Why, Thomas can't be a day over thirty. I was only seventeen, younger than you, when I met Daniel—and he was thirty-two."

"Still, GlennaMa, it's—" A ringing sound rose from below. "What's that?"

"The front doorbell. Probably a tradesman. Let it

be." But the ringing was insistent, and came a second and third time. "Perhaps you'd better see who it is, Stevie. It might be important."

Stephanie ran from the attic, down the grand staircase to the foyer, unmindful of the daring Empire gown she still wore. She opened the door to Thomas Hodges.

Two

Thomas Hodges had wrestled with the problem of Stephanie Summers for three years. She preyed on his mind, her remarkable hair, startling eyes and ripening figure indelible in his inner vision. She was going to be a great beauty, a prize of prizes for some man. And she was a girl with whom he had a close, indeed, lifelong, relationship. But it was hopeless, really. She was just a child, far too young for him, and she was family. He could be nothing more than a big brother to her. Surely that is what she considered him. Any other ideas about her were unthinkable, something to be purged from his mind.

He tried, but was not wholly successful. When he was with other women, he found himself comparing them to Stephanie, and not just in terms of her beauty, but in the natural, comfortable feeling he always had with her. Clearly he had to do something to rid his mind of Stephanie. He alternated between staying away, hoping to forget her, and believing that if he saw her again, he would no longer find her as beautiful as he envisioned. But on his infrequent trips East, she was always somewhere else. Then his Stepmother Moira wrote of Stephanie's plans to visit Grandmother Glenna. He eagerly accepted a business trip to New York, determined to see Stephanie and end his enamoredness of her once and for all. Thus, it was with nervous anticipation that he rang the doorbell.

Nothing had prepared him for the girl who stood in the doorway in the blue chemise dress. Stephanie Summers was a vision of feminity. Her nearly naked breasts seemed to leap toward him, and he was severely shocked. His aplomb deserted him and he could only gasp, "My God, Stevie, how you look!"

Not without dismay she realized then what she was wearing. Nor did she have to follow Thomas's eyes to realize what he was seeing. Instinctively she wanted to fold her arms across her chest to cover herself. A thousand nights she had dreamed of this meeting, but to be wearing this most womanly of gowns, revealing just how much she had grown up, exceeded all her dreams. She saw his admiration and delighted in it, in herself. Smiling, she said, "I hope I don't look too shocking, Thomas."

He raised his eyes to meet hers, marveling at the starburst in them. "Not unless being absolutely ravishing is shocking."

She laughed lightly and stood aside for him to enter, closing the door. She smiled again, couldn't help it, and extended both her hands for him to take. In her thoughts of him, she had tried to tell herself he would not be as handsome as she remembered. But he was—tall like his father, with soft brown eyes and reddish-brown hair worn natural, without too much pomade. He had a straight nose and a strong chin below a fine, wide mouth that Stephanie considered most attractive. The upper lip was firm, but the lower was fuller. A sensitive mouth, she thought, very appealing. He was not "pretty" handsome, as she thought of it, but more rugged, manly. Indeed, he seemed to exude masculinity.

She felt the gentle pressure of his hands squeezing hers. Sensation coursed up her arms.

"God, Stevie, you're so lovely."

Again she smiled. "You are, too, Thomas."

They remained there a moment longer, hands linked, eyes only for each other. Then she was swept deep within his arms, her body crushed against his and his mouth on hers, hard at first, then soft, opening, probing.

"God, Stevie, I said it would be a long wait, but—"

"It's been a thousand days—a thousand years."

They kissed again—and again. She felt buffeted with sensation as his mouth moved hungrily on hers, devouring. She leaned weakly against him. Her hands, seemingly of their own volition, clasped the back of his head and pulled him down to her, the kiss becoming more open, deeper, prolonged. As his tongue found hers, she heard sounds, and knew the moans were her own.

It must have been longer, but it seemed only a moment till he was holding her away, his hands on her upper arms. "Whew! I must say that was worth waiting for."

It had been her first real kiss. Sensation still raced through her and she dimly recognized her trembling awakening. At first she could only nod acquiescence, then she found her voice. "You shouldn't have stayed away three years."

"I didn't want to, Stevie." He looked into her eyes a long moment. Then he lowered his gaze. She knew what he was seeing. Strangely it didn't embarrass her. "You're fabulous. I've never seen such a dress."

She looked down at herself, her nearly exposed breasts delighting her. Then she laughed. "I don't think you ever will again, either. It's a costume. My mother wore it as Empress Josephine to a masked ball. I was just up in the attic—" Her hand came to her mouth. "Lord, I forgot GlennaMa! She's still in the attic."

She took his hand and began to run across the foyer and up to the attic. Thomas kept pace, but not without difficulty. It was not that Stephanie was too fast, but he could not take his eyes off her as she ran up the stairs.

Stephanie's ascent was also witnessed by Glenna, who had emerged, with difficulty, from the attic. It was a fetching sight to Glenna, Stephanie in that beautiful gown, running hand in hand up the stairs with Thomas, the two young people smiling at each other, mindful only of themselves. Thomas had always been one of Glenna's favorites; he was honest, trustworthy, loving by nature. So right for Stephanie. Seeing them together, Glenna once again felt a zest for matchmaking. It made her feel young.

Stephanie saw her now. "Oh, GlennaMa, I'm sorry. I—"

"Shush, child. I'm quite able to manage a few steps." She turned to her stepgrandson. "Thomas, how grand to see you again." As he came to her, she offered her cheek in greeting. "How handsome you look, Thomas."

"It's good to see you, Grandmother Glenna."

The trio went downstairs to the south parlor, a sunny room, warmed by the afternoon sun. Glenna had Stephanie serve a sherry for themselves, a whiskey for Thomas.

Their conversation was spirited. Glenna never missed a syllable, but she was also observant of every nuance between the young pair. She read their faces, the smiles, the frequent eye contact, the eager laughter, the attentive listening. Thomas seemed to take on verve, his voice a trifle louder; his discussion of his success in Chicago, while not boastful, was certainly full of pride. And Stephanie. She wore that bold gown as if it were an everyday garment. How different from her mother she was! Danielle at her age would have sat in the corner hoping to be struck dead from shyness. How animated Stephanie was, and so excited. Her complexion positively glowed.

"I have to say you look prosperous, Thomas. Chicago must agree with you."

He smiled. "Yes, grandmother, I do like Chicago. Oh, it's not as sophisticated as New York, but it's—I don't know, it's bustling, full of energy. Since the fire, it's just booming."

Glenna laughed. "I can tell you like it. Everyone in New York thinks anywhere west of the Hudson River is provincial. I'm sure Chicago is not."

"It can be quite rough in places." He smiled at Stephanie. "But we have our elegance, too. Some of the hotels and restaurants are quite good. Finest steaks in the world."

Stephanie reciprocated his smile. "I've heard Grandfather Hodges speak of Chicago as a masculine city."

"Yes, I've heard dad say that, too. I think he's right. You do feel like a man there."

Glenna laughed. "Perhaps that accounts for how very manly you look." She saw him blush. "You do, Thomas. It's the truth. You've gained a lot of confidence in yourself."

"Thank you, grandmother, but. . . ." He couldn't think of anything to object to.

"I know I've heard, but I can't remember. Do you have your own law firm there?"

"No, grandmother, I'm with American Western."

"That's railroads, isn't it?"

"And a whole lot more. Besides an operating line, we're involved with rolling stock, rails, just about anything connected with railroads."

Stephanie had never been more excited—Thomas coming, admiring her, his thrilling kisses. Indeed, her lips still tingled. Most thrilling of all, he remembered her, had waited for her to grow up. She had been so afraid he would forget her, but he hadn't. He was here, so handsome, looking at her, smiling at her, wanting her. She felt she would burst with happiness. But she restrained herself, wanting to act grown up. "What's rolling stock, Thomas?"

For him, it was a magical moment. Gone were the doubts and hesitations that had plagued him for three years. Stephanie was simply the loveliest, most desirable woman he had ever seen. He knew he was falling in love with her, hopelessly so. And he also knew he could now offer no resistance to that love.

He smiled at her. "Rolling stock is what it sounds like—that which rolls on the rails. We are one of the largest makers of locomotives and tenders. We also manufacture all sorts of freight cars, cattle cars, boxcars, tankers. Pullman does most of the passenger cars, but Mr. Kincaid hopes to expand into that field."

"Kincaid? It seems I've heard of him." Glenna was being deliberately obtuse. She remembered her late husband, Franklin Fairchild, describing Kincaid as one of the most selfish, ruthless capitalists in the country. He had called him a "Robber Baron."

"You probably have. Winslow Kincaid is—"

"Did you say Winslow?" For just a second Glenna's poise broke. She shuddered inwardly. As a young maiden in Ireland she had been brutalized by a man named Winslow. He had killed her father. His actions had led directly to her slavery and perilous adventures. Later he had followed her to America, determined to ruin her life. He had almost succeeded. To this day she could not hear the name Winslow without recoiling.

"Yes, grandmother, Winslow Kincaid. He's one of the wealthiest men in the country, and he's growing richer and more powerful each day. Before he's through, we will own or control all the western railroads, as well as manufacture and supply everything from spikes to locomotives, wheatfields to warehouses. Winslow Kincaid is a real go-getter, the sort of man who's making this the greatest country in the world."

"It sounds exciting, Thomas. What do you do for him?"

Thomas smiled at Stephanie. He seemed to be always smiling at her. "Not much, Stevie—" he laughed, "—and everything. I'm his aide, his adminis-

trative assistant you might say. He tells me what he
wants done, and I see that it is done." Again the smile,
the laugh. "I'd better or—" He dramatically drew his
finger across his throat.

"It sounds thrilling, Thomas. What an exciting life
you must lead."

"It is, Stevie, it really is. Why, just the other day Mr.
Kincaid asked me to. . . ."

Glenna only half-listened, her mind on Thomas. His
eyes were bright, his voice full of pride as he spoke of
Kincaid. Thomas seemed almost worshipful of his
employer, and yet Kincaid was the worst sort of man.
How could Thomas associate with him? His own father,
Moira's husband Lawrence, had spent his whole life
fighting corruption and greed. As a lawyer, he'd helped
break the Tweed Ring in New York. He'd helped to
expose Crédit Mobilier in Washington, as well as other
instances of graft. He had always taken the side of
progressive reform and free enterprise. How could
Thomas sit there and speak of this Robber Baron as
though he were some kind of god? Glenna was deeply
disturbed, but characteristically she bided her time
before speaking.

". . . this fellow wanted to switch to another railroad. But Mr. Kincaid had taught me how to handle
that. I cut the price way below the competition's, and of
course he changed his mind." Thomas laughed. "Later
we'll raise it—higher than before. That poor fellow has
a lot to learn about how to do business."

"And Mr. Kincaid liked what you did?"

"Oh, yes. Gave me a raise, in fact."

Stephanie laughed and clapped her hands. "Good for
you, Thomas."

Glenna now spoke, neither her countenance nor her
voice hinting of any disapproval of Thomas or Kincaid.
"I thought at one time you planned to enter law
practice with your father. Have you given that up,
Thomas?"

"I haven't really thought much about it lately, grandmother." He smiled at her. "I really like what I'm doing. It's exciting. I feel I'm part of a dynamic organization, doing something important. And I'm learning a great deal about the business world from Mr. Kincaid."

"If I may speak frankly, Thomas, I've heard my late husband speak of Mr. Kincaid as—well, a bit sharp in some of his dealings."

Thomas nodded. "I suppose that's true, grandmother. But you have to be on your toes in today's competitive world." He smiled. "Have you ever met him?" He saw her shake her head no. "If you did, you'd like him. He's all right, grandmother, believe me."

Glenna smiled. "I'm sure he is, Thomas." And she meant it. Thomas was right. She had never met the man and didn't really know him. His reputation was probably unfounded. All successful men are talked about, degraded by the envious. Thereafter she turned her mind to happier thoughts, these two young people reacting to each other. Why, they were already in love. The sexual attraction between them was so powerful Glenna could almost reach out and touch it. Very good. There could be no romance between two people without desire. Three great loves, three husbands, had taught her that.

A few minutes later Thomas looked at his pocket watch. "I'm afraid I have to leave. I've an appointment."

He rose from his chair and both women followed. Glenna spoke. "But you'll be back?"

"Not today, I'm afraid. I'll stop by tomorrow."

"But you're staying here, aren't you?" There was earnestness in Stephanie's query.

"I'm afraid not. Mr. Kincaid, or I should say American Western, owns a place, a house actually, off Madison Square. I'm putting up there."

Glenna said, "Must you, Thomas? You're welcome here."

"I know, but it's better there. No sense in putting

you out." Even as the women protested, he again pulled out his watch. "I'll tell you what. I'll hurry up this appointment. Then why don't I take you both out to dinner?"

Glenna laughed more heartily than was necessary. "Not this old woman, you won't. But why don't you and Stevie go?"

Stephanie felt a surge of excitement, saw the appeal in Thomas's eyes, heard him say, "Yes, why don't we, Stevie? We can do Delmonico's or some place splashy."

Stephanie glanced at Glenna, saw the smiling encouragement on her face. Then she looked back at Thomas. "I'd love to go, but I only came up here for a few days. I've nothing to wear—just a few skirts and blouses."

"Wear what you have on. You look grand."

She had forgotten her immodest attire. Remembering made her laugh a trifle nervously. "I'm sure—if Napoleon were still emperor. This is quite out of fashion."

"But—"

Glenna interrupted. "Don't fret, dear. I'm sure we'll find something for you to wear." Her laugh was full, excited. "Just accept Thomas's invitation and find out what time he's calling for you."

When he was gone, Stephanie turned to her great-grandmother. "What on earth will I wear, GlennaMa?"

"I had in mind the black satin."

"Black? In June?"

"Why not? It was about that time of year when your mother wore it. I'm sure you'll be as big a sensation as she was."

"But that was twenty years ago. The fashion is—"

"Whatever Pierre Chambeau declares it to be. His gowns are all classics—always in fashion, whatever the vogue. Everyone will recognize the gown as a Chambeau and envy you for wearing it."

Stephanie had a mental image of herself in the gown already. She was filled with excitement. Still, she protested. "But it's torn."

"Only the seam is ripped. You go fetch it, and the shoes that go with it. I'll see if I can figure out how to use this new model sewing machine Mr. Singer is producing."

Stephanie surprised herself. When Thomas, eschewing staid, old Delmonico's, took her to the posh, new Empire State Hotel, uptown on Forty-second Street, she made her entrance as though it were an everyday occurrence. On Thomas's arm she walked through the crowded lobby, head high, smiling and talking to her escort, pretending not to hear the babble of voices behind her. "Who is she?" "Do you see what she's wearing?" "I never!" As they entered the new restaurant—called a supper club, for it provided dancing as well as elegant cuisine—she seemed not to notice the stares, the hush in the room as the maître d' seated them.

A bit earlier Stephanie would never have believed she would do so well. As Glenna had measured and pinned, cut and finally stitched the gown to fit her slenderer figure, Stephanie's apprehension had given way to gradual despair. And when at last the finished product adorned her, she was appalled. She was clothed in thin, clinging black satin. It covered her arms to her wrists, as well as her back and shoulders. But the fabric was tight at her ribs and waist, and so snug at her hips she couldn't wear pantaloons or stockings or they would show. The skirt was narrow at the front, so her thighs were outlined with every step, though there was more fullness to the back, which fell into an elegant train. The dress gave the effect of concealed nakedness, which was greatly enhanced by the neckline. Below a collar, which acted as a demure choker, a wide triangle had been cut. When Stephanie held the garment against herself in the attic, she was aware it was décolleté. But on herself it was—she had no words to express her feelings. Her aureolae were barely covered. It was probably no more revealing than the Josephine costume she had worn in the afternoon, but the black satin was so thin, so stretched to cover her bosom, that her nipples prominently decorated the front.

"I can't, GlennaMa."

"Then don't, my dear. But does it help if I tell you—"

"That mother wore it? That I should have pride in being a woman?"

Glenna smiled. "Yes, that, too. But I was going to say how very lovely you are, how proud I am of you."

Stephanie heard the love, the sincerity in the older woman's voice. She glanced at her reflection in the mirror. "I'll be so nervous."

"No you won't. Just breathe deeply and try to relax."

Despite herself, Stephanie laughed. "If I breathe deeply, I'll come out of this dress."

The laughter really did not quell Stephanie's rising sense of panic as she stood before the mirror disapproving of this image of herself. Then she became aware of Glenna behind her. Her face was gray with fatigue. Stephanie turned at once to put her arms around her. "Oh, GlennaMa, you must be exhausted. Let me help you lie down."

"Yes, I think I will get into something comfortable. It's almost eight-thirty. That's not too soon for an old woman to go to bed." As Stephanie helped her undress and get into her nightgown, Glenna said, "I haven't had so much fun in a long time, Stevie. If I'm tired, it was worth it. You are so enchanting."

Stephanie pulled the covers over her. "Yes, GlennaMa—and thank you." She kissed her soft cheek. "Would you like some tea or hot milk?"

Glenna gave a weary smile. "Milk would be nice. Cora's back. Just ring."

"No, I'll go to the kitchen and tell her. Save her a trip."

As she walked down the second floor hall toward the stairs, Stephanie stopped before a large mirror with an ornate gilded frame. She didn't know this person at all, taller in heels, so slender in this formfitting gown, so bold in the display of her bosom. The face seemed strange, too, more made-up, her eyes somehow enlarged, her lips more sensuous with rouge. Only the hair, now burnished gold in the candlelight, seemed familiar. She still wondered if she shouldn't have a more elaborate hairstyle, but GlennaMa had recommended she leave it natural—just a smooth, wavy fall of red-blonde hair. Grandmother Moira still wore her red hair that way. Her crowning glory, she called it.

Again Stephanie's gaze lowered to the gown. Her mother had worn this. The thought warmed her and she saw herself smile a little. How beautiful she must have been, how desirable. If her mother could wear this. . . . Yes, why not? Then she remembered the other garments from the attic, all so daring, so revealing. Grandmother Moira had even worn that sheer blouse in public. Imagine! And the inaugural gown of GlennaMa's. This one was no worse than that. Her smile broadened. She had a reputation to uphold. A heritage had passed to her. Yes, this gown was right. Then she remembered. The gown had been ripped. Some man had been so enflamed he had torn it from her mother. An unpleasant image entered Stephanie's mind, but she quickly discarded it. Thomas would never do that. He was too considerate, too gentle. She remembered his impassioned kiss earlier. He just saw her and swept her into his arms. So nice, so very nice. She had felt herself surrendering. Surrendering to what? If there were more kisses like that, she would surrender happily. She took a last glance at the image. Yes, Thomas would like this dress.

She went to the kitchen to order milk for Glenna, enjoying Cora's admiration for her gown. Soon Thomas was at the door. The look in his eyes told her she had not overestimated his reaction.

It was a warm June night. A wrap was inappropriate; at least she was not compelled to wear one. Thus, head high, arms at her side, she walked through the lobby into the restaurant. She was proud of her appearance, of herself, of the heritage that she was beginning to fulfill this night.

Three

At age thirty Thomas Hodges was hardly inexperienced. Although he was far too busy to give a great deal of time to women, he had managed a reasonably active bachelorhood. Winslow Kincaid liked to surround himself with beautiful women. Many found Thomas attractive. He sometimes had a free evening.

But nothing in his past had prepared him for this moment. He was utterly captivated by the glamor of Stephanie Summers. The glory of her hair, her gemlike eyes, snowy skin, luscious lips, all ensnared him. And the gown, the gown! It was not just the opulent mysteries revealed, but the boldness of it that appealed to him, and the poise and confidence with which she wore it.

He had wanted women before, many times. But never had he experienced such desire as now. His business appointment had been a nightmare, endless time, for his mind was constantly on Stephanie Summers, that blue gown, exposed breasts—my God, such breasts!—and her passionate response as he kissed her in the foyer. Never had he been so impulsive with a woman, and she had loved it, wanted more. The conference at the bank mercifully ended. He rushed to Kincaid's house, bathed, shaved, changed, castigating himself for acting like a teenager in his eagerness to see Stephanie. His first glimpse of her in that black satin dress was like a stab in his loins. He had barely restrained himself in the carriage. He sat opposite her now, greatly aroused, roiling with eagerness.

"Why are you looking at me that way, Thomas?"

"Because I can't help it. I always knew you were going to be beautiful. I thought about you in Chicago, wondered. But I just can't believe how lovely you are. What is your hair called? I've never seen anything like it."

She loved his praise and her smile showed it. "I'm just a plain old strawberry blonde, Thomas."

And he smiled. "Oh, yes, very plain." He lowered his gaze. "And your gown. It's gorgeous. I thought you had nothing to wear?"

Laughter bubbled out of her. She was unmindful of the movement of her breasts as she did so. He wasn't. "I didn't. The attic, remember? This was mother's. She wore it twenty years ago. GlennaMa altered it to fit me."

"She did a good job." He tried to say it with a straight face, but couldn't hold it.

Her renewed laugh held no trace of embarrassment. "Is it too—?" She let her eyes speak the rest of the question.

"It's not too anything—unless it's too irresistible to me."

"I thought you might like it." Even as she spoke, she recognized the word she had been seeking to describe her feelings at being with him. She felt *comfortable* with him. She had worried that with the elapsed years, her growing up, they might have lost that special intimacy they had had when she was young. They hadn't, and it pleased her inordinately. She acknowledged once again his innate honesty, his candor, and her response to it. He thought her beautiful, wanted her, said so. She thought him handsome, wanted him, said so. There was no need for foolish, empty flirtations.

Champagne was brought, opened, poured. Thomas raised his glass. "To the most beautiful woman I've ever seen."

She tapped the rim of his glass with hers. "And to the handsomest, nicest, most honest man I know."

Affected, he said, "Is it possible I'm already in love with you?"

"Not already, Thomas. Hasn't there always been a special bond between us?" She laughed lightly. "No one read 'Goldilocks and the Three Bears' as well as you."

He joined her laughter. "That's because I always figured you were Goldilocks."

"I never thought of you as Papa Bear—more as the woodsman rescuing Little Red Riding Hood from the big bad wolf."

When their laughter faded, he said, "Do you realize I remember when you were born?"

She smiled. "I wish you didn't. All babies are ugly, I hear."

"You weren't. I was twelve, I think. Even then I thought you captivating. You've always been a beauty to me, the loveliest. I feel I've waited all my life for this moment—for you."

Eyes glistening with happiness and emotion, she was suddenly aware she still held the stemmed glass in her hand, untouched. She took a sip, wetting her lips, and set it down, watching him do the same. Then she gripped his fingers across the table, her left hand, his right. "I want to tell you something, Thomas. If you had kissed me three years ago, when we both wanted to, it—oh, I don't know. I wasn't ready."

"I know."

"I needed these years to think of you, to dream. I

thank you for giving them to me." She smiled, shyly, a
trifle embarrassed. "I was ready this afternoon."

He grinned broadly. "Were you ever!"

She laughed then, too. "But why didn't you kiss me
in the carriage coming here? I was so disappointed."

He grew serious. "I wanted to, believe me. But I
didn't trust myself."

She truly did not understand what he meant. In her
innocence she thought of her desire for him only in
terms of kisses. What else might transpire, leading to
his distrust of himself, was beyond the knowledge of a
Victorian maiden.

Their food came. Neither ate much, just poking at
their plates amid longing looks and knowing smiles.
They danced some. His arm around her back, his hands
holding her were like furnaces melting her. She had
eyes only for him—and a great longing to be deeper in
his arms, her mouth under his. She felt they were two
people alone in the universe. Once, fleetingly, she
thought of her mother. It must have been like this for
her, this dress, a passionate man, her own overwhelming desire. But the thought did not help her. She was
conscious only of the nearness of Thomas Hodges and
his heat that was making her smolder. Another thought
came to her. This whole day had prepared her for this,
the *now* of her life: the attic, trying on dresses, history
revealed, knowledge of mother, grandmother, great-
grandmother, awareness of the desire and love that was
her heritage. Her time had come. She knew, without
fear, she was ready.

He never asked. She never protested. He simply
ordered the driver to take them to the house owned by
Winslow Kincaid and the American Western Company
on Madison Square. It was only a few blocks from
Glenna's house.

He held her hand in the carriage, her tingling flesh
entwined within his. Strangely he still did not kiss her.
She waited, certain of its coming. He paid off the cab,
entered the gate, escorted her the short walk to the

door and brought out his key. The door opened. They entered. The door was closed.

He swept her into his arms. She was conscious of her breasts pressed against him, then her thighs.

"I've wanted to do this all evening. I could hardly wait to be alone with you."

The kiss drenched her in sensation and she leaned against him, fearful her knees were buckling. His mouth was open, his lips moving, and she felt she was being devoured. Then he was kissing her eyes, hair, ears, throat, before returning to her eager, aching mouth. She was flooded by his passion, trembling. But she had no capacity to restrain him or her own feverish turning of her head, searching out the contours of his mouth. Sensation flooded over her. Their lips were wet, hungering for each other. Nothing mattered but this—him.

He stopped and exhaled deeply in a prolonged "whew" sound. Still holding her, he said, "I'd better slow down, hadn't I?"

In her innocence she didn't know what he meant. But she said, "Yes, perhaps so." He was holding her so close. She had no idea where her own arms were. She had knowledge only of his body pressed against her, his eyes, bright in the dimly lit foyer, and the lips she so desperately wanted.

Thomas relaxed his embrace and turned her around. "Don't be afraid. We're alone. There are servants, but I gave them the night off." Arm around her, he led her a couple of steps, turning up a gas lamp. "I told them to put some champagne on ice. Let's see if we can find it."

They walked through the unfamiliar house, arms about each other. As she snuggled against him, Stephanie looked down at herself. The bodice of the black gown was in disarray, revealing an edge of bright pink flesh. She didn't know what to do about it.

He found the wine in the library, a small room, mercifully windowless. He deftly uncorked, poured, came to her, handed her a stemmed glass. Again she was conscious only of his nearness. He raised the glass in a toast. She didn't really hear his words. The desire he had created in her in the foyer had not left her. She was trembling again. Raising the glass was a major undertaking.

He saw and misunderstood completely, reaching out to take her shaking hand, steadying the liquid in the glass. His sense of honor surfaced. "Do you want me to take you home, Stevie?"

She looked at him, all eyes. "No."

"Does it bother you, our being family? I guess I'm sort of an uncle."

"No."

"I figured if Miriam and Morgan could, maybe you and I. . . ."

"I said it didn't bother me." She was surprised she could utter more than a single word.

He pursed his lips. "Then what's wrong?"

She looked at him, swallowing hard, then released his hand from hers, raised the glass, managing not to spill any, and sipped. The mechanical actions restored a feeling of sanity to her mind. Yes, she wanted to be here. Yes, she wanted his kisses, thousands of them. But that was not to be all. That she now sensed. As though speaking to the rim of the glass, she said, "I don't know what you're going to do."

His voice was husky. "Nothing you don't want me to do."

She looked at him then, holding him within her vision a long moment. Her words were almost inaudible. "Yes, I know. I believe you. I've always trusted you."

His lips, wet from wine, were like a magnet, drawing her. She came up on tiptoe toward him. He was under control now. The kiss was less ardent, less demanding, softer, tenderer, more lingering—and quite maddeningly tantalizing.

"Such lips you have, Stevie. I can't resist."

His words, his voice thrilled her.

Oh, how she wanted his kisses. "Then don't."

It was a real kiss this time. But as she clutched at him, her arms high around his head, her wine spilled down his neck. He jumped back from her and laughed.

"Oh, Tommy, I'm sorry. I've ruined your suit."

"Hardly."

She watched as he started to wipe his neck with a handkerchief. Then he removed his coat and vest, throwing them on a chair, undid his tie to dry inside his collar. How slender he was, yet such fine shoulders.

He looked at her, smiling. "Where were we?"

She inhaled sharply. "I think you were kissing me."

He came to her and she looked up at him, eyes wide, shimmering with expectancy. She saw his gaze lower, heard, "There's no figure like yours, Stevie. On earth there is no other." A reply formulated in the recesses of her mind, but she had no time for words as his hands found her waist. "God, my hands fit around you. How tiny you are." His hands measured her hips, returned to her waist, up her ribs. "How fragile you are." He caressed her back, her shoulders. "So delicate." Down her arms. "Such slender arms."

It seemed to her his hands, sliding over the black satin, created heat until she felt as if she were in an oven. She was being seared. Hands firm on her shoulders, holding her away, he bent to her lips, nibbling them, licking, his tongue laving the tender inner surfaces, probing the corners. She was quivering with sensation, couldn't help it.

He left her lips, bent lower, kissed the tip of her white triangle, slid his lips over the tops of her breasts, the sides of the valley, as far as he could reach. The action, so unexpected, startled her. A protest formed in her mind. But it went undelivered as he raised his head and pulled her to him in a long, deep embrace. His hand was in her hair, holding her head. She leaned against him, her heart beating wildly. Then she felt his hand at her breast, cupping, squeezing through the satin. Utterly shocked, she was about to protest, struggle, when his tongue suddenly came into her mouth, fully. She shuddered, her protest lost in the heavenly sensation of being filled. He moved his right shoulder, holding her head in the crook of his arm, and his hand entered the valley between her breasts, stroking, caressing, going within, finding. The thrilling touch of his hand, so smooth, cool, against her hot skin, made her shiver, and when his fingers found the hard buds she felt a sharp stab of pleasure. She trembled, almost unable to bear all that was happening to her.

Now it was he who was shocked. He moved his head back. "God, Stevie, such skin you have, such breasts. I've never."

She knew only the havoc his hands created as he tried to move to the other breast. He turned her and held her back to him, reaching over her shoulder, entering, finding. She looked down a moment, bewildered to see his hand within her dress, moving, but the sensation he produced overwhelmed her. Her eyes closed and she leaned her head against his shoulder, turning, seeking, demanding his mouth, finally finding, wanting more, so much more.

"How does this damnable dress come off?" he asked huskily.

"Buttons . . . in back." She felt him fumbling at her back and knew she wanted the dress to be gone, his hands on her. Yet, despite her eagerness, she knew something was not right. She opened her eyes. Books. "Not here?"

"No, by God." Then he was stalking from the room, through the dining room, foyer, pulling her by the hand, she running after him, heels clattering with the short, mincing steps her skirt permitted. She sensed her breasts were escaping from her bodice. At the foot of the stairs she stumbled, almost fell. In one motion he lifted her off her feet and she had a sense of lightness, floating. She put her arms around his neck, found his mouth, and pulled his tongue deep inside, sucking hard, desperate to be filled. But it didn't fill her enough. She wanted more—but what?

His passion was near the flash point, but as he carried her into the bedroom, kicking the door closed and returning her to her feet, he consciously calmed himself. His lifelong solicitude for her returned. Breath short, voice husky, he managed to say, "Do you want me to stop?"

She looked at him, but did not really see. She knew only overwhelming desire for him, a desperate need. She shook her head. Unable to speak, she meant it as "I don't know." He took the gesture as a negative.

"Oh, Stevie, my darling, I always knew it would be like this with us."

He kissed her, lovingly, tenderly, then began to disrobe her. Instead of ripping off the buttons as he longed to, he deliberately slowed his fingers, unbuttoning each small button carefully, pausing often to embrace her from behind, cradling her breasts within his hands, searching again and again within the fabric, kissing her back often. Amid it all were his words of wonder, "Such skin, so smooth, so soft, how lovely you are, unbelievably so."

She felt tingly all over, breathless. A strange heat radiated throughout her body, and her mind seemed disoriented. Opening her eyes she saw a masculine room, an unlit fireplace, a chest of drawers, a bed turned down. She stared at the furnishings blankly—they had no meaning for her, nothing did. She felt Thomas's lips hot at her neck and turned to give him access. As she did so she glimpsed a girl opposite her, a girl with reddish-blonde hair falling over one shoulder, a man behind her locking her in an embrace, his arms around her, his hands thrust deep within her black dress. Startled, she blinked. A mirror. In delicious confusion she was seeing as well as feeling what was happening to her. She gazed in fascination until, overcome with sensation, she closed her eyes.

There were many small buttons reaching from her neck to her hips. When Thomas had undone the last one, he reached within the parted dress, up her tiny waist, rising, searching, finally finding. It was as though his fingers were immersed in soft down, and he felt a pounding in his ears as his hands luxuriated in the fullness of her breasts, now in their natural state, squeezing gently, moving slowly outward until he found the hard, risen ends. "God, Stevie." He caressed the buds gently between his thumbs and forefingers. "Such a woman you are."

Marvelous sensations created havoc within her. Only his arms around her kept her from falling.

"Do you like this, my darling?"

"Oh, yes, yes." Her voice sounded strange to her ears.

He wanted his eyes to share the knowledge of his hands. He released her, slipping the dress forward from her shoulders, down her arms. It wouldn't come off.

"Buttons . . . at the wrists."

Maddened by the delay, eager to see her, he forced himself to undo the buttons of the sleeves. At last the dress slid from her.

When she turned to face him, she saw amazement in his eyes, heard him gasp. She thought he was surprised that she was naked beneath the dress.

"My God, Stevie, how you look!" In wonder his eyes measured her slender thighs, toured a strawberry meadow, witnessed diminutive hips and waist, fragile shoulders. But it was her breasts that leaped toward him, snowy, engorged, decorated with reddish-orange nipples, swelling with passion. "How beautiful you are!" He fell to his knees before her, arms around her hips, his face imbedded in the strawberry field.

She quivered all over, unable to control her body. She was aware of his head at her woman's place and could feel his hot breath as he rolled his face through it. And she felt his hands, sliding over her derriere, molding the half-moons, his fingers arcing jolts of pleasure through her at the joining. Then his hands were at her inner thighs, stroking her tenderly, yet the ache only increased, shooting down her legs. She felt each movement of his fingertips, shuddering as they separated, separated, found, found. She gasped and gasped again. She couldn't breathe.

She felt him rising up her waist, his head moving from side to side. She knew where he was going, and was eager for the arrival. He buried his face in her breasts. She moaned, both from the sensation and the intimacy of what he was doing. She saw his mouth open wide, taking as much of her within himself as he could, then felt him slide down the cone to the risen end. She gasped from unbearable sensation as he began to roll his head from side to side. Now he found her other breast, magnifying her pleasure. And all the while his hands, his hands, incessant, propelling. She shuddered under the onslaught of pleasure.

"Oh, please, I can't bear more."

He seemed to hear. She felt pressure against her inner thighs, and he simply stood up with her, carrying her across the room, his hands and mouth still at her most sensitive places.

She lay across the bed, moaning softly from the pulsating throbs where his hands had been. Through distorted vision she saw him undressing. Then he was naked to the waist, bending over her. He kissed her sweetly, then slid down her body, lingering at her breasts, then down, down. Nothing in her experience had prepared her for the pure pleasure of his head separating her thighs, his lips and tongue upon her. Her body seemed to dissolve. All she knew was the throbbing between her legs, quicker now, stronger, spreading upward.

Then he was gone. She lay there moaning from the throbbing, the ache arcing down her thighs and the incredible tension. Through slitted eyes she saw him hurrying, removing his trousers.

She felt herself being turned. The equilibrium of the

bed changed, his hands were on her thighs, spreading them. She opened her eyes, wide now, saw him on his knees above her. Then she couldn't hold her eyes open as she felt hardness where his tongue had been and a hot stroking bring on a sharp rise in her throbbing. There came a probing. She gasped. Another probe. Then she felt an exquisite stretching and cried out.

She was utterly filled, wondrously so, and she knew she had become part of him. They were as one. Shuddering, unable to breathe, she felt him rise up and descend into her again. A third and fourth time he filled her. She felt helpless, her whole being lodged in one enflamed area of her body.

She thought of it as an explosion, all noise, even light. It was as though dynamite had been detonated within an enclosed canyon, the sound and shock of it rolling along the length, then bouncing back, faster, faster, reverberating off the walls. She cried out from heavenly release, "Oh, oh, oh, Tommy, oh," as the echoes, some weaker, some stronger, spread along her cavern of ecstasy, never quite ending, thrilling her with pleasure.

"Oh, God, Stevie, you're so wonderful!"

He was still moving. She loved the sensation. They were in harmony, achieving an ultimate rhythm. Then she felt her throbbing heighten, her tensions rise, drowning out the echoes. For a moment she enjoyed the rocking of her hips, his repeated penetration of her body. Without willing it, she revolved her hips, once, twice, then it happened again, so quickly this time, the sharp ache spreading down her thighs, pulsating, the precipitous sense of fullness and bursting.

"Again? Oh, Stevie, Stevie. . . ."

She was shuddering, moaning, arching her back, straining against him, calling out, "Tommy, Tommy." Then her head came forward and her whole body collapsed as another devastation of noise and light, more ecstatic than before, deeper within, reverberated through her.

She was unaware of crying out or of the frenzied swiveling of her hips, was conscious only of his deep, rapid thrusts within her, filling, filling, the ache, throbbing, then a new detonation, so intense, shattering in its ecstasy. She heard him gasp, moan, and felt the deeper, propelling thrusts of his climax.

She lay there, utterly thrilled now by the slowly dying echoes. She heard him, "Oh, Stevie, I love you so." She opened her eyes, saw adoration and wonder on his face, then he came down over her, kissing her, softly, sweetly.

"Oh, Stevie, you were magnificent."

"Oh, yes, yes, it was so-o magnificent." She sighed. "It still is."

"Yes, yes." Then he kissed her, more ardently. She felt the sharp rise of his passions. Within her his manhood swelled anew, filling her again with exquisite sensations.

"Can you?"

"Oh, yes. Yes."

Four

She lay beside him, head on his shoulder, body pressed against him, her left leg crooked over his, her arm across his chest, enjoying his gentle stroking of her back. She felt utterly languorous, deliciously drowsy. A glorious sense of inner peace exceeded any she had ever known.

She first felt, then heard him laugh. "What's so funny?"

"In my whole life I've never let anyone call me Tommy."

"Did I call you that?"

"Over and over." His laugh grew. "I was hardly going to stop and tell you to call me Thomas."

She raised her head to look at him, smiling. "I'm glad you didn't—*Thomas.*"

He pushed her head back down to his shoulder. "God, Stevie, what a woman you are."

The words delighted her. "Really?"

"Yes, really. God, Stevie, the things you do."

"Me? You did everything. I hardly touched you."

47

She felt him trying to move, but held him in place. Then he touched her face, turning it so he could look at her. "You don't know, do you?"

"Know what?"

He caressed her cheeks, eyes, tenderly across her lips, then down her side, waist, her thigh across his. It felt heavenly.

"When I was inside you, you were so tight I could feel you climax. It was like, I don't know, moving contractions, spasms sort of. God, it was wonderful. What did you feel?"

She let out her breath in a long sigh. "I don't know. Explosions, I guess. They were so incredible. That's all I can tell you."

"How many did you have?"

"I couldn't think, let alone count. All I know is I got so tired, but they wouldn't stop till you did."

Both his arms came around her, holding her tightly. "Do you have any idea how remarkable you are?"

"I am?"

"Oh, yes. Darling, some women don't climax at all, most once. I knew one who did twice. But you—over and over. You're just incredible."

She raised her head, saw his bright eyes and beatific smile. "Really?"

"I wouldn't lie to you."

"And you liked it?"

"Oh, God, yes. Didn't you?"

She rolled more to her front and pushed up in bed, her leg higher on him, her arm over his so she could look down at him. "It was so . . . so *wonderful,* Tommy, so. . . . I never knew. Nobody told me."

"I feel—" He hesitated. Both his arms were around her shoulders, holding her close. "I feel positively, yes, *honored* to be the one to show you."

"Yes, yes, I wanted it to be you. Always I wanted that."

"Stevie, no man ever knows what a woman feels, except that it is something wonderful for her, thrilling.

For a man to know he is pleasing a woman means more to him than his own pleasure. And you! To have you, whom I've loved all my life, do it over and over, again and again—God, Stevie, I feel like praying in gratitude. I've just got to be the luckiest man in the world."

Her eyes misted over. "Oh, Tommy, what a thing to say."

Then he was smiling. "I feel reborn. This is the first day of the rest of my life. And I'm going to dedicate that life to loving you, always, never, never losing you."

"Oh, Tommy."

"To have known you all my life and loved you all my life, then to have you look like you do, dress like you do and make love like you do—" Grinning now, he squeezed her so tightly she could scarcely breathe. "What can I say? Never has any man been so fortunate —so blessed."

She swallowed, trying to remove the lump in her throat. "You're going to make me cry," she said softly.

"Then cry buckets, if they are tears of happiness."

"Oh, yes, Tommy, yes."

Then she was kissing him, lovingly and tenderly at first, then deeply, head turning over his, seeking the sensations that produced the sharp rise in her passion. She felt his hand searching out her breast and she moved to give him access, loving the pressure of his fingers.

"You know, don't you, I'll never be able to keep my hands off you?"

"I don't want you even to try to."

Again their lips and tongues joined, and she felt the sudden, dizzying propulsion of desire, the sense of fullness in her breasts, the sweet ache as his fingertips found her nipples. She felt him roll to his side, so he was above her, kissing down, she on her back. His hand moved down, down, slowly, lovingly. She spread her thighs, then quivered as his fingers separated, found, separated, found, entered.

"Can you?"

"If you want."

He didn't kiss her after that, just held her cradled in his left arm, watching her face as his right hand brought the passion, ache, throbbing. She wondered when he was going to move, enter her, fill her, then the thought was lost as, cradled like a baby, his fingers remained at her woman's place, sliding, sliding, smooth, liquid, incessant, insistent, building, building, until her whole body pulsating, she felt the inner detonations.

He watched in wonder as her head rolled from side to side and she gasped his name repeatedly. He observed all, letting the echoes linger. Finally he said, "Nice?"

"Oh-h yes . . . exquisite. But I thought you. . . . It was better . . . with you."

"I know, but I wanted it to be just for you." He smiled. "Call it a present."

She lay there in his arms. It was so heavenly, being held, so relaxed, his fingers, so gentle, producing precious sensations that radiated through her.

"God, you're wonderful, Stevie." Passionate now, he kissed her, adding to her pleasure. "Do you want to do it again?"

"If it pleases you."

This time he kissed her while his moving fingers wrote desire, compulsion, then fulfillment. Nor did they stop, not then, not until she saw, through slitted eyes, him rise above her, and welcomed him.

She awoke when he rose from the bed, saying he was going downstairs for the wine. She lay there, more tired than she had ever been in her life, unable to move, her body utterly satiated, drained. Yet it was such a lovely feeling of relaxation, of floating. Hers was a total peace, and she knew she was rapturously in love. Her mind sought to find some moment most precious in all they had done, and at first she could not. All the caresses, all the ecstatic sensations, never before known to her, had become a single entity. She knew the whole of love, not the parts. Then she remembered that which was most precious: his words. *I've just got to be the luckiest man in the world . . . I'm going to . . . love you always, never, never losing you.* Yes, oh, yes. And she was lucky, too.

She heard him entering the room and opened her eyes. He was naked, but neither that, nor her own nakedness embarrassed her. He carried a glass and a bottle of liquor. While he poured and took a generous swallow, she continued to admire him: flat stomach, nearly hairless chest, broad shoulders.

"You have a nice body, Thomas."

Lowering the glass, he smiled. "Not as nice as yours." His smile was both amusement and pure love. He offered the glass. "This will make you feel better."

"What is it?"

"The wine was flat. I brought brandy."

"Will I like it?"

"Probably not, but it'll perk you up."

She took the hand he offered and let him pull her to a sitting position on the edge of the bed. A momentary dizziness quickly passed. "Oh, Tommy, I'm so tired." She smiled wanly. "But deliciously so."

He sat beside her and put his arm around her shoulders, offering the glass. She took it, holding it in both her hands.

"Drink."

Again she smiled. "Yes, master." She raised the glass, sipped.

"More. A good swallow."

She obeyed and involuntarily shuddered as the liquid burned down her throat and into her stomach. "You're right. I don't like it." She heard his laugh. "What time is it?"

"A little after one."

"I have to go home."

"I know. We'll go soon. Can I see you tomorrow?"

Already she could feel the stimulation of the brandy. She smiled. "You'd better."

They made plans. He had conferences with lawyers, bankers. But he would come for her as soon as he could in the evening.

"I won't miss you all day. I'm sure I'll sleep."

She started to get up, but he tightened his grip, holding her. "Promise me you won't feel guilt or shame over this."

She turned her head. "I won't, Thomas. I won't let anything spoil it."

He held her with his eyes. "I love you, Stephanie Summers."

"And I love you, Thomas Hodges."

He kissed her then, softly, lovingly, the seal on what had transpired between them. "Tomorrow night we'll make plans to be married."

Her pulse leaped at the words, but she said only, "Yes."

At his urging she took another swallow of the fiery liquid, then said she had to go. She stood up and stretched.

"Lord, Stevie, such a body. It can't be you I'm to have."

She saw the wonder in his eyes, heard it in his voice and basked in it. Then she laughed. "I'm sorry, you can't return the merchandise if you don't like it."

She picked up her dress from the floor and stepped into it, turning her back for him to fasten the buttons. As he did so, she looked down at herself to see if the satin were wrinkled. "I'm going to have to be more careful with my garments around you."

"I just hope they have fewer buttons."

She felt the dress snugging her waist, up her back and looked at the result in the mirror on the wall. What she saw startled her. Her mother's dress. Her mother had worn this, wasn't it on that first night with her father? Yes, and in his passion he had torn it from her, and she had known the same ecstatic pleasures as her daughter had discovered this night. Oh, such a lucky dress.

"What are you smiling about?"

"You. Us."

Stephanie was about to enter her bedroom when she saw a shaft of light under the door to Glenna's room. At once she went there, rapped and on bidding entered. Glenna sat at her writing desk. She wore a robe, light blue in color. Her silver hair was plaited down her back.

"GlennaMa, it's two in the morning. What're you doing up?"

"I went to bed too early. I awoke and couldn't go back to sleep. I decided to get up and write to Moira. I'll doze off later." She set down her pen and turned in her chair to look at Stephanie more directly, seeing her hair, lips, the wrinkled dress. She knew instinctively what must have happened. But she only smiled and said, "Did you have a nice evening, dear?"

"Oh, yes, GlennaMa, yes." Stephanie came to her and bent to kiss her cheek, then stood before her great-grandmother, radiant with happiness. "Oh, GlennaMa, I love him so. And he loves me. We want to be married."

Glenna rose and embraced her. "Oh, my darling, I'm so happy for you."

"Is it all right, GlennaMa?"

Glenna stood back from her, hands on her shoulders, her eyes bright. "Of course it is. Thomas is fine, splendid. He has always been a favorite of mine. And you are just right for each other." Impulsively she hugged her great-granddaughter again.

"Thank you, GlennaMa, thank you. He's so wonderful and I love him so."

"I'm so glad, Stevie, so very glad." Glenna hugged her a moment longer, then sat back down in her chair. "Now, tell me all about your evening."

"Oh, GlennaMa, he—" Suddenly she stopped, her smile fading. There was nothing to tell, at least nothing she wanted to tell.

Glenna read her expression and understood. "Did you and Thomas . . .?" There was no need to finish the sentence. Again Stephanie's expression told all. "There's nothing to be ashamed of, dear. You love each other. It is only natural."

"Oh, GlennaMa, I knew you'd understand." Impulsively Stephanie embraced the older woman. "It was incredible. He was so wonderful. I loved it so."

Glenna smiled. "Bring over that chair, Stephanie, and let's talk." When the chair was moved, Glenna reached out to clasp both Stephanie's hands in hers. "You truly enjoyed it, dear?"

"Oh, yes, GlennaMa. He was so . . . so. . . ."

"Passionate?"

"Yes, and gentle. He thrilled me so. I couldn't stop."

"Of course you couldn't. It's always that way when there is love." She squeezed Stephanie's fingers. "I'm so happy for you—that you enjoyed it, that it was with Thomas. I saw today—or was it yesterday?—how much you love each other." Her smile was radiant. "I'm so happy that your first time was with someone you love and who loves you. It was that way with Daniel and me, so thrilling. It lasted all his life—and I still remember."

Stephanie was filled with emotion. "Oh, GlennaMa, you don't know what it means to have you say that, have you be this way."

"I think I do. I never had a mother, anyone to talk to. But I never felt it wrong—with Daniel, who loved me."

"I feel that way, too, GlennaMa. I know Thomas loves me."

Glenna's laugh was generous. "I know he does, too. And how could he help it?"

Stephanie reached across the short space that separated them and briefly hugged her great-grandmother. Then she sat back, a pensive look on her face. "GlennaMa?"

"Yes."

"He—he said I was remarkable."

"I suspect you were."

"When I was . . . with him, I felt . . . inside, a . . . a. . . ."

"An orgasm?"

"Is that what it's called?"

"Yes. And you had that?"

"Lots of them, GlennaMa. As long as he was. . . . I couldn't stop. They kept coming, one after the other. It was so . . . wonderful."

The older woman smiled. "And that's why he thought you remarkable?"

"Yes, he said other women don't."

"Perhaps not. But it's a family trait."

"I don't understand."

"Your mother's the same way. I know for a fact. She told me. Moira is, too." She laughed heartily. "And when I was young and in the mood I was that way with Daniel, and Cap'n Mac, too."

"Is it . . . all right?"

"Of course, dear. Didn't you say you enjoyed it?"

"Oh, yes."

"Then continue to enjoy it. It's the way you are and can't be helped." She smiled. "The problem is to find a man who understands and can satisfy you." Now she laughed. "You tell Thomas he's remarkable, too."

"He is, GlennaMa, he is, and I'll tell him." She sat there filled with happiness, at herself, at Thomas, her love, this beautiful old woman who understood her and approved of her. Suddenly she couldn't sit any longer and jumped up and did a pirouette. "I'm so happy, GlennaMa. I think I'll burst with happiness."

Glenna laughed. "I do get that impression."

"It's this dress, GlennaMa, this lucky dress. Mother wore it when she met father and—"

"No, dear. You're confused. Your father never saw your mother in that gown."

Stephanie stopped her whirling. "But you said father, dressed as a pirate, taking mother—"

"That was the blue gown you had on, the Josephine costume."

"Then when did mother wear this? Who tore it?"

"I told you, dear. It was Hamilton Garth, the man your mother lived with for a time—until she discovered who your father really was. Don't you remember?"

Stephanie felt a strange, abrupt change in her mood. "Yes, I remember now."

Always sensitive, Glenna read the change. "Does it matter, Stevie? It was a long time ago, all but forgotten —except by old women."

Stephanie managed a smile. "Of course it doesn't matter."

Glenna didn't believe her. "Are you sure?"

"Yes, I'm just suddenly very tired."

"Yes, you must be. And I am, too. We should go to bed. Do you want me to help with your gown?"

"No, I can manage."

In her room Stephanie stood before the mirror studying the image of herself in the black satin gown. Her mother had worn this with someone named Hamilton Garth, a man she had not loved. In his passion he had torn it from her. Then she had. . . . Visions of her own repeated orgasms fled through Stephanie's mind. Her mother was like that, too. And she had. . . . With a man she didn't love.

Exhaustion weighed heavily on Stephanie then. Slowly she raised her hands behind her neck and began to undo the buttons, one, a second, a third. Reflected in the mirror was the image of a girl, her nearly exposed breasts reacting lasciviously to the movements of her arms. Suddenly Stephanie gripped the edges of the fabric at the opening she had made. Shaking with anger, she was about to rip open the whole back of the gown when she stopped herself, lowering her arms, struggling for self-control.

She studied her image in the mirror a long moment, then at once understood. All Glenna had told her suddenly had meaning. Danielle Kingston, her mother, a girl of eighteen, so beautiful, but terribly shy, had been compelled to wear the Josephine dress, so shockingly décolleté, to a masked ball. A man dressed as a pirate abducted her, took her to a garret and . . . ravished her. Stephanie now understood, because of this night. Her mother had discovered her own body, its pleasures, her . . . capacities. It must have been so, yes. And she had fallen in love, just as her daughter had fallen in love with Thomas. But her mother didn't know who the pirate was, not then. She drifted into the arms of this man Garth, wearing this black dress, and he had. . . . Later she discovered who the pirate was, loved him, married him. But they got divorced.

"Oh, mother."

In the mirror Stephanie saw her own face screw up as she began to cry, for she had arrived at a point of instinctive understanding of her mother's deep unhappiness. *The problem is to find a man who understands and satisfies you.* Tears coursed down Stephanie's cheeks now as she wept for her mother, so dear, so beautiful, loving Walter Summers, Stephanie's own father, and only him, but divorcing him, then going from affair to affair, miserable, seeking, seeking, never finding. . . .

Five

The object of Stephanie's tears also looked at her image in a mirror. It was seven-thirty in the morning in London, and Danielle Kingston Summers, unable to sleep longer, had already arisen to begin her day. She sat at her vanity, rendering long, practiced strokes to her hair in preparation for arranging it. Ordinarily a maid would do this, but it was much too early to expect help now.

There had been a time years before when Danielle had hated mirrors, avoiding them and the image they reflected. She had felt she was looking at her inner self, peering deep into her soul, witnessing the unhappiness that lay there. But she had willed herself to stop such nonsense. Mirrors had no magical properties. They only reflected images. She used mirrors to do her hair, put on makeup, satisfy herself about her apparel, without permitting herself to analyze what lay behind the mirror-image.

Thus, she could now look at what she saw without feeling, a striking woman with Irish coloring, black hair, vivid blue eyes, bright mouth. Her skin was still snowy, but no longer flawless. Thirty-seven years had produced wrinkles at her temples and around her eyes, and the lines where her cheeks joined her mouth had deepened. No matter. She was still beautiful. But for how much longer?

She had already squelched that thought when she heard sounds from the bed across the room. She glanced over. James Lavelle, the seventh Earl of Wight, had merely rolled over to his left side. He would sleep another couple of hours. Danielle returned to the image and began to twist and wind her hair atop her head, pinning it. It would do for the morning. A more elaborate coiffure could be perfected later by Ruth, her maid.

Danielle rose then, stepped behind the vanity bench and removed her dressing gown. Once again the mirror refused to be her enemy. Despite thirty-seven years and two children, she had kept her figure reasonably well. Oh, her skin had softened and loosened somewhat, but her waist and hips were within an inch of what they had once been. She stood on tiptoe, stretching, then pinching above her hips. Yes. Being a little hungry all the time was worth it. Still on tiptoe she cupped her breasts, squeezing a little. They had grown a bit with age, but they were still firm, not too pendulous. Men still found them attractive, James Lavelle especially. She shook her head. Enough vanity. She dressed quickly then, donning a simple white summer dress. It was reasonably formfitting, yet suitable for the morning.

Downstairs Danielle was greeted by Wrigley, the butler, who offered breakfast.

"Just coffee, Wrigley. I'll have it in the morning room, if I may."

"As you wish, madam."

She smiled at his retreating figure. British servants were awesomely efficient, but they could be terribly stuffy. She looked out the window at the bright sunshine—the sun rose so early and set so late in these latitudes this time of year. A walk in the garden appealed to her, but no. She just had to write to Stephanie and Andrew; her mother, too. She had been gone over a month and had dashed off only a single, quick note to each of her loved ones. But she thought of them often. Stephanie would be with GlennaMa in New York. Danielle didn't worry about her. But Andrew. Danielle shook her head. She hadn't wanted him going off to Colorado to see his father, but had been unable to prevent it. Walter loved his children and had every right to see them. Yet she worried about what notions Walter might put into Andrew's head. Oh, well, there was nothing to be done. And Walter's taking Andrew for the summer had enabled her to make this trip to England.

She sat at the desk, retrieved paper from a drawer, picked up a pen and wrote:

Dearest Stevie,

Ten minutes later the page still contained those two words, for Danielle had succumbed to a turmoil of thoughts. Why was she in London attempting to *write* to her daughter? Why wasn't she with her, loving her, watching her grow into a woman, helping her? Stephanie was so beautiful, with such a luscious figure. Many men would want her, and she was so innocent, so terribly vulnerable. And here was her mother, an ocean away, involved in still another affair when she should be at Stevie's side, watching, advising, protecting the child she loved. She had failed as a wife. Was she now to fail as a mother? Why, oh, why, hadn't she talked to Stephanie, telling her about men, what they would want from her, how to protect herself, how to learn the difference between love and passion? A dozen times Danielle had wanted to talk to her daughter, but the words would never come out. And she knew why. She would be revealing herself, confessing to her daughter her own—Yes, there was a word for it. Accept it. Her own *promiscuity*. Self-loathing rose in Danielle like a ravenous animal.

But it was an old adversary. Danielle trembled from the effort, but fought the enemy, driving it back down into the dark place where it lived, snarling and growling, waiting for the next opportunity to pounce out and consume her. Through sheer will Danielle had learned to live with herself and her unhappiness. Her ally was self-realism, as she thought of it. She tried to be honest with herself and accept her own nature. Self-pity, self-hatred, self-delusion would destroy her. They must be allowed no place in her mind.

"Coffee, madam?"

She turned. "Yes, thank you, Wrigley. Just set it there."

"May I pour, madam?"

She smiled. "No, I'll do it, thank you."

When he left, she rose and poured herself half a cup, for her hand was trembling as she poured. Holding the saucer in her left hand, she raised the cup in her right. In fascination she watched her own shaking hand, the movement of the liquid in the china cup. She smiled at it. People thought her so cool, so calm and controlled. If only they could see her now. She managed to bring the cup to her lips, swallow, then swallow again. She tried to keep her mind empty, concentrating on the acrid taste of the dark liquid, refilling the cup. But it was no use. The thoughts were there, hovering, demanding admission to her mind. She knew she would fail to keep the demons out. She had not slept well. She was too tired this early morning to win this battle.

For nearly twenty years her own words had haunted her. In 1870 a man dressed as a pirate had abducted her from a masked ball in London, taken her to a garret, drugged her with aphrodisiacs, then ravished her. She loved it, the repeated, cataclysmic orgasms thundering through her body. She repeated the performance the next day without drugs. Then, before he took her home, the pirate asked if she was sorry. Had he harmed her?

Her reply still buzzed through her mind, like an endlessly stinging insect. "Yes, of course you did. . . . You have uncovered something in me, a sort of craving, something foreign to me, something animalistic which I'm not sure I like. I think I'm going to have a difficult time living with it. If that's not harming me, I don't know what is." He replied it would not be difficult if she found the right man. She answered, "So I will need a man now, will I? I didn't before."

Shortly thereafter she went to New York and drifted into the arms of Hamilton Garth. He was rich, ruthless and at times cruel to her, but—Danielle's self-realism would permit her to think no less—he had satisfied her lusts. Yes, *lusts*. That's what they were. Even in her fear and detestation of him, she knew what was happening. Even now, this episode was the dark place where the beast of self-loathing lurked.

She discovered that the pirate in the garret, her first love, was really Walter Summers. They married, had children, and she knew years of true happiness, living with Walt at Seasons in South Carolina. Walter Summers had loved her, understood her nature and needs, and reveled both in her and his ability to bring peace to her body. Her happiness was shattered virtually in a single night, when she discovered her husband was a hooded nightrider, a murderer, in the act of raising his rifle to murder his wife's dearest friend, Cassie Brown, solely because Cassie was a Negress. Danielle left Walter Summers abruptly, the image of his scarlet hood, the raised rifle, her screaming, leaping to knock it aside, indelibly etched in her mind. The image would not leave her, or the knowledge that she lived with a murderer. Her love for him died.

Was it true? Waiting in the wings, loving her, wanting her, had been old friend Benjamin Fairchild, grandson of Glenna's third husband, investment banker Franklin Fairchild. For over a year and a half Danielle resisted Ben, determined to be like her mother, who had endured seven years of widowhood despite her inordinate longings. But Danielle had finally given in to patient Benjamin, surrendering to her desires, his passionate admiration for her, her aching fulfillment. Tears of relief had coursed down her cheeks as she gave herself to a third man in her life. She divorced Walter Summers, planned marriage to Benjamin. His death in a train wreck had been a cruelty.

She drifted into affair after affair. The first frightened her, a married man who in a single night met her, bedded her and dispatched her into cascades of pleasure unknown since Walter Summers. But she awakened in terror. She didn't know this man. Yet she had disrobed for him and permitted him to plumb her deepest secret. What was to become of her? This course led straight to disaster. She never did it again. Yet that single night also formed the dark place where her self-loathing snarled.

In vain she sought virtue. In her self-realism she knew the effect she had on men, her beauty, snowy skin, lush figure, her aura of placidity, delicacy and fragility. She was, she knew, the epitome of still waters running deep.

She went from affair to affair. Discreet now, she selected men of substance, decent, honorable men, who loved her and wanted to marry her. She avoided the furtive, the hasty. Now her men were brought to family gatherings, meeting her mother and children. All were of long duration. Her affair with Aaron Hopkins lasted over three years. A hundred times he asked her to marry him. She put him off repeatedly, then finally broke off the romance. There was nothing wrong with Aaron Hopkins. He was an industrialist and philanthropist in his forties, scion of a splendid Baltimore family. He loved her desperately and would have been a superior husband and father to her children, offering her every comfort of wealth and respectability. But she couldn't marry him. She just couldn't. And she didn't know why. And it had been this way with each of Aaron's successors.

"So there you are. I wondered what had happened to you."

Startled, she turned, smiled. "Oh, James, I awoke early. It was such a lovely morning I decided to take advantage of it. Hope I didn't disturb you."

He came to her and kissed her lightly. "Only that you weren't there when I awoke. I fear you've ruined me forever for empty beds."

She allowed the kiss to be repeated, deeper, a trifle more passionate. "Then you had better give up double beds."

"Never, not as long as I have you." He bent toward her, then glanced over her shoulder. "Is that coffee I see?"

"Yes, but I'm not sure how hot it is now."

"I'll drink it even if it's frozen solid."

"That I wish to see." She went, poured him a cup, handed it to him. She watched as he inserted two lumps of sugar and added cream. The sweet concoction was repugnant to her—she liked her coffee black—but it was a trifle, of no real importance.

She had met James Lavelle, the Earl of Wight, six months previously, when he had come to Washington on a diplomatic mission. His was an old, aristocratic family of Norman origins, yet none of his heritage seemed to matter to him. She was attracted by his relaxed manner, his air of genteel self-deprecation. He was a widower in his mid-forties, extremely wealthy and, she thought again as he raised his cup to his lips, one of the most truly handsome men she had ever met. He was tall, lanky, with dark hair just beginning to gray, an aristocratic nose, fine blue eyes and a sensitive mouth below a generous but carefully trimmed brush mustache. Most appealing was his voice, deep, mellifluous, with the perfectly rounded vowels of the British upper classes. He used them now.

"So what are you up to this morning, my dear?"

She made a gesture toward the writing desk. "I'd hoped to write my children, but—" She smiled. "I fear I'm not very literate this morning."

He looked at her in careful appraisal, tenderness in his eyes. His voice conspiratorial, he said, "I'd hoped last night might make you more relaxed today."

More than any man since Walter Summers, Lord James Lavelle understood Danielle and her needs. He was not shocked by her, at least not after the first discovery. Rather, he seemed delighted, offering her admiration and approval. If at his age he was not as vigorous as she might have wished, he nonetheless found ways to satisfy her, delighting in the accomplishment. But far more important than her physical needs, he offered her emotional support. They seldom spoke of it directly, yet she knew he realized her unhappiness and its causes. In subtle ways he made her feel not just beautiful, but also intelligent, independent, courageous, accomplished. He was so very good for her.

He leaned forward now and whispered against her ear, "I know I feel ready to conquer the world."

She smiled and whispered back, "If last night is any indication, I suspect you will." She heard him laugh, joined in, then watched as he turned, adding a dark amber liquid to his cup. "You look very handsome, James. Are you off to the diplomatic wars?"

"Yes, confound it. The bloody Russians have come, and we are pulling out all the stops in hopes of an alliance. There are conferences and a lunch at the Foreign Office all day. Tonight Prince Edward and Princess Alexandra are holding a gala to honor the Prince's Cousin Nicholas. We are invited."

She smiled. "I'll do my best, James."

He held her with his eyes a moment. "You don't know what it means to me to be able to rely on your taste, your discretion. You will not only be the most beautiful woman there, but the ablest."

She smiled, delighted by his praise. "And I thought all Americans were savages."

"A few of you colonials learned from your masters, obviously." His laugh faded and he drained his coffee, setting aside the cup. "And what will you do with yourself all day?"

"Oh, I'll find something. I'm determined to write these letters. Then I may shop a little. I know, I'll visit the neighborhood where I grew up."

"A good idea, Danny. You'll enjoy it, nostalgia and all that." He grew serious, but masked it with a slight smile. "As for those letters, why don't you just say you are having a wonderful time in London, wish you were here? You might add that you are madly in love with a man who adores you." The smile widened. "Soul-searching is not always good for the soul, I hear."

She was affected. His ability to read her thoughts was uncanny at times. But she kept things light. "May I quote you? You did say adore?"

"You may even use the word *worship*, if you like."

He kissed her lightly, said he would see her no later than seven—he hoped—then left. She followed him to the doorway, looking after his retreating figure. He was, she knew, her last hope for happiness. He offered her everything she could ever want: wealth, elegance, respectability, even the title of Countess. Hers would be a life of importance and usefulness as the wife of a prominent diplomat. This very evening she was to meet the future King and Queen of Britain. As the Countess Wight she would manage this large house in London, the baronial family estate in Hampshire. They had gone there first from New York. She had been in awe of the grandeur of the estate, then found within herself the capacity to adapt and perform as expected. After a large dinner party at which she was introduced to his friends, James had repeatedly expressed his admiration for her. And his children seemed to accept her. At thirteen and sixteen they were perhaps a bit precocious in their formality and manners, at least by American standards, but she could see no hint of trouble there.

Yes, a splendid life lay ahead for her. And more, she

would have love. Beneath his British dignity Lord James Lavelle was a caring man, sensitive and deeply passionate. They had come to the London house, using the visit of the Russian Crown Prince as an excuse, to get away from his children and gain privacy, sharing a bed at night. Yes, he would make her a happy woman. This last chance must not be allowed to slip away.

Danielle turned back to the morning room and went directly to the desk. She now knew what to write. She would tell of this house and the country place, of meeting the Prince and Princess. She would finish tomorrow, after the event. Her family would be as thrilled as she was.

Six

All things considered, Stephanie Summers awoke rather early, a little after ten. She lay in her bed for a time, flooded with rapturous memories, reliving her frenzied passions and voluptuous fulfillments. She was aware of the dull ache deep inside her, but it was lost in knowledge of its cause. Oh, she loved him, how she loved him! Then she smiled, remembering his words. Aloud she whispered, "You are wrong, Thomas. *I* am the luckiest person in the world."

It was still hard for her to believe. Yesterday morning she had been a young girl visiting an aged relative. Bored, restless, she had gone to the attic to look at an old trunk. The doorbell had rung and she was transformed from a girl into a woman. A thousand girlish dreams were fulfilled in a single night, and in a manner exceeding her wildest imaginings. It was as if a fairy princess had touched her with a wand, making her beautiful and desirable, then providing her with the man of her dreams. She laughed aloud. But this was no fairy tale. Beneath the covers she raised her nightgown and ran her hands over her thighs, feeling her woman's place, where he had touched and, oh, yes, kissed the opening, still wet, where he had entered. Yes, life surely did exceed dreams.

Then she laughed again, this time at herself, and quickly pulled down the nightgown, threw off the coverlet and rolled to sit on the edge of the bed. The first thing she saw was the black dress where she had thrown it over the back of a chair. At once she remembered her mother. But there were no tears now. Sleep and daylight had brought a return to reason. Her mother was in London with that handsome, charming Duke. Oh, maybe not a Duke, but titled. He loved mother. He would be good for her. Mother would make a splendid Duchess or Countess or whatever. Surely she would find happiness now.

Then the black satin spoke another message to her. Heavens, she was to go out with Thomas again tonight —wearing what? She couldn't be seen in that dress again, but what else was there? Quickly Stephanie's mind raced over the attire she had brought, and she shook her head as she remembered skirts and blouses, a couple of simple shirtwaist dresses. Nothing. And Thomas would want her to be . . . after last night he expected—oh Lord, what was she to do? In panic she got up and went to the black dress, picking it up. Then she consciously calmed herself. She could wear this again if she had to. But there were all those gowns in the attic. GlennaMa could probably do something again. But she'd better hurry.

Stephanie stripped off her nightgown, then padded into the bathroom and started to draw a tub, not failing to be thankful again for Franklin Fairchild's nonpareil legacy, running hot water. While the tub filled, Stephanie went back into the bedroom, intending to run a brush through her hair and decide whether or not to shampoo. As she reached for the brush, she was conscious of the nude figure in the mirror and studied it unabashedly. She cupped her breasts from below, raising them, running a finger over the nipples now budding in the cooler air. Yes, she had a good figure. Visions flitted across her mind, the look in Thomas's eyes when he saw her, his words: *you can't be like this,* his kneeling, arms around her, licking her nipples. She felt heat spread throughout her body, striking her loins, and gasped at self-knowledge. Already she wanted him again. Was it like this for her mother?

By the time she had bathed, dressed and hurried downstairs to find Glenna in the sun parlor, Stephanie's desperation over her wardrobe had greatly mounted. A note from Thomas was delivered by messenger:

> *Darling,*
> *I have just learned I must attend a party at the Crosby Whitakers' tonight. It will be dreadfully stuffy, but it's business and I am compelled. I insist you go with me and the Whitakers expect you. Pick you up at eight.*
>
> > *All my love,*
> > *Tommy*

Her pleasure in the intimacy of the diminutive was quickly lost in her desperation. "I've nothing to wear, GlennaMa, nothing at all."

Glenna ignored her wail, for she was still reading the note. "The Crosby Whitakers. My, my, Wall Street would crumble into ashes were it not for him—or so he believes." She laughed. "But he and his wife are really very nice. You'll like them—and they'll adore you."

"But, GlennaMa, wearing what?" In dismay Stephanie realized she was near tears and sought to control herself by exhaling deeply. "Oh-h, I suppose I could wear mother's dress."

"Hardly, darling, at least not so soon. We'll have to think of something else."

Stephanie brightened. "The attic?"

"I don't believe the attic either, dear." Glenna smiled. "I think it's time you met Pierre Chambeau."

Stephanie gasped. Pierre Chambeau was the most famous dress designer in New York, and surely the most expensive. He dressed mother. "But he's very selective, GlennaMa. He only takes—"

"I know, but I'm sure he'll adore you."

"But, GlennaMa, it'll take weeks just to get an appointment with him."

Glenna laughed. "I'm not without influence, my dear. I'll write you a note of introduction." Soon she had penned:

> *My dear Pierre:*
> *This is to introduce my great-granddaughter, Stephanie Summers, Danielle's child. I know you will want to meet her. I also suspect she may inspire some of your finer efforts.*
> *Affectionately,*
> *Glenna Morgan*
> P.S. *Her French is quite good, I'm told.*

Armed with the note, Stephanie took a cab down to lower Fifth Avenue, entering a small, utterly unpretentious office on a second floor. There was not even an identifying sign on the door. She was greeted by a young, extremely effeminate-looking man. Ignoring his disdain, she handed him the note. He read the name on the envelope, gave a shrug and went through an inside door, closing it. He returned, sat at his desk and said nothing. She waited, wishing she hadn't come.

In a moment the door opened and a man stood in the doorway, staring at her. He was in shirt sleeves, a tape measure draped about his neck. He looked to be in his mid-fifties, although he was probably a little younger. Stephanie was startled both by the intense way he looked at her and by his face, heavily wrinkled, pock-marked. His was the face of utter dissipation. This could not be the celebrated Pierre Chambeau.

"*Ah, c'était vous!*"

She understood the words, "so it was you," but not

what he meant. *"Que voulez-vous dire?"* What do you mean?

The French came quickly then, but she managed to follow it. "So it was you who wore my dress last night. You had no right, not without my permission."

She spoke again in French. "How did you know?"

"Pierre knows everything. People saw you, recognized it as my creation. As soon as it was described, I knew it at once. I remember all my designs. I made it for your mother, not for you."

She felt crushed. "I'm sorry. But I found it in the attic. I had nothing to wear. GlennaMa—I mean my great-grandmother—altered it to fit me."

He stared at her a long moment, as though appraising her, then his expression softened, greatly aided by still-good teeth revealed in a smile. "Your French is surprisingly good. You learned from your mother, no doubt."

"Yes."

"I taught her. I taught her everything." He turned sideways in the door. "Come, *chérie.* Let us talk."

Still timorous, she entered his office, a squarish room, considerably larger than the anteroom, windowless, but brilliantly lit by a skylight. She saw a desk and chair, other pieces of furniture, a large drawing board with sketches pinned to it, a couple of dress forms. One had fabric draped over it. On a far wall were racks of fabrics. She looked at him. He was still appraising her face, her body. She was most uncomfortable.

"So you are Danielle's daughter. You have her delicacy, her complexion, but where did you get that hair?"

She told him, saw him nod.

"And those eyes?"

For the first time she found a smile. "I don't know. I just have them."

He nodded. "You are most fortunate."

Again he looked at her. It was as though he were whisking her attire away with his eyes.

"How is Danielle?"

"Fine, I guess. She's in London."

"I know. I made her wardrobe—or is it a trousseau this time?" He shrugged. "Did you know your mother was the first woman I ever dressed?"

"I did not, no."

"She made my reputation. I owe her everything. To this day I charge her only cost." He smiled. "And for what she wears in London, not even that. She carries my reputation to Europe."

He was looking at her with the greatest possible intensity. Stephanie didn't know what to say.

"Your mother is the only woman I have ever loved." He saw her shocked expression and smiled. "Oh, not carnally, *chérie*. I have loved her as the most beautiful woman in the world. Such coloring, such skin, such a figure, all delicacy and demureness, but within her burns such fire. She drives men wild. They do very foolish things to possess her." He shrugged, more heavily this time. "Alas, she is a *hausfrau*. She has wasted her life, her talents, in a hopeless pursuit of a love she will never find. Even now she does so. It is all a great pity. Such a foolish, foolish waste."

Stephanie had no idea what he was talking about, but was afraid to speak.

"So you are Danielle's daughter?"

"Yes." She was almost sorry she was.

He nodded two or three times. "You have a beautiful face, remarkable hair and eyes." He studied her a moment longer, making a "hmn" sound. "If you will disrobe, I will see what can be done with you."

She recoiled.

He sighed. "*Chérie,* I have seen a thousand naked women—no, ten times a thousand. I assure you, female nudity holds no surprises for me—and very few fascinations."

She looked around the room, desperate for a dressing room, a screen, something. There was nothing. But at least he had turned away from her, sitting at his drawing board. He raised a pencil, began to mark with it. With trembling fingers she undid her blouse and removed it, then stepped out of her skirt. Helplessly she appealed to his back. "Must I—" she forgot to speak French, "—take *everything* off?"

"Oui, chérie, complètement."

He seemed to understand when she had finished the task and stood there shamefully naked. When he turned around to look at her, his eyes widened. *"Ma chérie,"* he gasped. *"Impossible!"* At once he whipped his tape from around his neck and wrapped it around her waist. *"Mon Dieu!"* He measured her hips, then raised the tape to her bosom. "It cannot be!" He repeated the measurements, shaking his head, muttering to himself. Finally he draped the tape around his neck again and looked at her, astonishment still in his eyes. "I always believed your mother to have the finest figure I ever saw. But you exceed her in every way. The tape does not lie." He clasped her waist. "I did not know it was possible for the human waist to be so tiny. But it is." He raised his hands, cupping her breasts, raising, squeezing them inward. "And such breasts, so high, so firm and full."

"Please, oh, please."

He released her and stepped back. "Many men will do that, *chérie*, and you will adore it."

She tried to protest, but he silenced her with his hand. "You are young, *chérie*, doubtlessly innocent, but have you no conception of how you look? Such a figure you have." He motioned. "Stand on tiptoe." She obeyed. "Now raise your arms." Another motion. "Higher. That's it. Now turn sideways."

She did as he commanded, enduring a precarious balance, not unaware of what he was seeing. She was unprepared for his laugh, however. She blushed all over.

"I'm sorry, *chérie*. I'm not laughing at you, but at the note your grandmother sent."

"Great-grandmother."

"Oui, c'est ça. She said you would inspire my best efforts. Tell her for me that she is most correct and that I thank her for sending you to me. Will you do that?"

"If you wish."

"I will design a whole new fashion for you. You will be a sensation of sensations." In his excitement he clasped his hands together in front of himself. "Oh, *chérie,* I could cry. I am so *honored* to dress you."

Lowering her arms, returning to her heels, she stared at him. Honored? Thomas had used that word, too.

"We must go to work at once." He handed her a pad and pencil, instructing her to write the numbers he gave her. Then he began a series of precise measurements, her arms first, the length and various circumferences from wrist to armpit. Then her neck, shoulders. Soon he was taking intimate measurements of her breasts, circumferences, height, distances between her nipples and her shoulders and waist.

Her embarrassment was fortunately diminished by his prattle, interrupted only by the rendering of numbers he gave her. They were strange, for he used centimeters and millimeters. "Such a body is a gift from God, *chérie.* You must learn to take care of it. Eat sparingly, mostly fruits, vegetables and grains. You can have a little fish or fowl, but avoid red meats, all rich and spicy foods. My countrywomen pay a high price for their palates. Do you understand?"

"Yes."

"Never sweets, *ma chérie.* They are the devil's handmaiden for a figure such as yours. And you must exercise. It is vital to remain limber and keep the muscle tone. I will show you some exercises when you come again."

His measuring tape had passed down her ribs, waist and hips. Tapping gently, he had gotten her to spread her legs, and he was now on his knees, measuring her thighs.

"Since you have come to me, *chérie,* I assume some admiring gentleman has caught your fancy. I am certain he is unworthy of you, but it is good that you enjoy and gain experience. There will be many others. As I said, men will do very foolish things to possess you."

She felt heat throughout her body. How did he know about Thomas? And why didn't she stop him from saying such horrid things about him? She sought to change the subject. "How-how do you know m-my mother?"

He measured her other foot then. His task apparently completed, he sat back on his haunches and looked up at her. "It must have been twenty years ago. I had just come to this country, quite penniless, and found employment with a . . . a *barbarian* who called himself a dressmaker. Late at night we were summoned to the home of one—I remember, a savage named Hamilton Garth. Danielle was there. Obviously the savage had just finished ravaging her. She was numb with fear and shock, but so very beautiful. I felt sorry for her and later talked with her. She needed a friend to help her. I spoke to Garth and arranged to become her . . . her—well, I guess you would say I was her maid."

"Her *maid?*"

"Yes." He smiled. "Oh, *bien sûr*, everyone was shocked, but I was invaluable. I dressed her, did her hair, bathed her, massaged her, taught her everything she had to learn to become the magnificent woman she is today." He saw Stephanie's expression and laughed. "Don't be so shocked, *chérie*. It was an unusual arrangement, perhaps, but platonic, all quite proper. Quite different from the relationship she had with that creature Garth." He stood up, looking directly into Stephanie's eyes. "Your mother could have become the greatest courtesan the world has ever known."

She stared at him wide-eyed, shocked to her depths.

He shrugged. "Alas, she did not want it. She could have had the riches of Midas, the power of royalty, but she refused. Never could I convince her. She has wasted her life, her potential, her gifts from God, in a hopeless search for love. Love is worthless, *chérie*. Love is a chimera. Just as you think you have hold of it, it turns into something else. Love is a mirage, lying always ahead of you, beautiful to behold, yet it leads a woman like your mother—and you, I suspect—only to her doom."

She covered her ears with her hands. "Please, I won't hear any more."

"Of course." He smiled. "You are young—and your mother's child, I should imagine."

He returned to his work, draping various fabrics over her, for which Stephanie was grateful. "Your hair, your eyes are most unusual. It will be a challenge to decide which colors enhance them. But not black, I think. It displays your skin, but not your hair or eyes. No, you should not wear that black dress again."

"But I must." She told him of that evening's invitation. "I have nothing else to wear tonight."

"I see. What time is your engagement?"

"Eight o'clock."

"And it is now after two. That does not give us much time." He paused, looking at her closely. She knew he was thinking. Finally he spoke. "Yes, perhaps, just perhaps. It will be a challenge for Pierre." Instantly he draped a fabric around her and began to pin and mark, muttering about the choice of color and the best fabric. He worked rapidly, but it still was some time before he stood away, looking at her, nodding. She knew better than to utter a word.

"You must leave now. With these new sewing machines it is possible to work rapidly, but time is precious. I will bring the gown to your home at seven. Be ready for the fitting."

Gratefully she began to dress.

"How do you wear your hair?"

"Like this."

"I see, *au naturel*." He smiled. "You have good taste. An elaborate coiffure on one so lovely would be gilding the lily. Remember that—and do not be tempted to bedeck yourself with jewelry, either."

As she departed, he handed her a note in French for the proprietor of La Mode, four doors up the street. She was to purchase evening slippers. Since the heels would probably be higher than she was accustomed to, she was to practice wearing them.

Seven

When she returned home, Stephanie told Glenna of meeting Pierre Chambeau and of his making her a gown for this evening.

"I'm sure he will, dear, and it will be just lovely and you will be lovely. He really is a genius at dress design."

Stephanie hesitated. "I—I didn't like him, Glenna-Ma." Suddenly she was uncertain what to base her feelings on, then thought of something. "He—He made me . . . disrobe. I was—"

"Of course you were, darling. It's a terrible invasion of privacy. But he must take measurements. He'll have a dress form made, then it'll be easier."

"I hope so." Again Stephanie hesitated. "I don't know. I felt very—"

"You needn't be afraid of him, Stevie. He admires women, but they are only objects to him. He has no . . . no *physical* interest in them." She saw Stephanie's questioning look and wished the matter had never been brought up. "I've never understood that sort of

thing myself, but Pierre is . . . interested in men—"
she laughed nervously, "—preferably young and handsome ones."

Stephanie remembered the young man in the anteroom, his effeminate face filled with disdain. "You
can't be serious!"

"Does it shock you?"

Stephanie sighed and shook her head. "I'm beginning to believe nothing can shock me anymore."

Eagerly, Glenna changed the subject. "I gather
Pierre found your figure *eligible* to wear his clothes."

"Yes."

"He turns down most, you know."

"Oh, GlennaMa, he raved over me, said I had the
best figure he had ever seen, better even than mother's."

Glenna smiled. "I know, dear. I could have told you,
but I was afraid you wouldn't believe me."

Stephanie looked down at her hands. "GlennaMa,
he is a corrupt man. He says love is worthless, unob-
tainable." She raised her head, looking at her great-
grandmother intently. "I don't believe that, Glenna-
Ma. I love Thomas and he loves me. I know it's true."

"Of course it is."

"I don't want anyone but Thomas." Her voice was
nearly choking. "I won't have anyone else."

Not without effort Glenna rose from the chair,
leaning heavily on her cane, and came to Stephanie,
putting her free arm around her shoulder. "And so you
shan't. Pierre Chambeau will make you beautiful
clothes, but pay no mind to anything he says. He is, as
you say, corrupt. We need not purchase his cynical
view of life."

These words comforted Stephanie, and she spent a
few happy moments trying on her new shoes. They
were dark blue satin slippers, extremely pointed, with a
three-inch heel. "He said I would have to get used to
walking in these."

"It shouldn't take long."

Still wearing the shoes, Stephanie helped Glenna upstairs for her nap. When she had covered Glenna, Stephanie said, "That man Hamilton Garth, the one mother . . . knew. What did he look like?"

"Oh, he was handsome I suppose, very dark, with an almost swarthy complexion. I found out he was black Irish. In 1588 part of the Spanish Armada was wrecked off the coast of Ireland. Some of the Spanish sailors settled there. His original name was Garcia. It was altered to Garr and finally to Garth. I always thought the Spanish blood most evident in him." She hesitated. "Why do you ask?"

"No reason. I just wondered."

"He was ruthless and greedy, and that did him in. Lawrence Hodges, Thomas's father, found out he was bribing government officials. Garth was tried, put in jail and destroyed. He died a few years ago. You need have no fear of him."

"I don't." She smiled sweetly. "Just curious. Now you have a nice nap."

Alone in her room Stephanie surrendered to the images which had preyed on her mind ever since she left Pierre Chambeau: her mother, so lovely, so precious, giving her snowy body to a dark, cruel man named Garth. The couturier had implied their relationship had been somehow bizarre . . . sinister. Stephanie closed her eyes, trying to blot out the image, but it wouldn't leave. She raised her hands, covering her face, feeling the heat of it. Against her palms she said aloud, "Stop it, Stevie, stop it." Finally she was able to take her hands away, open her eyes. "Yes, I must." Deliberately she forced another image into her mind, her mother in the blue Josephine costume, Stephanie's tall, handsome, yellow-haired father taking her into his arms. "She loved him. I know she did."

Stephanie went downstairs and had a glass of milk and, mindful of Pierre's admonitions, an apple. Then she bathed, shampooed and generally pampered herself while awaiting the evening. This activity helped, but she could not shake her disaffections with the day. Pierre Chambeau made her feel—what? A word came to her. *Unclean.* Yes, he made her feel soiled.

It was actually a little before seven when Chambeau himself arrived, carrying a large dress box and a satchel. He made an elaborate but brief greeting to Glenna, who seemed greatly amused, then was alone with Stephanie in her room. She had hoped to have her great-grandmother there, but Pierre dispatched her, saying an artist must not be observed until his work is finished.

He instantly reverted to French and handed Stephanie a small garment. "These are an abbreviated pantaloon I have designed. See, there are no seams to mar the line of my gown. They will make you more comfortable."

Puzzled, she took them. Turning her back to the designer, she opened her robe and donned them, closing her robe afterward.

"Better?"

"Yes, thank you." She had been most uncomfortable wearing no undergarments the night before. She followed Pierre's instructions and sat at the vanity. He began to fuss with her hair, brushing, combing, patting.

"You have just shampooed, I see. Your hair shines brilliantly. Is this the natural wave?"

"Yes."

"How fortunate you are." A little longer he moved his hands over her hair. "Every few weeks I would trim it. Just a little, a millimeter or so. That will keep the ends from splitting."

Finished with that, he then produced several small jars from his satchel and began to make up her face. She watched in the mirror, fascinated, feeling his fingers, so gentle as they toured her face and throat. Then he began to achieve a miracle, a touch here, a dab there. The results were astonishing as he magnified her eyes, her lips, the snowiness of her skin.

"I never knew."

He smiled. "Of course not. Pierre Chambeau is a genius."

Quickly he tried to slide her robe from her shoulders. She clutched it above her bosom, stopping him.

"If you are to wear my gown, you must have makeup on your arms and shoulders." He sighed. "And you need not be such a silly *jeune fille* with Pierre."

She hesitated, then carefully, one arm at a time, clutching the robe, she bared her shoulders, but still held the fabric between her breasts, covering them. In a minute or two he had briskly rubbed cream into her arms, one at a time, then her shoulders and upper back, wielding a powder puff afterward.

"Your bosom, *chérie*. I must prepare it."

She looked at him in the mirror. His face seemed satanic to her. "No. I'll not let you touch me."

She felt him tugging at the robe, trying to pull it down, but she gripped tightly. Then he sighed deeply and shrugged. "Here, rub this into your breasts till it disappears, then powder lightly. I'll tend to your gown."

When she saw his back was to her as he opened the box on the bed, she lowered her robe and did as he instructed.

When he turned back to her, he said, "I fear you must remove the robe if you are to wear my dress." There was disgust in his voice.

She did so willingly, feeling a sense of triumph. He might have to see her naked, but she would never let him touch her.

The gown was astonishing and, considering how little time he'd had to create it, miraculous. It was made from a single piece of material, a thin, clinging silk satinet, of a light, almost silvery blue. It stretched from her bosom to the floor, wrapped around her with a single seam to the back. But it had been cut, in accordance with all those precise measurements, a millimeter here, another there, so it was extremely formfitting over her torso, waist and hips, before falling straight in front. The skirt was fuller in back, with an elegant train.

As she gaped at herself in the mirror, Stephanie uttered a single question: "How does it stay up?" There were absolutely no shoulders or arms.

Pierre's laugh was indulgent. "You will see when I finish hooking the back."

And she did. As his fingers moved upward from her waist, she felt the dress tightening around her. He had sewn strips of whalebone into the garment, running downward over her ribs and stomach to her waist. When he finished the last two hooks at the middle of her back, she felt a tight stricture under her breasts and at the side.

"You see, *chérie*, it is like a little corset. It will not come down." He was smiling proudly. "Actually this part took longer to sew than the rest of the dress."

She looked in the mirror and gasped. The bodice had begun modestly enough. Indeed, back in the couturier's studio, she had been relieved that he seemed to be draping fabric over her breasts. But Chambeau had left a fullness to the fabric in front, to which he attached yards of dark blue chiffon. It was draped from between her breasts, around the diminutive bodice and attached to the back. It fell as a long, wispy train from the top of the back to perhaps four feet behind her.

"You see, *chérie*, when you wish to sit or are walking on the sidewalk, you simply reach behind"—he demonstrated by reaching behind his own legs—"and bring the chiffon forward or to the side." He saw her looking at herself in the mirror and read her eyes, or believed he did. "I knew you'd like it. I puzzled over the color, then Pierre decided one cannot go wrong by matching the eyes. You see, the silvery blue is the starburst in your eyes. The dark blue of the bodice and train is there, too." He clasped his hands together in front of his chest. "I'm so proud I could burst," he cried.

Stephanie was still trying to come to grips with the

décolletage. Pierre had folded the extra fabric within and pulled it downward so sharply before attaching the chiffon that her breasts, pushed in and upward by the whalebone, seemed about to fall out of the dress. The entire valley of her breasts was exposed, even the inner, forward curves. Only the outer sides and the aureolae were concealed.

"You have never seen such a gown, *chérie.*"

She looked at her bare arms, her bare shoulders, the sharp rise of her breasts beneath. She shook her head. "That is for certain."

He went to the door, summoned Glenna. She entered, leaning on her cane, then immediately gasped, covering her mouth with her free hand in the feminine gesture of surprise. "Oh, my dear, you are so lovely, so lovely." She repeated the word several times, then turned to the couturier. "I salute you, Monsieur Chambeau. Do you realize what you have wrought is so utterly, utterly feminine?"

"I do, of course, *madame.* It was my intention."

The doorbell rang, and Stephanie knew it was Thomas. She wanted only to run to him, but heard Glenna say Cora would get it. She took a last, doubtful glance in the mirror and prepared to leave.

"*Chérie,* I have made you a small cape to wear on the street." The designer handed it to her. "And a small purse." She took that, also.

For a moment Stephanie looked at her great-grandmother, seeing the love and admiration in her eyes. But the only opinion she really wanted was Thomas's. Finally she spoke. "GlennaMa, will you and Monsieur Chambeau stay here? I want to be alone with Thomas for a minute."

"Of course, dear."

She deliberately did not put on the cape, but carried it and the purse in one hand as she walked down the red-carpeted grand staircase. Thomas might as well see this now. As she descended, Stephanie felt the pressure of the satinet against her thighs and knew their outline

was visible. She felt the gentle tug of the train against
her back as it fell behind her. But she had eyes only for
Thomas, standing in the foyer, near the door, looking
up at her. As she negotiated the last step and walked
the black and white squares toward him, she felt his
eyes on her nakedness, the revealed outline of her
figure. Closer to him, she saw the delight and awe
registered in his eys.

"Stevie, you're breathtaking."

Her voice little above a whisper she said, "Yes?"

He smiled, his eyes all tenderness and love. "You do
me—no, you do yourself proud. I just can't believe I'm
so fortunate as to love—and be loved by—you."

He embraced her then, holding her close, his lips
unmindful of her makeup. She didn't care, surrendering to the sweet message of his mouth. But only for a
moment. Against his ear she said, "I've had a terrible
day, Tommy."

He misunderstood. "Yes. It's been a thousand years
long, and I've died a hundred times waiting to see
you."

She stood back from him, hands on his upper arms,
feeling encircled by him. She searched his face, taking
in every detail. "Do you love me, Tommy, really love
me?"

He hesitated, then grinned. Imitating an Irish
brogue, he said, "Naw, sure I dun' like ye a'tall."

She was smiling then, dazzlingly. If he had sworn he
loved her, she might not have believed him. But his
teasing her as he had when she was a child reassured
her, and relief coursed through her. Her visions of her
mother, the cynicism of Pierre Chambeau were behind
her. She knew only Thomas Hodges and their love. She
had come home to where she belonged.

Eight

An ocean away Danielle Summers sat at her vanity brushing her hair while she waited for James Lavelle to come to her. She wore a white peignoir. It was tied demurely at her throat, but in the mirror she could see the pink of her nipples through the sheer fabric. She smiled, at least inwardly, then saw her eyes, bright, luminously blue. Was that anticipation, knowing what was about to happen? Was she filled with lust? She tamped down the ugly thought. No, not lust, happiness, genuine happiness. She had had a good day, the best in a long time.

The letters, once she got to them, had been therapeutic. In describing Downview, Lord Wight's country estate, and his London house to her children and mother, she had herself become convinced, not just of their beauty, elegance and history, but of the promise this life held for her. She had not written it, of course, but she sensed she would make an excellent mistress of these properties. Raised in England, this was the life of luxury and privilege she was born for. Of this she was now certain. Rather than pen these immodest words, however, Danielle had extolled the virtues of James Lavelle, his importance in foreign affairs, his many charities, his kindnesses to her. To her mother, Moira, she had written, "He is a very loving man."

Distracted by the letters, buoyed by their content, Danielle changed into a more elegant afternoon gown and visited the neighborhood where she had lived from 1861 to 1870 with Glenna, Moira and her brother Morgan. As she rode through the streets to her destination, Danielle became aware that she was looking at the upper floors of buildings. She knew why. Walter Summers had drugged and abducted a shy girl in a daring gown, kept her a night and a day, introducing her to the ways of love which had both pleasured and tormented her ever since. He had taken her to a garret in a building, but which building? He had blindfolded her and she had not known where she was. In the years of their marriage she had never thought to ask him where he had taken her. Then she consciously kept her gaze at street level. In a moment she smiled. She had thought of Walter Summers, delved into memories she had tried to suppress for years—and they had no effect. She felt neither joy, anger nor regret. It was just a curiosity, something that had happened to her long ago. Her smile broadened. Yes, Danielle Summers was making progress.

She did not actually enter the house where she had lived, didn't need to, for her memories of it and her happy life there were most vivid. Sitting in the cab, then walking around the block where she had played as a girl, Danielle enjoyed a flood of memories. In sorrow she thought of Joe and Jessie, the longtime servants who had lived with them. Both were gone now, Joe first. Wasted by cancer, he had nonetheless fought death hard, determined to stay at the side of Glenna, whom he had rescued from the jungle and protected all his life. Inevitably Joe had lost the battle. Then Jessie, so corpulent, yet beautiful, so loving, yet so sharp of tongue, had died soon afterward. The family grief was boundless. Danielle had never seen her mother weep so much as when Jessie died. And Danielle thought of her mother then, red-haired, voluptuous, passionate. Moira Kingston had endured seven years of widowhood before finding Lawrence Hodges. Moira had the same flaming desires as her daughter, perhaps even more, yet she had the virtue and courage to deny herself in order to set an example for her children. Danielle shook her head. An example not followed by her daughter.

None of these thoughts marred her day, however. They were just there, faced, recognized, accepted as the way things were. Perhaps they might have led to melancholy, except that an old tea shoppe that the family frequented was still in existence. She entered. Mrs. Smith-Abbott was still the proprietress and remembered her. For the next two hours Danielle sat over tea telling all that had happened in twenty years, regaling a benevolent old woman with tales of the family. It had been so very good to have someone to talk to, and Danielle promised herself to return often.

In the late afternoon she returned to Lavelle's house, bathed and dressed for the royal reception. She donned a Pierre Chambeau gown she had saved for a special occasion. It was a shade of blue she often wore, for it deepened and magnified her eyes, and was fitted at the waist. The skirt, while narrow in front, had a draped or sculpted look, with a short train in back. The bodice, with small sleeves worn off the shoulder, displayed her fine skin. Danielle had long before restrained Pierre in his more notorious excesses of decolletage, yet this bodice left no doubt of her womanliness.

James Lavelle had been most open in his admiration for her, and together they had gone to the ball. When introduced to the Prince and Princess of Wales, Danielle had curtsied deeply and exchanged a few words in the reception line. How beautiful and gracious Princess Alexandra was, her red hair still brilliant, and how regal the Prince was, with his beard and heavy figure. Too bad he had had to wait so long for the throne he deserved. Neither Danielle nor the royal couple remembered they had met before—at the infamous masked ball from which Danielle was abducted by Walter Summers. She had been too young and nervous to remember anything.

"You are an American. What fortunate reason has brought you to grace our city?"

For the merest of moments she realized the thought had been in her mind all day, unrecognized, unarticulated. Then the words were on her lips. "Lord Wight and I are to be married, Sir."

"Oh, my dear!" the Princess said.

"My heartiest congratulations, Lord James," the Prince offered.

She heard Lavelle enter the room, then saw him in the mirror, wearing a maroon robe. He stood behind her, hands on her shoulders, a serious expression on his face.

"Did you mean that?"

She met his reflected gaze openly, equally serious. "Yes."

"There is still time to change your mind without too much difficulty."

She looked at his image for a long moment, then said, her voice very soft, "I do want to marry you, James. I really am not an impulsive person."

And he looked at her, nodding slowly. "I love you, Danny. You have made me happier than I ever thought possible."

"I love you, too."

Suddenly he was grinning. "Did you really plan to announce it to the Prince?"

Images of the furor she had caused raced across her mind. She had almost broken up the receiving line as all came to congratulate her and James, even the Russian Crown Prince and Princess, who didn't know them at all. She laughed. "Hardly. But he asked me what I was doing in London. Suddenly I knew that's what I was doing here."

She was still smiling as she saw him bend, felt his lips at her cheek, ear, throat, hot, passionate. "The Prince has long had a roving eye. How he must envy me."

His hands found her breasts, cupping them through the fabric. She raised her hands beneath his arms and untied the peignoir, giving him access to her skin, pulling back the garment, letting it fall from her shoulders.

"You are so exquisite, Danny." His voice had a throaty sound. "You make me feel like a young man."

She watched his hands at her breasts, then closed her eyes at the sharp rise of familiar sensations. Such nice hands, strong, smooth, such a comfort. In a moment she felt the upward pressure and rose in accordance, stepping around the bench to face him. She saw desire in his eyes and smiled at it, aware of her own. Slowly she untied his robe and stepped within it, relishing the smooth warmth of skin against skin.

His arms were around her and he was looking at her with the eyes of love. "While I can still think, there is something I want to say."

"Yes?"

"I know Stephanie and Andrew are almost grown, but I will be a good father to them."

"I know. And I will be a good mother to your children."

He nodded slowly, a characteristic gesture. "Yes. They need you." His lips were descending toward her. "As I do."

For Stephanie the evening went beautifully. There had been forty, perhaps as many as fifty people at the Crosby Whitaker mansion. New York's finest were there. She had not known, but recognized the names of Astor, Vanderbilt, Belmont, Morgan. They were mostly an older crowd, but there were enough young people to keep Stephanie from feeling out of place. Actually

the evening was stuffy, the bilious soprano rather
screechy, the conversation at the sit-down dinner,
however grand and formal the service, considerably
over her head. But she did enjoy herself, basking in
Thomas's love and the attention she received, especially from men. And fortunately she was not called upon
to do more than smile, nod and be agreeable. The only
threatening moment came when the women retired to
leave the men to their cigars and brandy. Separated
from Thomas, Stephanie became apprehensive. But
when the ladies discovered she was the great-
granddaughter of Glenna Morgan Fairchild, they became very cordial and accepted her. Her gown drew
raves, and in answer to questions, she told them what
Pierre Chambeau was really like. She tried to be kind.

In their carriage leaving the party, Thomas had said,
"Are you tired? Do you want me to take you home?"

She had answered in the darkness, her voice husky,
"No. I want to be with you."

Now they stood in the library of the house Winslow
Kincaid owned in New York, sipping champagne.
Stephanie's heart was filled with love for Thomas
Hodges. His maturity, knowledge and love had made
this evening possible. Without Thomas at her side,
supporting her, guiding her subtly in what to say and
do, this whole evening could have been a disaster. How
fortunate she was to be loved by him.

She saw it in his eyes as he said, "I'm so proud of
you, Stevie, and that gown."

She smiled. "It's just a dress, Thomas. You should be
proud of Pierre Chambeau. He made it."

"He wasn't wearing it. Lord, Stevie, how you look,
what a figure you have! You dazzled everyone."

Again she smiled. "I only wanted to dazzle you."

"And you did—you do." He kissed her then, holding
his champagne away, pulling her to him, his mouth
hungry on hers. But only briefly. "You don't know
what you did tonight, do you?"

She saw him stand back, delight and pride in his eyes. "Should I?"

"I came to New York to try to negotiate a large loan, fifty million dollars, from a consortium of banks headed by Crosby Whitaker. I had written the prospectus for the loan in Chicago. Mr. Kincaid was impressed with it and, really on impulse, I think, decided to let me come here and see if I could pull it off. I honestly didn't think I could. The lawyers, Whitaker, the others on Wall Street, liked the prospectus, but I could tell they felt me too young. Kincaid himself should have come. I couldn't speak for him, however much I claimed to."

He raised his glass, swallowed. Stephanie waited expectantly.

"At that party tonight I suddenly realized I was on trial. And I also knew Whitaker was terribly impressed with you, Stevie. He couldn't take his eyes off you, and when he asked you to sit on his right, I was worried." He laughed. "Even jealous."

"You needn't have been."

"I know. You were fantastic. You charmed him to death. He kept watching you and the reactions of others to you. I just sat back and watched you weave your magic."

She opened her mouth to speak, but was silenced by his hand.

"You were the main topic of conversation over cigars and brandy. Everyone wanted to know who you were and where I found you. When I told them, there was a lot of talk about your mother, my mother, Grandmother Glenna. Someone said I'd better not let you get away. I said I was going to marry you soon." He saw her smile, try to speak, but again he stopped her. "Let me finish. After the cigars Whitaker took me into his study with some of the others. They had decided to grant the loan. No sense in keeping me in suspense till Monday, they said. Oh, Stevie, I know it was because of you."

"You're not serious!"

"I am. Oh, I know, the prospectus was good, Mr. Kincaid wealthy and powerful, but when they saw you, me with you, found out we are to marry, I—oh, I don't know. I think they decided I'm a very smart man, very lucky to have a woman like you, a man who is going places." He laughed. "A man to loan fifty million dollars to."

She laughed with delight. "I don't believe a word of it, but I'm so happy for you."

"Yes, Stevie, yes. When I go back to Chicago and tell Mr. Kincaid—God, Stevie, will my stock soar. I'll be on top of the heap!"

She had no chance to exclaim, for again he swept his free arm around her, pulling her body against his, probing her mouth. But then he drew back, frowning. "There's one problem. The job was done too quickly. I'll have to leave Monday, as soon as the papers are signed."

His words stabbed at her, but she managed a smile. "Then we'd better not waste a minute of this weekend."

Again he kissed her, longer, deeper, thrilling her. She leaned against him, feeling his manhood hard against her thigh, relishing what it foretold.

In a few moments he stood back and got rid of the encumbrances of their glasses. He was about to sweep her into his arms when he stopped, looking at her, all of her, running his hands over her shoulders, arms. "I want you so much, Stevie, I ache for you. But you're so gorgeous in that dress, I can't bear to see you out of it."

She smiled. "I'm disappointed in you, Tommy. All evening you never asked the obvious question—how does it stay up?"

"Well, how does it?"

She touched her sides. "There are stays built in. It's like a corset, very tight." She smiled. "If the choice is mine, I'm tired of wearing it."

Up in the bedroom it was not at all like the first time.

There were impassioned kisses, but not nearly so many, for they were not needed. Gone was the sense of discovery, replaced by certain knowledge and expectation. She instructed him how to unfasten the dress, for it was complicated, and he helped her out of it. Carefully she laid it on a chair—no heap on the floor this time. She let him observe and pull down her new, seamless pantaloons, then saw, heard his admiration for her. But this, too, was different. She now knew she had an extraordinary body and was certain of its uses. As he had before and she wanted him to do again, he dropped to his knees, enveloping her hips and derriere, fingers at her woman's place, mouth devouring her nipples. Again she felt the storm of sensation, her own onrush of passion, quivering under it. But this time she reached down, touched his hands, stilling them. With more air than sound, she said, "You have too many clothes on, Tommy."

A moment longer he held her breasts, pressing them together, sweeping his mouth rapidly from side to side, making passion ravenous within her. Then he stood up and removed his coat, vest, tie, studs.

"God, how I love you, Stevie. You're so magnificent."

She saw his adoration, reveled in it, but smiled. "You will be, too, if you ever get that shirt off."

He did, and she stepped into his arms, loving the feel of his bare chest against her breasts, his hands in her hair, stroking her back. And the touch of skin against skin seemed to enhance the passion of the long kiss they shared.

But she was impatient. She stepped back, running her hands across his chest. "You have such a nice body, Tommy, so smooth, such beautiful shoulders." Then she reached his belt, began to undo it, slide his trousers from him. His shoes were an encumbrance, but he leaned on her shoulders as she bent, removed them, his stockings, the unwanted trousers. He stood there in his underdrawers, the fabric strained in front of him.

He laughed nervously. "I don't know why, but this is embarrassing."

"I don't know why, either. I'm not embarrassed when you undress me." She unbuttoned the remaining garment, slid it from him. He tried to pull her to him, but she stepped back, saying huskily, "I want to see you."

"You already have."

She smiled. "Not really. I was too busy."

She looked at him boldly then, marveling at his manhood, which had so recently filled her, thrilled her. She raised her gaze to meet his, saw his eyes sparkling with emotion. "I think you're beautiful, Tommy." Then, because he had done it to her, she dropped to her knees before him, took his maleness in her hands and held it against her cheek, wondering at its throbbing heat. It felt almost as though it had a life of its own. She began kissing the length of it.

"Oh, God, Stevie."

She felt him trying to pull her up, but she stopped him. "I want to know the man I love." Above her she heard shortened breath, gasps. Soon she heard him moan, felt him shake, and knew she was pleasing him, as he had pleased her.

She leaned her head back and looked up at his face. His eyes were closed and his expression rapturous. Regaining his composure, Thomas glanced down at her, love in his eyes. In one movement he pulled her to her feet, swept her into his arms and floated her to the bed.

Nine

The next morning, Stephanie lay in bed, waiting for Thomas to return. He had gotten up, saying he was starved, put on his trousers and robe and gone downstairs to order breakfast.

Under the sheet she stretched, sighed and, without willing it, smiled. She was so tired, her body languid from a night of love, yet she felt so wonderful, so contented. Yes, a night of love. Oh, they had slept, but in each other's arms. So wonderful. So delectable.

She remembered all. He had placed her on the bed, then stood a moment, looking down at her. "Why did you do that?"

"I don't know. I wanted to. Didn't you like it?"

"You know I did."

"Wasn't it right to do it?"

He smiled. "Yes, but only if you want to."

She smiled, filled with desire. "I do, Tommy. I want to know all about you. I want to thrill you as you do me."

It seemed to her then that she was inundated in

intimacy. Their mouths found each other's secret places, they embraced within one another's legs, offering to each other exquisite private pleasures conveyed by gasps and moans and uncontrollable trembling. At first she had tried to concentrate on him, the explorations of her lips and tongue, the sounds of sensation she produced in him. Then she could not, for she was devastated by the electric, rhythmic movements of his mouth on her most sensitive places. As the now-familiar ache spread down her thighs, she was only dimly aware she was stroking his back, running her hands over him, faster, faster, frenzied, frantic. She wanted to keep on delighting him, but couldn't, as her own throbbing mounted. Then she couldn't move. Her mouth came open and she cried out as ecstasy reverberated through her. As her mind became clear again, she realized he had moved. They had been on their sides. Now he was atop her, his arms spreading her legs, embracing them, and she was opened wide to receive the wondrous laving of his lips and tongue. Again she found him and was filled, but she hardly had time to know his pleasure before her own response—deeper, longer, really a continuation of her former orgasm—swept through her. Then he was above her, on his knees between her legs, looking down. "Oh, Stevie, Stevie, I love you so." And she knew the blessed stretching, the precious fullness. There were repeated internal detonations of thunderous pleasure for her then, and between each one she was moved, shown a wondrous new way: on her side facing him, all hands and enveloping arms; above him, his hands on her breasts magnifying her pleasure; on her hands and knees, he curled over her, one hand at her dipping breasts, the other binding her writhing hips to the cause of her pleasure. There were other positions, many of them, and all seemed to work. She was aware of his growing urgency, as he cried out and knew shuddering release, and thought it would end. But the fullness returned, and with it the continuation of her ecstasy.

Through it all, amid the chaos of her mind, the weariness of her body, she was aware of what was happening to her. The very depths of her inmost being were plumbed. She was being peeled away, stripped to the very essense of herself, and for that loved and loved and loved. What was happening to her passed beyond sensation to something elemental, transcending pleasure to create an ultimate joining. She was being welded to him mind and body.

She lay there in the morning light, smiling from memories. She had awakened in the middle of the night, on her side, back curled against him, snuggling within his arms, his hands enveloping her breasts. So delicious. And it had come from so far away, so slowly, shattering sleep until she turned within his arms to kiss him. Again this morning. She had come atop him, for she liked this position best, able to control her movements, see the desire and love in his eyes, speak of the wonder of it all, feel her breasts overflowing his hands.

He entered the room and stood over her, smiling. "Good morning, sleepyhead."

"Not me. Sleep is hard to find around you." She smiled and reached out her hand, taking his. "Oh, Tommy, did we really do all that?"

"I do believe we did." He sat beside her and bent to kiss her lightly. Then he folded down the sheet to see her breasts, now rounded hillocks, falling to the side. "Strawberries in a field of snow," he said, bending again, kissing once, twice. "I love you, Stephanie Summers, soon to be Stephanie Hodges."

She was thrilled by his actions, words, the love in his eyes. "Yes, I want to be."

"Do you know what you are? Unbelievable. How can you do it so often?"

She smiled. "You have an awful lot to do with that."

Again he kissed her lightly. "I held off as long as I could, wanting to find if there is an end to you. I never found it." He kissed her then, tenderly, more open and deeper. Then he stood up. "Breakfast will be coming soon. We've got to do something about making you decent."

When the butler, Combs, wheeled in the laden table, she was enveloped in Thomas's robe, he dressed in shirt and trousers. A gray-haired Negro, Combs merely acknowledged the introduction. To her gratitude he seemed thoroughly unimpressed to find a young woman had spent the night with young Mr. Hodges.

Stephanie and Thomas were both starved, and ate the eggs and sausage and rolls with gusto, mostly in silence. She realized how very much she felt like a bride on her honeymoon. Then her eye was caught by her gown, resting on the chair. "We have a problem, Thomas. I've nothing to wear but that dress, and I can hardly wear it on the street on a Saturday afternoon." She thought a moment. "I know. I'll write a note to GlennaMa, asking her to send some things in a bag. One of the servants will deliver it, I'm sure."

He looked at her sharply. "I should have taken you home, Stevie. How will I ever explain to Grandmother Glenna?"

"She knows I'm with you. She hasn't worried."

"But what'll I tell her . . . about us, what we did?"

Stephanie grinned. "She already knows."

"You *told* her?"

She saw his aghast expression and laughed. "Glenna-Ma has lived so long and done so many things, she can read minds. Nothing surprises her. Just say nothing and act natural." She patted his hand. "Everything will be all right, believe me."

"But what will she *think?*"

"She'll think I'm a lucky girl. See how smart she is?"

The note was sent, the suitcase of clothes returned. There began for Stephanie a weekend to be remembered, all freshness and innovation, cast in the innocence of unique and rapturous happiness. Winslow Kincaid's New York house also had modern plumbing, and they took a bath together, lathering each other; then, unable to deny themselves or want to, slipping and sliding as they made love among the bubbles. They dried each other, relishing the opportunities for exploration. When he powdered her, she exulted in her femininity, absorbing the marvel in his eyes, his words of admiration. She had never felt more beautiful. Shyness at her nakedness never entered her mind as he brushed her hair, stopping frequently to fondle and caress her.

"I warned you I won't be able to keep my hands off you."

She reached behind her back to clasp him. "You're not the only one."

Having him dress her—helping him—was nearly as much fun as the disrobing the evening before, so romantically intimate. Together they went out, she in a blouse, skirt and summer straw hat, he in a striped blazer and boater, to walk in the park, laughing, talking, feeding the birds, licking ice cream cones while strolling hand in hand. She saw people staring at them, smiles on their faces. And why not? She was in love, radiant with happiness.

She insisted they visit Glenna, laughing at his objections. "What are you going to do, hide the rest of your life?"

"No."

"And I thought we weren't going to have any shame or guilt."

That convinced him, but when he greeted the smiling Glenna, he blurted, "I love her, grandmother."

"Of course you do, Thomas." Glenna smiled at Stephanie. "How could you not?"

It was not enough for him. "We're going to be married as soon as we can. I have to go to Chicago. I'm going to finish up what I have to do, find a house for us, then take my vacation. I should be back within two weeks. We'll be married then."

Glenna managed to put her arms around them both. "I'm so happy for the two of you."

After tea with Glenna they returned to Thomas's

place, made love, lying in each other's arms afterward talking of themselves, making plans for the wedding, their life together. Then they dressed for the evening, Stephanie in her shocking sleeveless Pierre Chambeau gown. She sensed Thomas wanted to show her off and she obliged, making sophisticated, eye-stopping entrances in Delmonico's, the Hoffman House, Henry Hill's, other posh places. She arrived back at Thomas's bedroom utterly exhausted.

"Are you too tired, Stevie?"

"Yes." She smiled. "But in my whole life I will never refuse you or fail to respond to you."

"Promise?"

"Try me."

She fulfilled her promise but, after a single, shattering climax, fell deeply asleep in his arms.

The next morning they took Glenna to mass, then to lunch at a quiet restaurant in the neighborhood, Thomas expounding garrulously on the joys of life in Chicago to a strawberry blonde with shell-like ears. After taking Glenna home, they rode up to Central Park for a promenade, band concert and a leisurely, wine-filled supper in a garden restaurant. They returned to Thomas's place, two tireless, seemingly insatiable young people squirreling away love for what both knew would be two weeks of discontent. When, on Monday morning, Thomas returned her to Glenna's before heading for Wall Street, Stephanie Summers knew she had experienced to fullest measure the meaning of happiness.

She was determined not to pine for Thomas while he was gone, but to use the time to prepare for her wedding and married life. She filled her time writing endless, marathon letters to Thomas and shopping for her trousseau. There were long, daily fittings with Pierre Chambeau. He was preparing her a magnificent wardrobe. The couturier believed with all his heart that Chicago was inhabited by Huns and Visigoths, but if that was where Stephanie was determined to go, he would set the barbarians on their collective ear. He truly did invent a new fashion for her. In his daytime dresses particularly, he designed a long line, with narrow skirt, fitted to the torso and accentuating her tiny waist. "The corset-makers will love me," he said, "and the surgeons will grow rich treating ruptured spleens and livers as women cinch themselves in trying to imitate you, *chérie.*" The illusion of height and slimness was enhanced by exaggerated pads, elevating the sleeves, sometimes two or three inches above the shoulders. The evening gowns he made for her also accentuated her petiteness, while perpetuating his reputation for exotic display of the female bosom. Stephanie was delighted. Thomas would love them.

But try as she would, Stephanie could not keep from missing her fiancé. Increasingly, memories of Thomas, their lovemaking, intruded on her mind. She felt a strange heat often, almost an incipient irritability. She knew what it was. She wanted him already, needed him. Was it to be this way all her life? She smiled inwardly. She would just have to find a way to keep him close to her.

She and Glenna were in the parlor, Stephanie at the desk, writing a guest list. She had already decided to be married in New York and have the family come up from Washington and Maryland.

"It'll be like a family reunion, Stevie—such fun."

Stephanie pursed her lips. "Not quite, GlennaMa. Mother won't be here, and I so wish she could be."

"I know, dear. She'd want to be here right now, sharing all this with you."

Stephanie's frown deepened. "Could I—could I cable her or something, tell her about Thomas, the wedding, how happy I am?"

"Of course. It's a splendid idea. Why don't you do it right now?"

Quickly Stephanie procured a new piece of paper and began to draft the cable. But the words wouldn't come. She had filled pages to Thomas, but all of a sudden she couldn't think of what to say to her own mother.

"What's wrong, dear?"

"I don't know. I can't seem to find the right words."

"Certainly you can. Just say you and Thomas love each other, plan to marry June twenty-third and then live in Chicago."

She tried that, but again set down the pen in frustration. It was too abrupt, just a setting down of facts without feeling. Then she turned to her oldest relative. "GlennaMa, were you this happy when you married great-grandfather?"

"Daniel? Oh, yes, indeed so." Glenna smiled. "I know, dear, you feel so special in your happiness, and you should. But, believe me, every bride knows the feeling. A pity if she does not."

"And you and great-grandfather had . . . before—?"

"Yes. It doesn't matter. There really can be no love without physical attraction." She laughed. "At least no love worth having."

"And grandmother? Did she and Grandfather Kingston . . . ?"

Glenna remembered a moment. "As a matter of fact, no. Ned knew of her affair with his brother. He felt, and quite correctly, the way to win Moira was to let her come to love him first. He was so right in that."

"And mother? Oh, yes, you told me that story—the pirate, the garret—" Stephanie sat pensively a moment, staring at the blank page. "Was mother happy when she finally married father?"

"Excessively, just like you."

Stephanie turned her head, staring at Glenna, awareness seeming to bolt into her mind. "But they didn't stay married. What happened?"

"Surely you know, Stevie."

"I know something—or is it nothing? I'm no longer a child. You said mother was like me—or I'm like her. We have the same . . . desires, the same. . . ."

"I remember our talk."

"Then how could she leave father, if she loved him so? I'm dying now to have Thomas's arms around me, hold me, and it's only been three days. How could mother bear it?"

"It has been difficult for her, Stevie. I can only hope she is finding happiness with her Englishman. He seems right for her."

Stephanie persisted. "Why did she leave father?"

Glenna sighed. "I believe it's called irreconcilable differences."

Agitated now, Stephanie said, "Oh, please, Glenna-Ma, talk so I can understand."

"Walter Summers, your father, was a southerner, a Confederate officer in the late war. He was a good man. He loved your mother extremely. But he bore within himself his upbringing, the southern attitudes toward the war, the former slaves. When he and Danielle were married and went to live at Seasons, his prejudices surfaced. Danielle could not bear them. She possesses no racial hatred. How could she? Joe and Jessie practically raised her. The Morgans were always abolitionists. And your mother grew up in England, where there is little prejudice." Glenna sighed, finding this narrative most unpleasant. "When your mother discovered your father was a nightrider, shooting and lynching colored people—oh, I doubt if he ever actually killed anyone, but he was there—" Glenna gave a deeper sigh, "Danielle left him. They have never been able to patch it up."

Stephanie thought about it a long moment, visualizing her mother, her father. Another time Stephanie would have been greatly disturbed to learn this about her father's nightriding activities. But now her thoughts lay elsewhere. "She didn't know this about father before she married him?"

"His racial hatred?" She saw the girl nod. "No. How could she? It never came up till they moved to South Carolina."

Stephanie stared at Glenna wide-eyed, shocked at her own thoughts. She rose from the desk and walked across the room, looking out a window, her back to Glenna. "Isn't there an expression, something about marrying in haste?"

"Yes. Marry in haste, repent at leisure."

A moment longer Stephanie stared out the window, seeing nothing, her mind turned inward. "I'm not going to marry Thomas yet, GlennaMa." There was conviction in her voice.

"You can't be serious, Stephanie. You love Thomas, he adores you."

"I know. All that is true. But so was it for mother and father."

"What are you saying, child?"

Stephanie turned to face Glenna. "I love Thomas, I know I do. But I've got to be absolutely sure. I'm going to Chicago and live with him. When I am sure of him, myself, our love and happiness, then we will marry. I will not repeat mother's mistake."

Part II

Chicago

Ten

Winslow Kincaid was in an expansive mood. And why not? He had just completed a business coup that would soon rank him with Rockefeller, Carnegie, Armour, Vanderbilt, Morgan and Gould as a leading captain of industry. He would have the wealth of Midas and power undreamed of by Alexander, Caesar or Napoleon.

He was sitting now behind his immense polished desk in his twelfth-floor office atop the American Western Building on Michigan Avenue, conducting his regular Friday afternoon meeting with his managers. As usual the meeting had an aura of informality, with the dozen or so men lounging on the sofa, seated around the small conference table in the corner or in chairs brought in for the occasion. But the informality was an illusion. Grown men had been known to shake in terror before these meetings, for Winslow Kincaid demanded hard figures, and would brook no excuse for failure. Nor did he hesitate to find the roots of a man's failure in his character and antecedents. Personal ridicule was a weapon Kincaid used like a rapier.

He engaged in none of this today, much to the relief of those assembled. Indeed, he wasn't even listening to the reports, although none of those present realized it. In his expansiveness, he had passed out cigars and told his men to help themselves to his brandy. Perhaps the liquor, as much as his exaltation in triumph, contributed to his woolgathering.

He could remember the exact moment when the conception had come to him. He had been walking over the viaduct leading to the main West Side locomotive works when he suddenly stopped and looked down at the tracks. It was a blustery day, he remembered, and he was cold. Yet he stood there shivering, looking at nothing really, just ribbons of steel, a few boxcars on a siding. The men accompanying him also stopped, looking dutifully where he looked, seeing nothing either.

The idea had come full blown to Winslow Kincaid at that moment, and he at once recognized it as a conception of genius because of its simplicity. What good were all those shining rails if there was nothing to run on them? If he could control all the rolling stock, the tens and tens of thousands of boxcars, ore carriers, coal hoppers and tank cars, he could control the nation. No kernel of grain, no head of cattle, no lump of coal, no manufactured product would move over those parallel silver ribbons except on the terms he dictated.

He did not inspect the West Side works that day, but wheeled, returned to his office and at once began to put his plan into operation. He had not started from strength. He had inherited from his father, John Kincaid—a two-fisted Irishman if there ever was one—a small foundry manufacturing axles and wheels for railroad cars. In twenty years of unrelenting risk-taking, Winslow Kincaid had expanded that plant and acquired others, cutting prices to a near-ruinous level, until he was a significant manufacturer of rolling stock and a moderately rich man. If he didn't dominate the industry, he at least had a reputation as a hardnosed, resourceful man who knew how to make money.

This reputation he proceeded to use that blustery day. Within six months he had formed the Railway Car Trust, convincing other manufacturers it was self-defeating and ridiculous to continue their cut-throat competition. The combination was made effortlessly, the individual corporations exchanging their stock for shares in the Trust. Heads of the member corporations became Trustees, deciding industry-wide policies on manufacturing, pricing and so forth. Winslow Kincaid had no difficulty getting himself elected chairman of the Trustees. It was a bad day for the manufacturers who did not join the Trust. They were forced into either joining the Trust or going into bankruptcy, until a railway wanting to purchase a piece of rolling stock had no choice but to acquire it from the Trust at whatever prices it set.

But why purchase a boxcar or coal hopper? The answer to that question formed the second and crucial part of Kincaid's plan. He said to the operating railroads: "Why *buy* rolling stock? Why invest so much money in ownership and repair? Why not simply lease the cars from the Trust, which will assume full responsibility for maintenance and repair?" To back up his logic Kincaid offered to buy back all the existing rolling stock—surely the operating lines could use the capital.

This very week, following a round of negotiations, the Southern Pacific, Union Pacific and other major western lines had agreed to his proposal. This fueled Kincaid's expansive mood. With the major lines in the fold, the lesser westerns would soon follow. Then he would attack the New York Central, Pennsylvania, Baltimore & Ohio and other eastern lines. Within a year he would own and control every railway car in the United States, save for George Pullman and his passenger cars. And it wouldn't surprise him if Pullman made an overture to join the Trust one of these days.

"The men are talking strike, sir, not just on the West Side, but in Joliet and St. Louis, too. The layoffs, Mr.

Kincaid, and now the ten percent cut in wages, have the men worried. They're listening to hotheads, getting belligerent."

Kincaid looked at Rawlings, manager of the main plant, whose words were intruding on his reverie. Here was the crux of his whole scheme. The western railroads had bought the leasing arrangement because the terms were favorable, ridiculously favorable from Kincaid's standpoint. American Western and the Trust would be ruined if these prices continued. But they wouldn't. By curtailing production, "accidents" and other events, Kincaid planned to create an artificial shortage of rolling stock. Then the rail lines would pay *any* price to get a railway car.

He glared at Rawlings. "Hotheads, you say. You mean anarchists. I didn't become head of this company to let a bunch of socialist terrorists tell me how to run it." He turned sharply to his right. "Hodges, you had better have injunction papers prepared, just in case. If they want to strike, we'll show 'em a thing or two."

"Yes, sir."

Kincaid leaned back in his swivel chair, hands clasped behind his head, his expansiveness coming to the forefront. "Gentlemen, this has been a banner week for our company, the beginning of a bright new future for us all. You have all worked very hard, and I want to thank you for it. I'm proud of you." He saw the smiles of appreciation. "Tonight we play a little—and we've earned it. I expect to see you all at the Palmer House. We'll send those railroad officials home with the knowledge they are dealing with first-class people."

He listened to the hubbub of voices and watched the men begin to file out. "Hodges, if you will wait a minute."

Thomas turned and came to stand before the immense desk. "Yes, sir?"

Kincaid smiled up at him. "You look tired."

Thomas was bone weary. "I am, a little, Mr. Kincaid —but exhilarated."

"And well you might be. The money you brought from New York made all this possible, you know." It wasn't true, of course, but the fifty million had helped.

"Thank you, sir."

Kincaid rose from his chair and walked over to a cabinet on which a tray of liquor bottles rested. He replenished his own glass and poured a little into Thomas's. "This will perk you up."

"Thank you, sir."

The motions of a toast were made. "You will have the energy to come tonight?"

"Of course, sir."

"And you're bringing that little lady of yours?"

Thomas smiled. "Yes, she's looking forward to it."

"Good."

The mere thought of Hodges's "doxy," as Kincaid thought of her, roiled his loins. This week of wheeling and dealing had left him greatly stimulated, and he needed a woman badly. Ever since he'd laid eyes on the little strawberry blonde, Winslow Kincaid had wanted her. Lord, such a body! Much too good for this lovestruck young swain. She belonged with a man of experience. And he would have her. At fifty-five his hair might have turned iron-gray, but he still had his vigor. She might think him a trifle short and heavy now, but when he got her into bed, she'd find out what a good man was—and what real money would buy.

"Yes, a fine-looking woman, Thomas. I understand she's creating quite the sensation here in Chicago."

Thomas smiled. "I suppose so, sir."

"Good. Tell her to keep it up. Helps the company image." He laughed. "Matter of fact, I'll tell her so myself when I see her tonight." He set his glass down, a gesture of dismissal. Thomas followed suit, said his goodbyes and left the office. Kincaid looked at the young man's retreating back. He would have to send Thomas Hodges off on a business trip, and soon.

* * *

Stephanie surveyed the results in the mirror with approval. This was a special gown, a favorite since the first fitting with Pierre Chambeau. She had saved it for a special occasion. The ball this night at the Palmer House surely qualified as one. She turned, looking over her shoulder at the back. Her wardrobe had created a furor in Chicago. She had even been interviewed by a reporter for the society pages of the *Tribune*. This gown would hardly damage her reputation.

Pierre Chambeau had outdone himself. He had finally found the "perfect" color for her, satin of an old gold color, burnished with a hint of red, almost metallic. In this light her hair seemed to match the gown. Throwing fashion to the winds, Chambeau had designed a gown that he knew would become one of his celebrated "classics." The skirt was extremely narrow, enveloping Stephanie's hips and legs, but gathered in back to create a generous train and the illusion of fullness. It fit like a second skin over her torso, hugging and accentuating her tiny waist. There was no back at all to the gown, just narrow, ruffled straps at the shoulders. Not long before, Stephanie would have considered the décolletage of the bodice disreputable, but now it enthralled her. Using his new technique of built-in stays, Chambeau had thrust her breasts up and together, leaving them all but exposed. Stephanie smiled in approval. Thomas would like it—and the sensation she would create.

She knew she was dressed ridiculously early, but when Thomas came home, she wanted to spend time with him, fuss over him, not have to closet herself in the bedroom to do her toilet. Besides, and she smiled at the thought, Tommy liked having her dressed provocatively when he came home from work. In her brief "marriage" she had learned that.

Stephanie had worried through every clack of the rails from New York to Chicago. She knew her decision to live with Thomas was hastily made. But she hadn't wanted to think about it. Impulsively she ran from the house and wired Thomas that she was coming. The very next day she was on the train for Chicago.

But as the dreary miles sped by the windows of her Pullman Palace Car, she was consumed with misgivings. What would people think of her? What would her mother say when she found out? And Grandmother Moira? Stephanie had already seen the hurt, the doubt in GlennaMa's eyes. She had said nothing, but Stephanie knew what she was thinking. Glenna simply was in no position to scold her. Nor were her grandmother or mother. All three had lived out of wedlock with men. They lived in glass houses and couldn't throw stones. Stephanie was doing nothing they hadn't done. Indeed, she was better than her own mother. She loved Thomas and he loved her. It was a far cry from that wicked Garth her mother had given herself to. Or even her latest English Duke, for that matter.

Again and again Stephanie told herself she was not going to feel guilty about anything she and Thomas had done or would do. Their love was beautiful, not tawdry or wicked. *Then why don't you marry him?* Try as she would, she could not quite still this inner voice. Her answer was always the same. *I will not marry in haste and repeat mother's mistakes. It isn't fair to myself, Thomas or children we may have. It is better to be sure first.* The answer, oft repeated, reassured her— almost.

Less easily put aside was her knowledge of sin. There could be no escaping it, and she spent much of her time on the train with her hands inserted in her purse, secretly saying her rosary. She begged forgiveness of the Virgin, whispering the *Memorare* over and over. And she promised to go to mass regularly. She would marry Thomas soon, not delaying a moment longer than necessary. And on the day of her marriage she would go to Confession and thereafter make amends her whole life.

Her biggest worry, however, had been Thomas. In

her telegram telling him of her arrival, she had conveyed the idea she couldn't be apart from him, which was true, of course. But how would she explain her real reason without making it appear she distrusted him or believed there was some flaw in his character? A score of times she had rehearsed what to say. Then, when she was in his arms, it came so naturally. Yes, he understood. They had no need to be hasty. And he was family, after all. He knew of Danielle's unhappiness and could understand Stephanie's fear of repeating her mother's mistake.

"I'm not testing you, Tommy. You do believe that, don't you?"

He smiled. "Did it ever occur to you that I might be testing you? I've worried you might turn into a termagant."

And she had laughed. "I promise not to do that." And she had hugged him as proof.

He had grown serious then. "There is one problem, Stevie. Chicago is a big city, but people are bound to find out about us. Lots of eyebrows will be raised. It won't bother me, but I don't want you—"

"I know. I've thought about it." She smiled. "Mother, grandmother, GlennaMa—especially her—were all talked about—still are. Lots of people were scandalized by them. I guess it's my turn now."

"Are you sure?"

Her smile had been dazzling. "Yes, I'm sure. It won't bother me—at least not very much. The women in this family have always thrived on shocking certain people. I guess the heritage has passed to me."

Yet she still had lingering doubts that their "living in sin" bothered Thomas. She knew it did her. More than once she wished they were married and could shed this stigma over their relationship. But she was determined to give the arrangement at least two months. They were halfway there.

She was blissfully happy. They both were. They had

moved into a French flat, as Chicagoans called it, on the eighth floor of a new building on Lake Shore Drive. The view of Lake Michigan and Lincoln Park was breathtaking, and Stephanie had thrown herself into decorating the apartment and settling down to domestic bliss. By her choice they had no servants. She didn't want intruders. She wanted Thomas all to herself. So she cleaned, sent out the laundry and was beginning to learn to cook. Mercifully they ate out a lot. There were times when she would have liked a personal maid, but the intimacy of Thomas brushing her hair, helping her into and out of her gowns far exceeded the ministrations of any maid. Besides, with no servants both felt free to roam the apartment naked. More than once she had greeted him that way when he came home from work.

Their lovemaking remained at white heat. She felt as though she were an instrument, quivering with the music he made. When they were together, they were in a nearly constant state of arousal, and even when he was at work her mind was mostly on him, eager for his return. She believed their physical intimacy to be the truest thing she had ever known in her life. When they shed their clothing, they also shed all sham and shame, all pretense and deception. He loved her, delighted endlessly in her body, wanted her. She loved him and found both delight and complete fulfillment in him. Each did to the other whatever they wanted when they wanted, never seeking permission or doubting approval. Repeatedly he had plumbed her innermost depths. She understood his fascination with her capacities, his determination to explore her limits. On two separate weekends he had taken her on a voyage of discovery, but neither one had reached their journey's end; they had merely passed into the unknown. Even this week, when he worked such long hours and was so tired, Thomas still found energy to make love to her even as he was falling asleep. Thomas Hodges was making her into a wholly sensuous woman. Of that Stephanie was certain. With equal certainty she knew she loved the transformation.

Part of her happiness lay in the fact that she liked Chicago, much to her surprise. It was now second in size to New York, and in many ways superior. With much of it destroyed in the fire of 1871, Chicago had been rebuilt as a more modern city. Oh, it still had fetid slums, where immigrants and the poor were overcrowded into shacks and ramshackle wooden buildings. And the odors from the stockyards, soap factories, packing plants and the Chicago River deservedly earned it the reputation as the "smelly city." But at its best Chicago was an inspiration. Michigan and Wabash Avenues were lined with fine buildings, architecturally impressive and thoroughly modern. Many were of twelve and fifteen stories, and Chicago surely had more elevators in service than New York. After the fire new utilities were laid. Most downtown office and apartment buildings, including theirs, had modern plumbing, gas and electricity, even telephone service.

She was also surprised at the elegance of the city. The homes on Prairie Avenue—one even had three taps, hot water, cold water and champagne—were as pretentious as any in the East. She had not yet seen them, but she understood the suburban homes on the South and West sides, linked by commuter railroads charging a nickel, were equally grand. The Palmer House and the Grand Pacific were the equal of any hotels in New York, and the soon-to-open Auditorium Hotel promised to rival them both. Why, the barber shop in the Palmer House was floored with silver dollars. Imagine! Supplementing the fine hotels were many excellent restaurants and supper clubs. Stephanie particularly enjoyed shopping, if only for a loaf of bread, in the many gourmet delicatessans, often run by Germans, Scandinavians and other ethnic groups. She also took pleasure in an occasional evening at the theater, the opera or the ballet.

There was an air to Chicago which attracted her, a kinetic energy, masculinity, a can-do atmosphere and a sense of freedom. It was a far friendlier and open city than New York or Baltimore. At dinner parties, for example, women were not segregated following the meal, as in the East. And Chicagoans, burgeoning with wealth, had a thirst for culture and sophistication. The new park system, virtually surrounding the city, was to be envied, as were the new museum and opera house. The finest thespians, from Edwin Booth to Lily Langtry, played long engagements in the city. And the residents were much given to elaborate parties and balls, either in their homes or hotels. The social life in Chicago could be exhausting both to person and purse.

To all this Stephanie was welcomed. Her beauty and the daring Chambeau wardrobe made her an instant celebrity, to be ensnared by any fashionable hostess. Oh, she was aware of snubs and hostile stares from some women, but was determined not to let it tarnish her happiness. Instead, she basked in the favorable attention and did her best to earn it, as with this golden gown she now wore. But, with Thomas's help, she would not let her head be turned. Her body had more important uses than simply wearing gowns, however alluring.

When Thomas came home, he was gray with fatigue. As he embraced her, Stephanie felt his weight heavy against her. "You poor darling," she said. "You're exhausted." Arm around him, she led him to a Morris chair, where he simply collapsed, head against the back, legs astraddle, while she fixed him a whiskey.

When she turned to take him the drink, she saw him eyeing her. "God, Stevie, how you look!"

Ever since that day when she had greeted him in New York wearing the Josephine costume, that expression had become a touchstone of their lives. He said it innumerable times, and she never tired of hearing it. At this moment she knew she dressed not to impress others, but to please this man she loved.

"I'm about to take it off, stay home and put you to bed."

He sighed. "Don't I wish, but we have to go. Mr. Kincaid is expecting us."

"Then I'd better help you get ready." She handed him the glass. "Here, drink this while I draw you a bath. Then you're going to lie down a while."

"With you?"

"Not on your life." She smiled and bent low to kiss him lightly. "But I like your ideas—although you're not being particularly sensible."

Forty-five minutes later he was lying atop the bed, quite naked, while she sat beside him, gently massaging his temples, the back of his neck. "Just go to sleep, darling. A half-hour will make a new man of you."

"Yes, got to regain my strength."

She felt his hand at her cleavage, stroking, squeezing. She didn't mind. "Indeed," she whispered, maintaining the gentle, rhythmic movements of her fingers, feeling him relax. His hand fell away from her. She thought he was sleeping.

"The hard part is over, Stevie, for now. I won't be so busy for a while."

She had no idea what he meant but said, "Good."

"Mr. Kincaid asked if you were coming tonight. Says you're doing a lot for the company. He . . . he plans to tell you . . . tonight."

A little longer she massaged him. "Go to sleep, my darling." When she heard his regular breathing, she silently got up, closed the bedroom door. In the kitchen she indulged herself in a cup of tea. The thought occurred to her she needn't have dressed so early. She could be doing it now, while he slept. But no—she smiled—he would have stayed awake to watch her. He loved doing that. And it was nice to be sitting alone with a cup of hot tea.

She thought of what Thomas had just said and slowly

shook her head. If there were a serpent in her Eden of happiness, it was Winslow Kincaid. She simply didn't like him, but really had nothing overt to base her feeling on. She had seen him frequently, at parties at his house, balls, company social affairs. He was unfailingly courteous; indeed, solicitous of her. Yet she could not escape her intuitive repugnance. In part it was the way he treated Thomas, like chattel, a man employed to serve him, not an equal. But, she had told herself, he treated all his people that way, not just Thomas. Apparently that was the way he was. And he paid well, even generously. Thomas was getting rich through stock options. And Thomas didn't seem to mind Kincaid. So why should she?

But it wasn't just Kincaid's treatment of Thomas that fueled her antipathy. There was something about the man and the way he reacted to her. The word *lecherous* entered her mind, but she had never looked it up and wasn't sure precisely what it meant. When she was gowned as she was now, Thomas made her feel beautiful, proud of her womanliness. But Kincaid. . . . She felt he was undressing her with his eyes, scrutinizing her body, making her feel unclean. And he touched her too often, holding her hand too long within his, taking her arm, rendering "fatherly" pats to her cheek or bare shoulder. Whenever there was a party at his house on Prairie Avenue, there were unfailingly at least a half-dozen stunning young women, revealingly gowned. His companions, obviously. Then why did he pay her so much attention, commanding her to his side, introducing her to people? It was almost as though he were showing off his . . . *possession*.

In her heart of hearts Stephanie knew what he wanted. Admitting this to herself, she shuddered. She would die first. More than once she had thought of speaking to Thomas about Kincaid's attitude toward her. But she could never quite get the words out. What had Kincaid actually done? Nothing, save treat her with elaborate chivalry, offering lavish attention. Thomas would not want to hear her girlish intuitions. Heavens, he might even think *she* was interested in that fat old man. Oh, he wasn't exactly fat, but burly, massive in the shoulders and chest. Repugnant, that's what he was. No, she should say nothing. Why upset Thomas? Kincaid was his employer and Thomas idolized him. Why he did that, Stephanie couldn't understand. Suddenly, wearing this bold gown of gold, she knew she wasn't looking forward to the evening that lay ahead.

Eleven

As Stephanie entered the Palmer House on Thomas's arm, she was once again impressed with how grand it was, all tessellated marble and gold trimming, resplendent with sumptuous furnishings. As she mounted the splendid staircase she absorbed the eyes she knew were upon her, and she felt a resurgence of pride in herself.

American Western had taken over the entire ballroom. The governor and mayor were present, along with the leaders of the business, social and mercantile life of Chicago. The guests of honor were the heads of the western railroads, who had just begun to enhance the wealth and power of Winslow Kincaid.

It was indeed a lavish affair. The immense buffet groaned with suckling pigs, whole lambs, buffalo, antelope, roasts large enough to feed a block in the slums for a week, birds in their plumage; indeed, every culinary delicacy. Festooning the tables were, if it could be imagined in July, ice statues, including one of the American bald eagle, looking for all the world as though it were about to cast its cold body on an unsuspecting pheasant nearby. The ladies were gowned to the nines, dripping jewels.

Had Stephanie been uncertain of her charms, Winslow Kincaid left no room for doubts. He walked halfway across the ballroom to greet her and Thomas. As he bowed, kissing her hand in a much too florid European manner, Stephanie felt her breasts, just at Kincaid's eye level, being consumed by him. Then, as photographers took their picture, sending up clouds of flash-powder smoke, Kincaid continued to hold her hand. There was not a blessed thing she could do to extricate herself. He was taking advantage of her and that's all there was to it.

When the photo session had ended, he turned to her. "My dear, my dear." He was smiling at her benevolently. Or was his expression supposed to be fatherly? "If I may use the word, may I say you look absolutely ravishing."

She didn't like the word at all, but could only say, "Thank you, Mr. Kincaid."

He lowered his voice, seeming to become serious. "While I have a moment, I'd like to say to you"—he glanced at her escort—"and Thomas that I thank you both. This is a glorious night for American Western and all who labor in her vineyards. Thomas has exceeded himself, as I always knew he could, and you, my dear"—he patted her hand—"have been of inestimable value."

Ordinarily she would have been thrilled by the words of praise for Thomas, but now all she could say was, "Me, sir?"

"Yes, you, Stephanie." He gripped her hand more tightly. "Business deals often rest on intangibles, my dear. Thomas told me how invaluable you were to him during his negotiations in New York, and his success there was the crux of all we celebrate tonight." His smile was pure condescension. "I don't expect you to understand, Stephanie. It is not worth bothering your pretty little head about. I just want to say that since you have arrived in Chicago, you have aided us immeasurably with your beauty, charm and sophistication."

She saw his eyes lowering to her bosom. She was extremely uncomfortable. Mercifully she was now able to extricate her hand from his. "Thank you, Mr. Kincaid, but I still don't understand what I've done."

Kincaid laughed, his mirth apparently genuine, and glanced knowingly at a smiling Thomas. "My dear, there is a tendency among people, particularly easterners, to view Chicagoans as barbarians. I think they come here expecting covered wagons, Indian attacks and men in buckskin suits. When they meet someone as stunning and charming as you, they realize that we at American Western are not cowboys and Indians. Am I not right, Thomas?"

For the merest instant a thought flashed across Thomas's mind: Why was Kincaid making all this fuss over Stevie? He didn't with the wives of other employees. Then Thomas dismissed it. Kincaid was just being gallant. "Yes, indeed, Mr. Kincaid."

Thomas's employer smiled broadly and reached out to clasp Stephanie's upper arm. "Having so spoken, allow me to introduce you to some of our distinguished guests."

For most of the evening she was compelled to remain at Kincaid's side, only the presence of Thomas making it bearable for her. Again and again she was introduced, the names and titles a blur in her mind. "May I present *our*—" Such a word! "—charming Miss Summers, who is betrothed to *our* corporate counsel, Mr. Hodges." It was an elevation in rank that neither Thomas nor she knew was official.

She smiled, shook a hand if offered, endured the inevitable lowering of gazes, accepted the encomiums to her beauty and costume. At age eighteen it was all extraordinarily difficult for her. She felt she lacked the poise, maturity and sophistication to be constantly charming to worldly men, many old enough to be her father or grandfather, and their suspicious, hostile-eyed wives. Again and again she fell back on her small repertoire of questions and remarks: "Where are you from?" "I hear it's lovely there." "It must be important work you do." "Do you know my grandfather Lawrence Hodges, the Washington attorney?" "Yes, Glenna Morgan is my great-grandmother." "Yes, she is the widow of Franklin Fairchild."

She was asked to dance often. The whole evening the effort to be constantly charming, more sophisticated than her years, was exhausting. She received only brief respites, a dance or two with Thomas. He tried to bolster her. "I'm in awe of you, Stevie. You're doing fabulously, a regular *tour de force.*"

"Am I, Thomas? And why do I have to do it?"

Worst for her were the times when she was embroiled in business discussions, of which she had absolutely no knowledge. She would try to nod where it seemed appropriate, or look knowing or smile or laugh when it seemed the thing to do. Inevitably the moment came when her opinion was solicited. She saw the curious faces, the attention focused on herself. Barely concealing her panic, she fell back on naivete and native honesty. Smiling, she said, "Mr. Kincaid, how would I know? I've never even seen one of your factories."

Kincaid smiled, his gallantry surfacing. "Gentlemen, I think we are most unchivalrously inflicting our business preoccupations on this bewitching young woman." There were nods, words of agreement and apology. But Kincaid turned to a particular man, beckoned him peremptorily and commanded, "Rawlings, at your first opportunity I want you to give Miss Summers a tour of the main works. Answer all her questions."

Rawlings bowed to her. "I will do so happily, sir."

In the wee hours of the morning, as they rode home in a hansom, Stéphanie snuggled beneath Thomas's arm, her fingers entwined with his. She was tired, yet exhilarated. Mostly, however, she was confused. This entire evening, the attention lavished on her by Kincaid, being thrust forward to meet people of importance, struck her as bizarre. She was, she knew, a mere girl of eighteen, dressed up in a revealing gown, involved in situations far beyond her experience. Why? How had it happened?

"Do you have any idea, Stevie, what it means to a man to have a wife like you?"

"That's just it, Thomas. I don't know."

"Lord, Stevie, with you at my side there is no limit to how high I can climb. Do you believe that?"

She turned her head, seeking his face in the darkness. "Of course, I believe in you. I just don't understand what I have to do with it." She heard him chuckle. "I'm serious, Tommy. I don't understand."

"Surely you see how impressed Mr. Kincaid is with you?"

Perhaps it was the darkness that made her speak her mind. "He is impressed that I am young, attractive, wearing this striking gown. All he was doing was showing me off—like I was some kind of possession, a toy, a doll. I didn't like it, Thomas."

"Of course you didn't. But it's important, Stevie. You don't know how much you helped me tonight. That talk of general counsel. I suspect he'll make it official one of these days."

She squeezed his fingers. "I hope so, Tommy, for your sake." They rode in silence a minute or so. Again the darkness encouraged her. "I don't really like Mr. Kincaid, Tommy. Sometimes I think he's—well, *interested* in me."

Again Thomas felt the prick of a doubt, but again he denied it. "Certainly he is."

"You know what I mean. He's—"

"Mr. Kincaid has an appreciative eye for a beautiful woman—and you certainly qualify as that. Why, you made every woman at that party tonight look dowdy. But he means nothing. Why, he's old enough to be your father."

"Grandfather is more like it."

"Have no fear of him, Stevie. He just likes you, admires you. He won't bother you—that way."

"Is he married?"

"Not for a long time." Thomas laughed. "Actually he's married to American Western and the Railway Car Trust. That's the main reason you need not worry about him."

She felt reassured.

Upstairs in their apartment Thomas poured himself a whiskey and asked if she wanted anything. She didn't, but she wanted to share all things with him. "A little sherry might be nice."

When he brought it to her, he kissed her lightly. "Have I mentioned—what's that new expression?—oh, yes, what a knockout you are in this dress?"

She smiled. "I don't believe you did."

She felt his free hand on her arm, her shoulder, down her bare back, cool, smooth, sending shivers through her. Then he kissed her, lightly as before, and bent lower to brush his lips over the tops of her breasts, the deep valley between, returning to nibble gently at her moist lips.

"Are you too tired?"

"Yes." She smiled. "But let's."

She turned her back for him to unfasten her gown. He downed his whiskey, got rid of the glass, and began his task at the back of her dress.

"Tommy—" the mere use of the nickname was part of their intimacy, "—explain to me what tonight was all about. What was being celebrated?"

"One of the biggest business deals in history, that's all."

"What kind of a business deal?"

He stopped his fingers and looked over her shoulder at her. "Do you really want to know?"

"Yes. I felt so foolish not understand what was going on."

He returned to the hooks at her lower back. "All

right, I suppose you should know. But it's rather hush-hush. Can you keep this to yourself?"

"You know I can."

"Mr. Kincaid is moving to corner the railway cars of the whole country. Tonight's affair marked the first step. The main western rail lines have agreed to sell their rolling stock to Kincaid and the Trust, then lease them back. When the eastern lines agree—and they will—Kincaid will own virtually every freight car in the country."

"Why does he want to do that?"

"Why not? He'll be the most powerful man in America. Nothing will move over a rail line without his approval. He'll be able to charge whatever the traffic will bear. Can you imagine how much money there is to be made?"

As the hooks gave way beaneath his hands, Stephanie felt a blessed relief from Pierre Chambeau's torturous built-in corset. "I'm sorry, Tommy, but I still don't understand."

He laughed. "You are hardly alone in that. Few do. I didn't myself for a long time, but doing so much of Kincaid's legal work enabled me to catch on. I guess the key to it is the Railway Car Trust."

"What's a Trust?"

"It's a business arrangement, a combination. All the makers of railway cars stopped competing with each other and got together. They traded individual stock for shares in the Trust. If a railroad wants to buy rolling stock, they can only go to the Trust. Kincaid is the head of it."

"There are no other manufacturers?"

"None worth mentioning."

Free of the fasteners at last, she turned, slid the straps from her shoulders and stepped out of the gown. In a moment she was naked before him, except for her high-heeled slippers.

"God, Stevie, how you look!"

She smiled, delight in her eyes, but stepped back as

he reached for her. "You've too many clothes on, Tommy." As he began his more involved, time-consuming act of undressing, she said, "Isn't there a word for what the Trust is doing? Isn't it bad?"

"The word is monopoly. And I don't think it's bad. A bigger company just has to be more efficient. Big business is good for the country."

"How can that be?"

"Look, it's happening in every industry you can think of. Rockefeller has formed the Standard Oil Trust. He controls just about every drop of kerosene and oil produced or sold in the United States. The same thing is happening in steel, copper, meat packing, sugar. The gas and electricity in this flat is controlled by the Chicago Gas Trust. Even the telephone over there on the wall is being combined into the American Telephone and Telegraph Trust." He laughed. "Everything in life, from cradles to coffins, is—or soon will be—controlled by some Trust or other. Mr. Kincaid is a very smart man. He may have the most important Trust of all, for he will control the transportation system for all the other Trusts."

She watched him pull his shirttail out, take off the garment. "Is it legal?"

"Sure. There are no laws against it."

She stepped forward to undo his belt. In a moment she stopped. "Sit on the sofa. I'll take off your shoes first." He did as she directed, and she squatted before him to remove his evening slippers and black silk stockings. "It doesn't seem right, Tommy, a few big companies freezing out all the others. What about free enterprise?"

He laughed. "That's palaver for politicians. The little fellows can't compete anymore, Stevie. They're too small, inefficient. They can't raise the capital. Big business is the way things are now."

She unbuttoned his trousers, and he raised his hips for her to slide them from him. She bent low, pulling the garments off over his feet. When she finished, he lay slouched on the sofa, hips resting on the forward edge of the cushion, his head on the back, eyes closed. She smiled. His manhood was awake, anyway. She bent down, clasped, kissed him. In a moment she felt an upward pressure on her arm, heard him say, "Come here."

She knew what he wanted. They had done it before. She knelt on the cushions, knees and arms straddling him. Arching her back, she began to sweep her breasts over his face, cheeks, eyes, forehead, around his chin, back and forth, finally entering his open mouth. Sensation flooded through her, and as his hands caressed her waist, hips, rounding her derriere, stroking her thighs, entering the strawberry meadow, she relished the sharp rise of her passion.

But her mind would not quite be stilled and, reluctantly, she moved away from him, huddling on the edge of the sofa, and willing her desire to be still. "Being a monopoly means you can charge whatever prices you want, doesn't it?" she asked, resisting his efforts to pull her back to him. "I don't think I like the idea of Winslow Kincaid setting prices, controlling everything. Do you?"

"Sure, why not?" Thomas replied, pulling her back firmly and consuming her right nipple with his tongue and teeth. A moan of pleasure escaped her, and Thomas released her momentarily. "After all, he pays for all this." Thomas made a lazy gesture around the room. He didn't want to think about the issues Stephanie was raising. He only wanted her.

She felt the pressure of his hand against her back, pushing her further to where she wanted to be. As his mouth came to her and his fingers made her gasp and tremble with heightened pleasure, whatever thought she'd had was lost in her sudden surge of desire.

"Oh, Tommy, such a lover you are."

She arched her back and began to sway her body,

throbbing even before a new sensation separated her legs. For a moment she was hardly able to breathe; then, with a cry of longing, she widened her knees and settled over him. As he rolled her to her back on the couch and came atop her, a final lucid thought came to her. How nice not to have servants.

Twelve

Danielle Kingston Summers had never fought anything so hard in her life as her fear of marriage to James Lavelle. She thought of the fear as a malignancy, evil, growing, a disease threatening her very life. In increasing desperation she had done everything she could think of to quiet, exorcise or at least place in remission this rage within her.

The fear was an old adversary. Several decent, loving men had wanted to marry her. She had considered at least three, but had refused them on the point of acceptance, overwhelmed by the fear of failure. This time, with James Lavelle, she had lured herself into a trap. He was so fine a man and she cared so much for him and the life he offered, the fear had not surfaced. Marrying him, becoming a Countess, finding happiness had seemed so right, and in an impulsive moment she had announced her intentions to no less than the future King and Queen of England. The fear began almost at once. The very night she had accepted James, Danielle lay awake beside him, her body satiated, and felt the fear. It was as though a bad seed were planted in good soil, bursting forth, an ugly vine of unhappiness, growing rapidly, twisting throughout her. There were times when she was so full of terror she had difficulty breathing, and her stomach ached until she had no appetite.

She fought the fear with the only weapon she knew, surrendering to him, giving herself in an unstinting effort to be all that he wanted her to be. If she could just forget herself and concentrate on loving him, she could win this battle. If that failed, perhaps if she were tired enough, everything would be all right.

Their engagement caused a minor sensation in London, and Danielle was instantly immersed in a social whirl of receptions and balls. Everyone wanted to meet the beautiful American fiancée of Lord Wight and congratulate the handsome couple. Even the press visited. Badgered by questions, half-blinded by flash powder, Danielle set an early date for their wedding, August eighth, his lordship's birthday. This led to a flurry of activity for the wedding and reception, guest list, invitations, church, minister, trousseau, all the quagmire of details for even a "small" upper-class British wedding.

They divided their time between Downview in the country and the London house, and Danielle sought to assume her role as mistress of both places. She gave a significant ball for acquaintances and several dinner parties for intimate friends, while at the same time accompanying James to state dinners and other diplomatic functions.

When at Downview, she threw herself into stepmotherhood, giving generously of her time and attention to Allyson and young Jamie Lavelle. She tried with all her might to love them. She talked at length with Allyson, showing her how to fix her hair, some tricks of makeup to enhance her appearance, then took her shopping, so that the ungainly girl actually began to feel beautiful and graceful. Young Jamie, destined to be the next

Earl, was easier. Just a smile, a few words, the touch of her hand, were enough to make him adore her. Both children did.

But their reaction was as nothing compared to James Lavelle's downright worship of her. None of her efforts as mistress and hostess, mother and helpmeet, were lost on him. He was open in his admiration, unstinting in his appreciation. But it was as the woman he loved that she enthralled him. As she gave of herself and became strung more tightly with fatigue and strain, she became even more beautiful. She might be losing weight, but it made her more delicate and fragile. And in her submission to him and the course she had chosen, she became more feminine. Her aura of vulnerability deepened. Seeking to please him, her attire became more provocative and alluring. And with gesture and smile, touch, word and thought, she gave him an intimacy of mind exceeding even that of her body. And she gave all virtually as a sacrificial offering. Danielle Summers became wholly orgiastic, the embodiment of glamorous temptation, stunning Lord Wight both with her capacities and her expert arousals of him until, filled with wonder and love, he said, "Danny, I feel drenched in your femininity."

None of it worked. She had only made matters worse.

She sat now in the darkness of their bedroom in the London house, shivering despite the warm robe she had donned. Fear raged within her, fear such as she had never known, not when she was a naked captive of a retarded giant in Colorado, not when she and Moira had faced rape and death at the hands of kidnappers in Maryland. Those were dangers of the flesh. She now knew her sanity was in peril.

She couldn't keep this up, going without sleep, eating hardly at all, pushing her mind and body by will alone to be what others wanted—what she ought to want. And she did, she did. Then why was she so afraid? Again and again she told herself it was just the natural fear of a woman with one failed marriage. She had loved Walter Summers, but had seen poverty and fear and hatred of Reconstruction in South Carolina erode that love, until it was killed in a single night of lanterns and guns and hideous hooded riders, one of them her husband. Why was the image of that horrid night preying on her mind so? James Lavelle was not Walter Summers. There was no racial hatred in him. He was not a man with a secret streak of violence in him. Why was this image returning so often after all these years to fuel her fear and drive away this last chance for happiness? Why was she so afraid?

She had received a letter that afternoon from Stephanie. It was long and intimate, the first she'd had since arriving in London, and it had not helped a bit. It had in fact rendered a series of shocks that had propelled Danielle to desperation.

Stephanie told of visiting Glenna, going up to the attic, trying on old dresses. That was the first shock. Danielle hadn't known her beloved GlennaMa had saved the old gowns. Why on earth had she? The idea of her little girl dressing up in that horrid Josephine costume—Danielle shuddered even now at the thought of what had happened when she wore it—appalled her. And "accidentally" wearing it to answer the door, confronting Thomas. As Danielle read the letter, her hand shook violently when she learned of her daughter's wearing the black satin Chambeau gown out in public. She remembered it as a hated garment. Hamilton Garth had torn it from her shortly before the train wreck. How had GlennaMa gotten hold of it? Why, oh, why, had she saved it? The thought of her sweet, innocent Stevie wearing that dress filled her with loathing.

She read on, the contents of the letter coming as a series of shattering blows. Stevie and Thomas in love. They couldn't be. She was too young. The words were etched in Danielle's mind: "We are madly in love, mother, and he is so wonderful. We didn't do wrong. I

know you will believe me." Danielle wept uncontrolla-
bly, and through streaming eyes, tears dropping on the
page, she had barely been able to read: "In your black
satin I had such a sense of you all evening, mother, of
being with you. And later, when GlennaMa talked to
me and I learned you and I are alike, sharing a capacity
for enjoyment and pleasure, I felt blessed to be your
daughter." Danielle had doubled over, face pressed
against her knees, racked with sobs. She felt she
couldn't bear more, but she did. A Pierre Chambeau
gown, a description of it. So beautiful. Bitterly Danielle
imagined the gown and hated the little Frenchman for
making it for her child. He had no right. She read on.
An ecstatic weekend of love, just like being married,
which she and Thomas were going to be. Then came
the cruelest shock of all. "I love Thomas with all my
heart and I'm certain of his love for me, yet I have
decided to wait a little while. I want to be absolutely
sure of him, of our love. I am positive there is nothing
about him that I will not adore always, but I know you
can understand, mother, that I want to avoid making a
mistake. Meanwhile, we are ecstatically happy here."
The descriptions of their apartment and life in Chicago
were lost as Danielle reeled under the heavy, hurting
blow. Her daughter, her adored Stevie, was living
unwed in Chicago with Thomas Hodges simply because
she feared becoming like her own mother. Stephanie
had tried to be tactful, but she might as well have
printed in bold letters: I DON'T WANT TO MAKE
YOUR MISTAKE. I DON'T WANT TO BE LIKE
YOU, MOTHER.

By sheer willpower Danielle had come to grips with
the letter, gone to the reception and acted properly. It
had strangely—or was it so strange?—acted as a fuel to
the erotic excesses just concluded in the bed she shared
with James Lavelle. Danielle had managed to convince
herself not to worry about Stephanie. She was eighteen, a young woman who had to make her own way in
life. Danielle could remember Glenna telling Moira the

same thing when Danielle was eighteen, and Moira had been so overprotective and worrisome. And Danielle was able to tell herself she was not neglecting Stephanie by being away. Had she been there, the course of events would not have been altered an iota. Likewise, she made peace with Thomas Hodges. He was a good, decent, loving man, not a cad, or rake. Yes, they would love each other, perhaps always had. Danielle remembered Thomas's brotherly kindnesses to Stephanie as a child, her girlish crush on him, his appreciation of her budding maidenhood. Yes, their love was probably inevitable. They would be good for each other. It was right.

Then why was she sitting here in the darkness, shivering with fear for them, for herself? Suddenly Danielle bolted upright, her back ramrod-straight. The image of that night near Charleston sped across her mind: guns, hooded men by lantern light. Her hand came to her open mouth and she bit hard against the white knuckles, tears scalding her eyes. It had all been an excuse. She had used it all these years. Benjamin Fairchild had been waiting in the wings, declaring his love for her. She had even kissed him in the moonlight, telling herself it meant nothing but friendship. But it had meant everything. Walter knew, knew her nature, what kind of a woman she was. Back at the house, his rifle and nightrider costume discarded, he had reasoned with her, but she would not listen. He had grabbed her, forced down her throat the last of the aphrodisiac, the same love potion he had first used to seduce her in the garret. He had taken her, oh, how he had taken her, climaxes thundering through her, wild, compulsive, never stopping until both of them had passed out. She had called it rape and left him. He had prostrated himself, begging forgiveness, asking her to return and start over. She wouldn't listen, sure of her righteous anger. "Is there someone else?" he asked. She lied. But there was someone else, Benjamin. After him another and another. Always there was someone else.

She liked men, lots of men. She liked this life. It was what she wanted. Walter Summers knew. Pierre Chambeau had known, urging her to be a courtesan. She wasn't even that. She was just a common whore. Even her own daughter knew and feared it in herself.

The beast of self-loathing had sprung from its dark, inner place, free of all bonds, and was in the process of devouring her.

"What's the matter, Danny? Why are you crying?"

She sat on her vanity bench, back to the mirror, bent over, hands covering her face, her body heaving with sobs. Lord James jumped from bed and came to her, kneeling, both arms around her.

"What's wrong, Danny?"

Her answer was a continuation of her deep sobbing. She gasped for air, emitting a deep sob. He held her for a time, patting her back, uttering nonsensical, soothing words. When she didn't react, he was frightened, and he left her to turn up the gas lights.

"You've got to tell me what's wrong, Danny."

Finally she raised her head from her hands and, blinking against the light, looked up at him, unmindful of her tear-stained face. Her mouth opened, but only the sounds of labored breathing came out, until at last she managed, "Home . . . I . . . I want . . . to go . . . home."

"The letter you got today. It upset you." He saw her shake her head. "It was from Stephanie. Is something wrong?"

She could only stare at him, mouth agape, then, through swimming vision, she saw him trying to smile.

"One of the things I love about you, Danny, is that you are such a caring mother. But Stephanie is eighteen, very well brought up. Unless she's hurt or ill, I'm sure she'll be all right."

Danielle could only shake her head.

"What's wrong? What did she write to upset you?"

"The letter . . . has nothing . . . to do with it. I—I can't marry you. It's . . . it's hopeless."

He looked at her a moment, then a soft smile spread his lips. "It's a bad thing, Danny, for a prospective bride to get up in the middle of the night, worrying. You've just got a case of the jitters."

"No, James. I'm . . . unworthy of you. I'll just . . . ruin your life."

Now he laughed. "And I'll enjoy every second of my ruination. Come back to bed, let me hold you."

"James, no. Listen to me. I've tried these past weeks, harder than I've tried anything in my life—tried to love you, your children, your way of life. And I do. That's the awful part. I love it all."

She was making no sense to him. He could only laugh. "And you've succeeded, Danny. We all love you—whether you've tried hard or not."

She shook her head in frustration. "You don't understand." Her sigh was deep, marred by the remnant of a sob. "I'm afraid, James. I've been living in fear all these weeks, trying to forget it in loving you, being what you want me to be. And I didn't even know what I was afraid of—until now."

He grew somber. "All right, what are you afraid of?"

"Of myself, the way I am, of ruining your life, ruining myself. We must stop now, before . . . before *more* damage is done."

He sighed. "Danny, you have made me happier these past weeks than I ever thought possible. The children adore you. All who know you adore you."

"And I'm sorry for that. It just makes everything harder."

He stared at her, utterly confused. "I'd best get the doctor. You need a sedative."

"No, James. I don't need anything except to go home—where I belong." She shook her head in frustration and clasped her hands in front of her, bringing them to her chin. "James, I know this is hard for you. I know I've made you love me, made you think of me as a certain sort of person. But I haven't been the real me. You don't love *me*."

"Let me be the judge of whom I love."

"No, if you knew what I'm really like, you—you'd never love me."

"Danny, I—"

He was interrupted by her actions. In one motion she untied her robe and slid it back from her shoulders. "You're not the first, James."

"I know you've been married before."

She held the robe wider, seeing his eyes fixed on her nakedness. "And almost married and almost married and—and in between unable to resist. There have been so many men I—I can't remember them all." His gaze was locked with hers now. She saw shock register in him. "What I . . . did with you tonight, I've done countless times, innumerable times. I—I can apparently do it with anyone."

He was not a man easily rattled. He swallowed, not without difficulty, and said softly, "None of us are candidates for sainthood, Danny."

She closed her robe, cinching it around her waist. "Can't you understand what I'm saying? I'll do it again, James, and again. You can't want that?" She saw him shaking suddenly from the effort at self-control. "I don't want to hurt you, James. It's better this way, believe me."

"You don't know what you're saying."

"I do, James. Time and again decent, loving men have wanted to marry me. And each time I couldn't. A terrible fear would drive me away. I never knew what it was till tonight." She shuddered. "There have been too many men, James. I'm used, jaded, soiled." She saw him trying to speak and raised her hand to stop him. "Don't you see? I've enjoyed every one of them. James, I'm virtually a whore."

The word stunned him. He trembled, couldn't help it. "What are you . . . going to do?"

"Go home. If there's virtue to be found, I'll seek it."

A long moment he stared at her, trembling, shaking his head as though to negate all he'd heard. Obviously struggling for control, he turned from her, went to the nightstand, opened a humidor, retrieved a cigar. In a moment he was crumbling it in his hand. "It's not that easy to walk out now, Danielle—the children, my friends, the wedding, gifts—"

"Embarrassment. Yes, I know. James, I'm filled with self-loathing, consumed by it. A little more won't matter." She buried her head in her lap to avoid his gaze, and once again burst into heartrending sobs.

Thirteen

About the last thing Stephanie Summers wanted to do on Saturday night was to dress up and go out. She longed for a quiet evening with Thomas, just the two of them, perhaps dinner at their favorite restaurant, a stroll beside the moonlit lake, coming home to love each other. But no. They were invited to the ostentatious home of Marshall Field at 1905 Prairie Avenue for a gala summer ball. They had no choice but to attend.

Stephanie's yearning for a quiet evening had been with her all day. She slept late, awakened with a sense of loss. Thomas was not in bed with her. Then she remembered. He'd said he had to go to the office. Why did he have to work on Saturday? Couldn't Kincaid give him the weekend off? She thrust the thought aside, remembering their lovemaking. Such a lover he was! The things he did! How right they were for each other. How she loved him.

She arose, did her exercises as Chambeau had instructed, then languished in a perfumed bath, shampooed and massaged an ointment into her wet body, also according to the dressmaker. The very act aroused her, and she wished Thomas were there. He loved doing it. Back in the bedroom she looked at herself boldly, standing on tiptoe, sucking in her waist. She now knew she had a spectacular figure. And she also knew the uses of her body. How could Thomas make her climax so often, then leave her still wanting more, like now? She smiled. No matter. She was just a lucky girl.

She dressed, dried her hair, then went out to do a little grocery shopping, wishing they were staying home. She just had to improve her cooking. It was a pleasant afternoon. She enjoyed chatting with the shopkeepers. Thomas arrived home a little after five. She recognized at once something was wrong and asked him about it.

"Nothing—" he smiled wanly, "—and everything."

"What is it, Tommy?"

"Mr. Kincaid has put me in charge of determining the price for acquiring the rolling stock of the western lines. I'm to get an exact tally, determine the condition of the cars and negotiate the price. It's a very important and responsible assignment."

"That's good, isn't it?"

"Yes, that part is." He smiled, or tried to. "The bad part is I have to go away a few days—out West, inspect the yards, oversee the whole shebang."

His words stung her. "How long is a few days?"

"I should be back inside a week. You know I won't make it a second longer than I have to."

"Can I go with you?"

He sighed. "I wish, how I wish, but it wouldn't work. I'll be on the move constantly, probably sleeping in cabooses and such. It's best you stay here."

"When do you leave?"

He pursed his lips, looking at her forlornly. "Tomorrow, midday. Have to be in St. Louis early Monday."

She nodded, aware of a sinking feeling in her stomach. But she forced a smile. "I never thought I could keep you with me *all* the time." The smile widened. "Wives of important businessmen have to expect these separations."

"Yes." Then he swept her into his arms. "Oh, God, Stevie, I love you so. When can we get married?"

"I really don't know what we're waiting for. Let's get married as soon as you return."

"Do you mean it?"

Her smile was now dazzling. "Maybe it'll make you hurry home."

More than ever she wanted the quiet evening with Thomas, but she dutifully dressed for the Marshall Field gala. At Thomas's request she wore the first, silvery blue, bare-shouldered gown Chambeau had made for her. She had not yet displayed it in Chicago.

Stephanie did her best, and it was good enough to keep anyone from noticing anything amiss, but she really did not have a very good time the whole evening. She realized she had seen most of these people the evening before, and if that were true, they had all just seen each other. How bored they were! She was looking at frozen smiles, listening to empty, meaningless chatter. The women, dressed in fine clothes and jewels, were there to be seen and admired, their husbands and escorts exulting in the evidence of what their money could buy. And Stephanie was no different, dressed for exhibition, her breasts thrust forward, all but exposed for public admiration. She battled such dark thoughts all evening.

Winslow Kincaid was there, and he didn't help Stephanie's mood one whit. His eyes, seeming to devour her décolletage, were lecherous. She had looked up the word and now knew its meaning. And his hands, too, often found her arm, her waist.

"How utterly enchanting you look tonight, my dear Stephanie."

"Thank you, Mr. Kincaid."

He glanced up at Thomas and smiled. "You don't suppose we could get her to call me Winslow, do you Thomas?"

"You might try, sir."

"I'm afraid I'm going to have to call you Mr. Kincaid this evening. I'm quite angry with you for sending Thomas away."

"My dear, I am sorry, but business is business and man's work is never done, that sort of thing." He laughed. "Am I not right, Thomas?"

"Regrettably you are, Mr. Kincaid."

To Stephanie, Kincaid's laugh sounded too hearty, forced. And why didn't he instruct Thomas to call him by his first name, as he had her?

"I quite understand that you'll be lonely while Thomas is gone." Kincaid patted her arm. "But we'll just have to see that you're not *too* lonely." He smiled up at Thomas. "I know, we'll start tomorrow. The White Stockings are playing baseball in the afternoon. I have box seats. Why don't you come as my guest, Stephanie? Should be a good game. Have you ever seen the major leaguers play?"

She shook her head.

"Then it'll be great fun for you. What do you say?"

Her mind was formulating a tactful refusal when she heard, "Yes, why don't you go, Stevie? You'll love it."

She was aghast. Thomas had no right to answer for her, but she couldn't countermand him now, could only smile and mumble her acceptance.

Kincaid was bowing. "And now, if you'll do me the honor of this dance, Miss Summers."

She was out on the dance floor with him then, and he was holding her a good deal too close. There was nothing she could do about it without making a scene. Quite improperly he kept her for a second dance, then held her arm at the elbow to introduce her to some friends. Mention of her relationship with Thomas was avoided. Kincaid was claiming her as his own.

To get away from him Stephanie excused herself and

went to the powder room on the second floor. A couple of other women were there. Stephanie nodded, smiled, agreed to a pleasantry about what a grand ball it was. Not until they were gone could she vent her frustration and anger. Kincaid had no right. He was taking advantage of Thomas, of her. It was unfair, unjust, unkind, uneverything! Then she gritted her teeth and sighed. Consciously she willed herself to relax. There was nothing to be done. She had to be pleasant to Thomas's employer. All right, she would be. But she would also be careful.

"Have you noticed Kincaid?"

The voice startled her, for it was male. She turned around sharply, fearing someone was in the room.

"Naw, I only saw the blonde. What a body!"

A second voice, smirking with laughter.

"She's Hodges's doxy, and Kincaid's practically frothing at the mouth to have her. Can't say I blame him."

On the wall near the floor she saw a grill. The voices must be coming up through the heating system.

"If that's Tom Hodges's girlfriend, Kincaid hasn't a chance. Tom's crazy about her." Laughter. "And I imagine he keeps her plenty happy."

Stephanie knew she was blushing, and was relieved when the voices were lost in the sound of running water. These men, whoever they were, must be in another lavatory someplace.

But the water was shut off. "Besides, Kincaid's got his hands full with his deal he's trying to pull off."

"Cornering railroad cars? Do you think the government will let him get away with it?"

"I think he may have done it before they even realize what's happened or know what to do about it. His real problem's the workers. I hear there's going to be a strike."

"You don't say?"

"Yes. He's already had a big layoff, now he's cutting wages ten percent."

"That doesn't make sense. I'd think he'd have his plants going full blast."

"So would I, but we're not Kincaid. Don't you see what he's doing? He's creating an artificial shortage of freight cars to drive the prices sky-high. It's a smart move, if it works."

The party finally, mercifully, ended, and Stephanie was back home with Thomas. She went at once to the bookcase and dictionary.

"What're you looking up?"

"A word I heard tonight?"

"What word?"

Quickly she flipped pages, ran a finger down a column, read. Ordinarily she might have become angry, but the words, leaping from the page, hurt too much. Her eyes smarted, filled with tears.

"What's the matter, Stevie?"

Slowly she raised her head and looked at him. "Is that . . . what I am? A—a woman of . . . of loose morals. A p-prostitute. Mistress."

"What're you talking about?"

"D-doxy." She had trouble even uttering the word. "I—I went to the . . . the ladies' room—on the second floor. I heard men . . . talking."

"Men!"

"Oh, they weren't there. They were someplace else . . . in another room. Their voices . . . came . . . through the heating pipe . . . or something."

"What did they say?"

"Oh, God, they said . . . they said I was . . . a . . . a *doxy.*" She was crying openly now. "Oh, Tommy, is that what I am?"

He had her in his arms even before she finished the question. "Oh, Stevie, you know you're not."

"Do I?"

"Yes. I love you, we love each other, we're going to be married." He kissed her then, wet cheeks and eyes, hair, lips, rapidly, comfortingly.

"They said . . . Kincaid is . . . frothing at the mouth . . . to have me."

"He probably is, but what does it matter? You belong to me."

Amid his kisses, she said, "Yes, yes. They said you were crazy in love with me." And, as he devoured her mouth, she knew for certain he was.

Against her ear he said, "It was just talk, Stevie. Don't pay attention to it—" he laughed, "—except the part about my being in love with you."

"Yes." And she turned her head, eager for his mouth, his kiss. But it did not last too long. Neither was quite ready yet. He released her, poured two brandies, handed her one.

"You all right now?"

She sighed. "Yes. I'm sorry. I shouldn't have been so upset, I guess, and wouldn't have been if I hadn't been so tired. I hated the whole evening. I was on edge. I wanted to be alone with you."

"I know. I felt the same way."

"And tomorrow. Oh, how I dread your leaving." She remembered. "Why did you say I'd go to the ball game? I don't want to—not with him."

He pursed his lips into a frown. He didn't like her going with Kincaid, either. But what could he do? "He's my employer, Stevie. He pays me well and I've got a great future. I just have to—*we* have to—put up with a certain amount of . . . of inconvenience."

"I know." She smiled. "And I'll be good. But that doesn't mean I have to like him."

"Just be nice to him—pleasant. He won't bother you, Stevie, I'm sure of that. He simply admires a beautiful woman—and you're surely the most beautiful woman he's ever seen."

She smiled at the compliment. She really didn't believe Thomas, but let it go for now. She'd have to deal with Kincaid in her own way.

Glasses were raised. They held each other with their

eyes, declaring their love without words. Finally she said, a little above a whisper, "I'll die till you get back, Tommy."

"Me, too."

Their free hands found each other, fingers clasping, entwining, relishing contact, wanting more. He caressed her bare arms, shoulders, throat. "What a body you have, Stevie."

She smiled. "So I heard—through the radiator."

"That again. You can't blame them for—"

"It's all right. I'd heard it before—from you."

The caresses continued, back to her throat, under her chin, cheeks, across her lips, sending shivers of sensation through her. It was a prolongation of their desire, a postponement to magnify their passion. "What else did you hear up that damn heating duct?"

"Oh, some not very nice things about your employer."

"What now?"

"Something about cornering railroad cars and—oh, yes, cutting production to create an artificial shortage to drive prices up."

"I see."

"Is it true?"

"Probably."

"They said there's going to be a strike."

"Maybe. It won't matter if there is."

He was back at her breasts now, and suddenly she wasn't in the mood. She lifted his hand away, holding it, staring at him.

"What now?" He was smiling.

"Isn't it . . . well, terrible, Tommy, putting men out of work, cutting wages just . . . just out of greed? Isn't that what it is? Pure greed."

"I think it's called good business."

"He's already rich, Thomas, terribly rich. Why does he need more money?"

"I don't think he does. He wants power."

"To put men out of work? What kind of power is

that? Just today, when I was in the bakery, Mrs. Johanssen said bread had gone up two cents a loaf. She blamed it on transportation costs for flour and such. I didn't know what she meant—then. I do now. Kincaid is doing this."

"So?"

"So two cents a loaf doesn't mean anything to you and me, but—" She was agitated now. "Tommy, there are people I'm sure who can't afford that two cents—especially if they're out of work. They'll go hungry."

He smiled. "I doubt it, Stevie." He sought to return his hand to her breast. She had a fleeting instinct to step back from him, but she had never in their whole relationship refused his caress.

"I'm serious, Tommy. I don't think what Kincaid's doing is right." His fingers stroked the inner sides of her breasts. A finger sought, found a nipple beneath the fabric, sending shivers of sensation beneath her skin. "Do you?" He set their brandies aside, then brought both hands to her breasts, doubling the sensation, further increasing it by running the tip of his tongue over her lips. "I'm . . . serious, Tommy. Do . . . you . . . think it's . . . right?"

He came away. "I don't think about whether it's right or not. I just know it's damn good business—and that I adore you." His kiss, deep, probing, passionate came as punctuation.

She responded. Always she responded to him, feeling the quick leap in desire, the delicious ache in her thighs. But when he came behind her to unfasten her gown, her mind cleared. "Tommy, there has to be a right and wrong to everything."

"In business the only wrong is not making a profit—and the bigger the profit, the greater the right."

She shook her head, trying to understand his words. "Can that be true?"

The dress was gone from her before he spoke again. Then he said, "God, Stevie, how you look!"

She heard his words, a touchstone of their lives.

Ordinarily it would have signaled embrace, immersion in expression of their love. But now, something wasn't right. He was not being honest with her. "I asked you, Tommy. Can that be true? Can profit be the only consideration?" She saw him hesitate. It was a question he didn't want to answer. "Why is Kincaid so important to you, Tommy?" Again she saw his hesitation. Suddenly she was aware of her nakedness. Involuntarily she looked around for a robe, something to cover herself with. She had never felt this way with him before. Why now?

Thomas was uncomfortable, too, but for a far different reason. Hers were questions he had refused to ask himself. Oh, they were there in his mind, festering below consciousness. For a long time he had felt a sort of lingering unease about his work. He found it difficult to talk to his father about it and avoided the subject. Now, to have this girl whom he adored and wanted above all things in life confront him this way. . . . He couldn't let it happen.

"I told you, Stevie. He's my employer. He pays well."

She stared at him. "Anything for money, Tommy? You said the bigger the profit, the greater the right. Your father isn't that way. He has his own law firm. He takes cases he believes in. And he has money, too."

The lawyer in Thomas surfaced. She had given him a way out. He took it. "I believe in what I'm doing, Stevie."

Her eyes, gemlike, held him. "Do you, Thomas—truly?"

His facial expression gave no indication of the quick, savage skirmish between his lifelong instinct to tell the truth and his desire for this girl. She was all that mattered. He must never lose her. "I do, Stevie. I feel I'm doing something important—helping to build this country, making it richer and more powerful every day. And it's exciting, Stevie, being part of it all."

She heard the excitement in his voice, saw it in his

eyes. "Yes, I suppose it is—for a man." She smiled. "I'm sorry. I guess I'm sounding like a nagging wife."

And he smiled. "No. You have every right to ask. You're part of my life." With inner relief he could now accept the truth and utter it. "Kincaid isn't *that* important to me, Stevie. You are. All I know is that I love you—more than anything else in life—and that I'm going away tomorrow. I won't see you for a week."

His reminder stabbed at her. "Oh, Tommy, I'll never make it that long."

She stood naked before him, devoid of embarrassment as he looked at her, for she knew that was part of their love.

"Stevie," he said softly, "I think about you all the time when we're apart."

"I know. I think of you, too."

"I try to remember your body, your breasts mostly, so voluptuous, so perfect, rising from your slenderness." He smiled, just a little. "But I can never quite visualize you perfectly. I'm always surprised, delighted anew at how lovely you are."

Her eyes were bright. But when he reached out to touch her, she took his hand. "You've too many clothes on, Tommy. I want to touch you, too."

There soon came what she believed to be the most precious of all the exquisite moments they had had together. They stood in their living room, a little apart, simply touching. Never had her skin seemed so sensitized. Never had her fingers felt so alive as she touched him. "God, Tommy, that feels so good."

"Yes."

"I've never known your touch to be this way."

"God, yes. Your skin . . . I've never. . . ."

Both wanted to leap into each other's arms, but neither could relinquish the touching. They stood there, running their hands over each other, slowly, savoring electric sensations, seeking, finding the most sensitive places, reaching behind to caress back, bending to thighs and legs, even ankles, returning again and again to the most erotic places. Stephanie felt suspended in time, steeped in peerless pleasure, as their hands wrote a silent language of love. Her whole body throbbed. Her breasts felt so tight they might burst each time he found the risen, burning ends. He turned her, his arms enveloping her from the rear, kissing her back, sliding his face over it as his hands, his hands, kneaded, stroked, caressed her breasts and found, found her inner thighs, the tender, throbbing place. She heard the sounds of her own moaning as she arched her back, straining to feel more of him, reaching behind, filling her hands, hot, pulsating.

Finally she turned. For just a moment she was aware of being totally enveloped within him, her body pressed hard against his, each of his arms almost encircling her. How wondrous. She felt him, hard against her thigh, and moved, ensnaring him, moving her legs, squeezing, massaging.

"God, Stevie."

She was looking at him now, seeing the torment, the pleasure in his eyes. "I'll not let you forget me, Tommy."

She felt him bending his knees and understood. She rose to tiptoe, spread her legs and in a moment cried out from the ecstacy of the spreading, filling.

"Oh, Tommy, Tommy."

She felt she had become part of his body, pressed hard against him, encircled within his arms, pulled off her feet, their mouths and hips joined, herself utterly filled and, as he thrust hard within her, she felt her whole body disintegrate amid the rolling thunder of her passion and its release. Kincaid, her doubts, her fears, all were forgotten as she lost herself in passion for Thomas Hodges.

Fourteen

Stephanie told herself she might have enjoyed the baseball game if she were with Thomas, or even her brother Andrew, her Uncle Morgan—anyone but Winslow Kincaid. But that's whom she was with, and the result was an insufferable afternoon.

Her troubles, aside from not wanting to go at all, began with her realization that she had no idea what to wear. In the end she donned one of Pierre Chambeau's new fashions, a gown of white dotted Swiss. It was demure enough, with long sleeves and a collar to her throat, but more formfitting than she would have liked, especially since she was so uneasy about Kincaid. But she wanted to keep up appearances, and the fashion, accentuating narrow waist and height with the exaggerated shoulder pads, was already sweeping Chicago. Her outfit was completed with a matching parasol and a wide-brimmed chapeau. As soon as she arrived at the ball park near the lake at the foot of Randolph Street, she knew she was overdressed, attracting too much attention.

A greater source of dissatisfaction was that she was alone with Kincaid. She had expected, when he mentioned a box, that there would be a party of people in attendance. But there were just the two of them, and no escape from him. Other than the strain of smiling and talking to him, she was not worried about his actions at the stadium. There was an immense crowd for the game between the White Stockings and some team or other from New York—perhaps as many as eight thousand people. Kincaid was forced to keep his hands, if not his eyes, to himself.

There was one good thing. The game itself gave her something to talk about. She did not understand it one whit and could care less; grown men, wearing funny uniforms, hitting a ball with a stick, then running around to no good purpose. It was silly and excruciatingly boring to her, but she asked questions, never once bothering even to try to understand the complicated, nonsensical explanations. Ultimately her attention focused on a couple of the players who were obviously inebriated. She really wasn't interested in them, but it was something to look at.

The Chicago team apparently won, for Kincaid was ebullient as they left the stadium. "A very good game," he said. "I hope you enjoyed it, Stephanie."

She smiled. "Yes, it was most absorbing, Winslow." She hated calling him by his first name, but he insisted, leaving her no choice.

"Good. I can't tell you how pleased I am to take you to your first baseball contest."

"Thank you, Mr.—I mean Winslow."

As they climbed into his carriage, a handsome victoria drawn by a pair of caparisoned black bays, he said, "Now where would you like to have dinner? I had in mind. . . ."

She tuned out his choice, concentrating on the words she had planned for hours. Smiling wanly she said, "I'm sorry, Winslow, but I have a fearful headache."

"Oh, my dear, I hadn't realized."

"I thought it would go away, but the sun, the excitement." She patted his hand with her glove. "Would you mind just taking me home? I hate to spoil your evening, but I'm afraid I won't be much fun. I'm just not up to it today."

She saw disappointment, even a glint of anger in his eyes, but she had left him no choice but to take her home. She managed to leave him in the lobby, successfully insisting she didn't need a doctor, just a good night's rest.

To her relief she didn't hear from him all day Monday or Tuesday. It surprised her, and as Wednesday wore on she even began to believe she had perhaps misjudged him and his intentions. She busied herself with housecleaning, writing letters and daydreaming of Thomas. God, that extraordinary feeling of oneness that last night. How she loved him! She read herself to sleep at night to keep from thinking about him too much.

The phone rang late Wednesday afternoon. Her growing confidence in Kincaid was shattered the moment she heard his voice. "How're you feeling, Stevie?"

The question momentarily stymied her, in part because she was outraged at his familiarity in the use of her private diminutive. Then she remembered her nonexistent headache. "Better, Mr. Kincaid. Thank you."

"Winslow, please."

"I'm sorry. I quite forgot." But she deliberately declined to say the name.

"There's an important party at the Philip Armours' tonight. I'd like for you to attend as my guest."

Her reply was speeding to her lips even before he finished. "I'm sorry, Mr. Kincaid, but I—"

"I won't take no for an answer, Stevie. There will be important cattle shippers and meat packers there. It is crucial to our company interests. Thomas would want you to attend in his stead."

Panic rose in her. She felt a trap closing, but fought it. "I can't possibly take Thomas's place, Mr. Kincaid."

"Oh, but you can—and you will." He laughed. "I assure you, Stevie, you will be far more fascinating to potential customers than Thomas."

She was affronted by his disparagement of Thomas.

"So I'll not take no for an answer. I'll pick you up at eight."

She grimaced, but said, "All right, Mr. Kincaid. If you think it's important."

"I assure you it is—and my name is Winslow." There was a pause on the line, strangely nervous. "I'd like to ask a special favor of you, Stevie. Would you wear that, ah, lovely gold gown you had on the other night?"

It was an outrage. "Really, Mr. Kincaid, I—"

He laughed. "I know, I have no right to ask, but just this once. I have a good reason, which I'll show you when I see you. Goodbye, Stevie."

By the time eight o'clock rolled around, her rage had subsided, or nearly so. She was dressed in the backless, excessively décolleté gown he had requested. With all her heart she had wanted to spite him by wearing something else. But she willed herself to put on the dress she now hated. Kincaid was Thomas's employer. There was no point in alienating him. Thomas would expect her to handle this situation. And she ought to be able to.

One of the attractions of their new apartment house was that it boasted—quite literally, in the advertisements—a new communications system offering heightened security. The receptionist in the lobby could buzz any apartment, then actually speak over a wire, saying who was in the lobby asking to come up. Thus, Stephanie stood waiting for the buzzer and the voice over the intercom, intending to meet Kincaid in the lobby.

She was startled by the ringing of the doorbell. Puzzled, she opened the door on a smiling Winslow Kincaid, a bouquet of flowers in his hand. She could only stare. No one was supposed to get by the reception desk in the lobby. Yet apparently Kincaid had not found it difficult to do so.

"Forgive me, Stevie, but I convinced the doorman I wanted to surprise you."

"You certainly have done that." Quickly she forced herself to warm the coldness of her greeting with a smile. "Now that you're here, won't you come in, Mr. Kincaid?" Another smile. "Oh, yes, it's Winslow I'm supposed to say." She stepped back, letting him enter, aware of his eyes upon her. "I'm all ready. Just let me get my wrap." She hoped she did not sound as nervous as she felt.

"No rush at all, Stevie." He produced the bouquet. "I hope you like red roses."

She had to accept. "Why, thank you. I adore roses." Then came the business of unwrapping the tissue, exclaiming over the flowers, finding a vase, water, arranging the blooms, exclaiming over them again. She knew he was watching her, and she felt like a mouse with a cat. No, the prey of a vulture. "Two dozen. You shouldn't have."

"You're right. I should have made it three."

She smiled, tried to laugh, poked at a wayward stem. "They're breathtaking." She reached for her cape, which lay over a nearby chair. "I'm ready when you are."

"I came early. I want to have a chat and—" he smiled broadly, "—I've something I think you'll like."

"Really?"

"Yes, I said I had a reason for asking you to wear that gown—" again the broad smile, "—aside from how very fetching you look in it."

"Thank you." She waited, certain she had turned to wood on the way to petrification.

His smile now turned to a laugh. "Don't be so nervous, Stevie. I won't bite. And you might offer me a drink."

She was fully flustered. "I'm sorry, of course." Somehow she made her way to the buffet, the tray of bottles. "What would you like, brandy?"

"If you will."

She poured the spirit and a small sherry for herself, brought his to him. He raised his glass in a toast. His dark eyes were like two holes in the mask of his face.

"To an extremely attractive young woman who does not realize her inestimable value to our enterprise."

"Thank you, but I'm afraid I do not." She was about to say she was just a girl about to wed his employee Thomas Hodges, when she was distracted by the movement of his hand, reaching inside his dinner jacket, extracting a long, narrow box.

"This may help you understand your role better."

She set down her sherry, untouched, took the box, opened it and gasped. Inside the box was a necklace, fashioned of heavy gold, made into squares linked together. In the center of each square was a star sapphire, graduated in size to the center one, which had to be over a half-inch in diameter.

"Now you know why I asked you to wear this gown. The other evening I saw you wore no jewelry. I thought at once of something like this. At first I had in mind diamonds. Then I realized it had to be star sapphires, to match your eyes. I had it made for you."

She was aghast, astonished, dismayed. "I—I can't . . . accept this."

"Of course you can. It becomes you."

"I can't accept this." She raised her head from the gems, turned, saw his beaming countenance. "I can't. I'm engaged to Thomas. We're to be married when he returns."

"Of course, my dear. No one will realize the value of this trinket more than young Hodges. He will consider it a most suitable bonus for his efforts, which it is, of course."

She stared at him. "Do you mean that?"

"I do." He laughed. "I not only pay his salary, but if I wish to give his bonus to his attractive fiancée, that is my prerogative."

"It's a bonus for Thomas?"

"And for you—for gracing our meetings, enhancing our public image."

She felt confused, dazed, uncertain.

"Why don't you try it on?"

The box was in his hand and she was lifting out the necklace, reaching behind her head to fasten it.

"Let me do that for you."

"I can manage."

"Don't be silly. The giver of jewelry gets to put it on."

She turned her back to him then, lifted her hair to the side, let his hands come around her neck. It was intimate, much too intimate.

"It's lovely on you, Stevie, just lovely."

She went to a mirror. Instantly she hated the bauble, garish, ostentatious, destroying the effect of her gown. Pierre Chambeau had been wholly right in his caution about gilding the lily. She turned back to Kincaid, her mind racing for some way to refuse. For once he was not looking at her. His head was tilted back as he drained his glass.

"May I help myself to another?"

"Of course." Warily she watched him go to the bar, refill his glass. He seemed to look around for the first time.

"An attractive flat, very modern. You have excellent taste."

"Thank you."

He seemed to pick out a chair, then sat in it. "We have plenty of time, Stevie. Please sit. Let's have a chat."

On guard, she sat in the Morris chair, several feet away from him.

"Your sherry, my dear." He rose, retrieved her wine and brought it to her.

"Thank you." She was relieved when he resumed his former seat. How could he be so relaxed when she was wound tight as a mainspring?

His smile was actually benevolent. "My dear Stevie, I don't know when I've met a young woman so endearing and exciting as you are. Thomas is very fortunate to have you as his wife, as he soon will."

Some reply was in order, but she could think of nothing.

"Yes, Thomas will go a long way with you at his side. His future at American Western is brilliant. His abilities, his conscientiousness insure that. And to have a companion, a wife like you"—his smile was cagily expansive—"why, the sky's the limit for him."

She heard his words, but still no thought, no word would come to her.

"Of course, he's young, untried, inexperienced, but he's learning. Mistakes are unavoidable, quite often threatening. As his wife"—again the expansive smile—"I should say as his prospective bride, you will want to do *everything* to prevent such a mistake, won't you?"

It was a question. He was looking at her, expecting an answer.

"I—I don't understand what you mean."

"I think you do, Stevie." His face grew somber, his voice a trifle hard. "You are a most attractive young woman. Quite a remarkable figure. As I said, you are exciting. I'm sure you'll want to do whatever is required to insure the continued success of the man you're about to marry."

The meaning of his words was so plain he might have bludgeoned her with them: Still, she said, "You're not serious!"

"I'm afraid I am, my darling."

She stared at him, unable to believe her ears. Suddenly his face was an apparition. She could not bear to look at it and rose abruptly, turning her back. Mindlessly she strode to a table near the wall phone, leaned both hands on it, trembling. Silence rose in the room like a physical force, until she filled it. "You want me to go to bed with you?"

"Yes."

"And that is the price of Thomas's success?"

"I'm afraid so." He laughed. "I should say, I hope so."

She turned to face him. "And if I refuse?"

His reply was a small smile and an elaborate shrug of his shoulders. His eyes seemed fastened to her, mesmerizing. She turned away, desperate for escape. Her wrap on the chair back. "Hadn't we better go to the party?"

"There is no party at the Philip Armours', Stevie. The only party is this one—just the two of us."

From the corner of her eye she saw him rise, come to her. Then his hands were on her upper arms, turning her, making her look at him. "Oh, please. . . ." It was a plaintive wail. His face was coming toward her to kiss her. She felt his hot breath, smelled the brandy. At the last moment she turned her cheek. *"Oh, please . . . don't!"*

"Oh, come now, Stevie, don't act the innocent maiden. You and Hodges have—" He laughed. "It's time you knew an experienced man. You'll be better for it. Hodges will thank me."

Her whole body trembled. She couldn't breathe, think. Her head was reeling.

The buzzer.

The sound screamed through her and she leaped backward. Frantically she searched the wall, found the button that activated the intercom, pushed. "Yes?"

"I let the gentleman come up, Miss Summers. Was it all right to do?"

The words, distorted as they came from the wall speaker, had no meaning to her. All she wanted to do was scream for help, but she didn't know how to.

"There's another gentleman here to see you, miss. A Mr. Hodges."

That had meaning. *"Thomas!"*

"No, miss, a Mr. Lawrence Hodges."

Oh, God, grandfather. "Send him up at once, *please."*

Fifteen

Larry Hodges, Thomas's father, stepgrandfather to Stephanie, was now sixty-one, but looked and acted a good ten years younger. Age was kind to him, for he remained tall, slender and in good health. His brown hair had become salted, white at the temples, but the heavy brush mustache he affected remained a rich brown, showing up well against his ruddy complexion. He was a distinguished-looking man, his appearance enhanced by his relaxed informality and the poise gleaned from a life of association with the great and near-great of America.

Stephanie was waiting in the open doorway when he stepped off the elevator. She ran into his arms before he had made two strides. Lawrence Hodges was a bit startled by the greeting, the tears of joy that came into her eyes, but then she had always been an affectionate child. No, hardly a child anymore. As he held her away, smiling, he was momentarily stunned by her beauty, the glories of her figure revealed by the gown. But his discomfort was fleeting. After twenty years of marriage to the still-glamorous and lusty Moira Morgan Kingston, his long association with the beautiful women of this family left him with few surprises.

"How gorgeous you look, Stevie. But you're going out. I'll only stay a minute."

His words flustered her. "No, no, I'm not going out—the party was canceled." Fright in her eyes, she rose to tiptoe and whispered in his ear, "Stay, please. You must stay." Then, aloud, as though for other ears, she said, "It's so good to see you, grandfather. Do come in."

As she took his arm, leading him to the apartment, he said, "Is Thomas here?"

"He's away on a business trip, grandfather. I'll explain everything."

Larry's surprise and puzzlement at seeing a short, burly man in the apartment, a brandy snifter in his hand, was genuine, although it would have taken a keen and knowledgeable observer to detect it.

"Grandfather, this is Mr. Winslow Kincaid. He's Thomas's employer."

The second half of the introduction was unnecessary as Kincaid strode across the room, smiling, right hand extended. "And you must be Thomas's father. I can't tell you what a pleasure it is to meet you."

The Washington attorney took the proffered hand, shook it firmly. "Mr. Kincaid, I'm pleased to meet you. American Western, isn't it?"

Kincaid was grinning, acting as if what had almost happened had never entered his mind. Stephanie couldn't believe the change in him.

"I want to tell you what a fine boy you have. He has a brilliant future with us. One might even say dazzling—as I was just telling Miss Summers—wasn't I, Stephanie?"

His hidden meaning thrust into her. She couldn't speak.

"Yes, Thomas is a fine young man, invaluable to me."

"He's not here?"

Hodges spoke to Stephanie, but Kincaid answered. "He's off completing the purchase of a few railroad cars for us."

Larry smiled. "Oh, yes, so I've heard—only I believe it's more than a few."

For the first time there was a hint of nervousness in Kincaid, as he laughed. "Perhaps it is. But I believe a company inventory can never be too large." Awkwardness, uneasy, discomforting, rose as a miasma then. Kincaid acted to ward it off. "I'd best be going. I imagine you two have a lot of catching up to do." Nervously he went to retrieve his top hat, gloves and stick. "I just dropped by to see how Stephanie was getting along, didn't I, my dear?"

She heard the threat in his voice and somehow found a reply. "Yes, of course. Thank you, Mr. Kincaid." She even managed to show him out the door, not missing the hard glint of warning in his eyes as he said goodnight.

None of this was lost on Larry Hodges, although he was greatly puzzled as to its meaning. His instant decision was to say nothing. Rather, when Stephanie closed the door and turned around, he offered, "Stevie, you look positively devastating."

The exaggerated compliment unnerved her. She looked down at herself, seeing her near-nakedness. "I'm sorry, grandfather. Give me a minute to change."

"You'll do no such thing." He laughed. "When you get to be my age, Stevie, the charms of a beautiful young woman are some of life's higher pleasures." He saw the doubt in her eyes, almost pain. "I mean every word, Stevie."

She ran to him then, throwing her arms around him. "Oh, grandfather, I'm so glad you're here!"

Remembering Kincaid, like Stephanie dressed for the evening but going nowhere, he had an idea just how glad she was. "And to think I almost didn't come. I was in Springfield, meeting with the governor, some legislative leaders. At the last moment I decided to come up here and see how Thomas is doing—and you."

Suddenly fearful, she stood back, looking up at him. "Grandfather, you don't mind . . . us? You don't . . . disapprove of . . . of Thomas and me, do you?"

"Do you love each other?"

"Oh, yes—madly."

His grin couldn't have been more avuncular. "Then I think my son is extremely fortunate." He kissed her forehead. "I really am surprised at his good sense."

"Do you mean it, grandfather? I love him so."

"As I said, he is most fortunate."

"And I am, too, grandfather."

His smile faded just a little as he nodded, said, "Yes." The change in mood was not lost on her as she asked if he wanted a drink, then fetched him a whiskey.

"Why did you really come here, grandfather?"

"To see Thomas and you."

"I know that. But why? This is a little more than just a family visit, isn't it?"

He smiled. "Among the reasons Thomas is so fortunate in you is that you are perceptive, Stevie." He motioned to a chair, as though asking permission to sit. She nodded. When he was seated, his long legs crossed, his whiskey tasted, he said, "As a matter of fact, I'm worried about Thomas." He saw her reaction. "I don't mean his personal life—although I do wish you two were married."

"We're going to be very soon, grandfather. As soon as Thomas returns."

"Glad to hear it. I'm sure you'll help him come to his senses."

"About what?"

He looked up at her a moment. "Why don't you sit, Stevie?" He waited till she was arranged on the sofa, a little sideways, facing him, her legs tucked under her. He smiled at her. "Would you mind if I had a cigar?" She didn't mind, and the business of lighting took its leisurely time. Finally, through a cloud of blue-gray smoke, Larry said, "I was pleased to meet Kincaid a few minutes ago. Gave me a chance to sort of get the feel of him." He rendered a sort of half-snort. "I gather, though, you were not glad to have him here. I rather had the feeling I was rescuing you." He watched her eyes and knew he was right.

"I did nothing, grandfather, he—"

"I know. Just be careful with him, Stevie, very careful." He sighed. "I only wish Thomas would be."

She waited, watching him puff on the cigar, sip his whiskey. He would speak in his own good time.

"Kincaid is playing a very dangerous game—dangerous for him, the country, the people of this country. And it is dangerous for Thomas. I hate to see my son involved. I hate it more than I can tell you."

Still she waited.

"This business of cornering railroad cars is bold, risky. I'd admire the pure brigandry of it, if it weren't so potentially lethal for the country." He looked at her sharply. "Do you have any idea what I'm talking about?"

"Yes."

He didn't believe her. "He's trying to buy up all the rolling stock, then lease it back to the operating railroads."

"I know that. I've been uneasy myself."

"He's already moving to create an artificial shortage of freight cars. He'll drive the cost of transportation in this country sky-high."

"Yes. Men are already out of work because of it. The price of bread just went up two cents."

He stared at her in disbelief, then he grinned. "You're not only gorgeous, but smart, too. Does my son realize what a prize he has in you?"

She ignored the flattery, her mind on what caused her fear. "How is Thomas in danger?" Then she waited out the recrossing of his legs, the cigar, the lifted whiskey glass.

"Kincaid will not get away with this, any more than

Fisk and Gould did when they tried to corner the gold market in Sixty-nine. It's too bad Grover Cleveland was defeated for reelection last year. But even so staunch and conservative a Republican as Benjamin Harrison will be forced to act to save the country from what amounts to piracy and blackmail." Another puff on the cigar, a long ash unrolled. "Men like Kincaid—and there are lots of others—rich, powerful, ruthless and becoming more so all the time, bent on acquiring more and more power. Actually they are robbers, stealing from the people, their own workers, their stockholders, the whole country. They seem to be creating wealth, but they are actually destroying it, denuding forests, squandering precious resources, polluting everything they touch, and all in the name of personal aggrandizement. They are robbers. Indeed, the term is being used. Kincaid is a Robber Baron."

She heard his eloquence, but cared only for one thing. "What of Thomas?"

"We're getting a late start, Stevie. By *we* I mean those of us in government and elsewhere who are concerned about what is happening and trying to stop Kincaid and the others—Rockefeller, Armour, Carnegie, Vanderbilt, the rich thieves among us. I was just in the state capital talking with the governor and legislative leaders about Kincaid. They're worried and want to enact laws to stop him." He sighed. "But the states can't do much. Kincaid will just incorporate in New Jersey or some state that coddles these people. It'll be business as usual. Only the federal government can act. And the Robber Barons are spending fortunes to see that Congress fails to act. But the people are concerned. Congress will be *forced* to act. Right now I'm employed by John Sherman of Ohio and a group of other senators. They want to push through some antitrust legislation to curb men like Kincaid."

"Tell me about Thomas, grandfather. I don't understand."

"Kincaid must be stopped, by whatever means we

have at hand. We can't wait for legislation. I'm preparing a dossier on Thomas's employer and his activities. At the very least we will expose him to the public. But I'm hoping for some kind of criminal charge. We suspect he has bribed some public officials here in Chicago. A couple of recent train derailments look extremely suspicious. I hear he has a goon squad wrecking trains. In his greed he'll do anything to force up prices. But we'll get him. You just watch."

"But Thomas?"

He looked at her a long moment, remembering just in time to catch the long ash on his cigar. "Surely you understand, Stevie. If we bring down Kincaid, or just succeed in holding him up to public calumny—well, I'm terribly worried about what will befall his chief errand boy and hatchet man. Or whatever title Kincaid has given Thomas."

"Chief counsel, I think."

"That's even worse. Can you imagine my being in court fighting my son? What would it be like for me to testify at a trial that ruins Thomas's career, maybe puts him behind bars?"

She sucked in her breath, making an audible sound. "You can't mean that?"

"I'm sorry, Stevie, but it's a distinct possibility. Kincaid must be stopped. I would not hesitate to bring down my son, if that is what is required." He watched her eyes, seeing the fright in them. In compassion he softened his voice. "Do you have any capacity to reason with Tom, get him to leave Kincaid while he still can?"

"I—I don't know."

"I certainly can't get through to him. I opposed his coming out here in the first place. And I've worried myself half-sick over the meteoric rise he's had. Now he's deeply involved. Can't he see what sort of man Kincaid is?"

"I d-don't think so."

He looked at her sharply. "But you know, don't you?

Did Kincaid . . . was he trying to . . . to take advantage of you?"

"Yes. That's why I wanted you to stay." Her voice was little above a whisper.

In his anger Larry Hodges leaped out of his chair. "Lord, such a man! He is totally without principle or decency. We've got to bring Thomas to his senses. You will tell him, of course."

"I—I don't see how I can. He'll lose his job. I'll just have to . . . deal with it, somehow."

"Stevie, tell him, let him have it out with Kincaid. Anything to get him to leave this scoundrel."

She looked up at him, her eyes meeting his levelly. "It won't work, grandfather. Kincaid will say I'm imagining things, or that it was all a misunderstanding. He'll even say I enticed him here. If I tell Thomas, all I'll do is drive a wedge between us. He'll come to distrust me."

Larry stared at her a long moment, then wearily sat back down. "You're right, I suppose."

"Thomas believes everything Kincaid says. He worships him as some sort of—I don't know, god of success, I guess."

"Yes, that says it pretty well." He sighed, then drained the last of his whiskey. "What bothers me is that it is so foreign to my son's real nature. He wasn't brought up this way by me or your grandmother. There is nothing in the whole family association to make him suddenly so greedy for money, mad for power."

"I don't think he is, grandfather, at least not personally. He's just . . . enamored of the whole process of big business, of wheeling and dealing. I think he wants to participate, see if he can do it. It's a game to him."

"A deadly game."

"Thomas says there is nothing wrong with making money. It makes the country great."

"Of course there's nothing wrong with it, and he's right about our growing national wealth. But it's the way the money is made. Right here in Chicago you have a man, Cyrus McCormick. He manufactures farm machinery, his famous reaper and such. A giant company, really revolutionizing farming. And McCormick is a fabulously wealthy man. But he's done it by making a good product and selling it. He hasn't entered into monopolistic Trusts. He hasn't squeezed out competition by price-cutting, demanding rebates from railroads, sabotage and the other methods of the Robber Barons. McCormick has shown what big business ought to be. We need more like him.''

There was a lengthy silence between them then, as they each thought their private thoughts. Finally Stephanie said, "I'll try to talk to Thomas, grandfather. Maybe it'll help."

"I'm sure it will. He couldn't resist you—I'll never believe it, Stevie.'' Smiling, Lawrence Hodges stood up. "I'm tired. I'd better go to my hotel."

"Oh, please stay. You can sleep here.'' Then she remembered. They had not furnished the other bedrooms. "I—I can sleep on the couch. You can have the bed."

He laughed. "No, I'd better go to the Palmer House. Besides, I hardly think Kincaid will bother you any more tonight."

"But tomorrow, I—"

"I really should get back to Washington." Hodges smiled. "But I doubt if civilization would end if I took a day off to allow a pretty girl, my future daughter-in-law, to show me the sights of Chicago."

"Oh, yes, yes."

"Will that help? I can only stay the one day."

"Yes, I'm hoping Thomas will be back on Friday."

Thursday was a thrilling day for Stephanie, sightseeing, lunch, dinner, talking, laughing, hearing of the family from a courtly older man who showed her only affection and admiration. He made her feel not just beautiful, but intelligent, too, a worthwhile person. At one point, over dinner, she said, "If Thomas, when he's older, isn't as handsome and full of grace as you, grandfather, I'll have made a terrible mistake. I know now that's why I'm marrying him—in hopes he'll be like you."

Larry could only laugh.

"No wonder Grandmother Moira loves you so."

An image of Moira crossed his mind, her fiery red-haired passion, pent up while he was away. "It will be good to get home," he said softly.

Sixteen

Thomas did not get home on Friday. Instead, Stephanie received a telegram, hastily sent from Denver. He was on his way to San Francisco and couldn't possibly get home before Wednesday. He loved her and missed her.

Stephanie read the telegram both in sadness and fear. Kincaid would surely come after her now, demanding satisfaction. But, thanks to Grandfather Hodges—she was going to have to learn to call him father, not grandfather—she knew what she had to do. She would refuse Kincaid, spurn him, fight him and, if necessary, call the police. If he took it out on Thomas, demoting, even firing him, so much the better. Thomas shouldn't be working for a man like Kincaid anyway. And he didn't need him. As grandfather had said, Thomas was a good enough lawyer to make it on his own. And there was always a place for him in grandfather's Washington law firm. As soon as Thomas came home, she was going to convince him, if it was the last thing she ever did.

But having made up her mind about what she must do with Kincaid did not make the doing of it easy to contemplate. Nevertheless, when he telephoned at midday on Friday, she was iron-willed. He was picking her up at seven. They would have an early supper, then he was taking her to the Orpheum Theater to see Mlle. De Lacour's troupe of cancan dancers. Stephanie knew it was a naughty show, not at all a respectable place to take her. But she acquiesced. This night had to be, no matter what. Mr. Kincaid, dear Winslow, was in for a surprise. Yet her determination could not quite quell a lingering fear. Kincaid was a strong man. Perhaps it would have been better to tell him on the phone. No, there had to be a face-to-face confrontation.

The phone rang again. She lifted the receiver and spoke into the mouthpiece, detecting once again the odor of hard rubber.

"Miss Summers?"

"Yes."

"This is Gerald Rawlings." She was still casting for recognition when he aided her. "The manager of American Western's main works."

"Oh, yes, Mr. Rawlings. I remember you."

"Do you recall Mr. Kincaid's asking me to give you a plant tour? Would this afternoon be all right?"

She had quite forgotten Kincaid's impulsive order at the party, and touring a factory had no appeal for her. But it was something to do, and it would give her something to talk to Kincaid about. Might even take his mind off his lust for a while. "I'd love to, Mr. Rawlings. This afternoon is fine."

"I'll send someone to pick you up. Would three be all right?"

"Certainly. I'll be ready and waiting in the lobby."

Stephanie had no idea what to wear on a factory tour and figured whatever she chose would be wrong. After trying on three different outfits, she selected a fourth—for comfort. It was a stifling day in Chicago—sultry, temperature in the nineties. She settled upon her coolest garment, a light blue, thin cotton. It was formfitting with a narrow skirt, and the neckline, scooped front and back, was not as modest as she would have liked. But she decided the décolletage was not too extreme and the open throat would surely be cooling. Best, the gown was sleeveless, afternoon modesty being preserved by fabric draped capelike over her shoulders and upper arms. Deliberately she wore no chemise or petticoat, just Chambeau's abbreviated undergarment. This way she felt able to combat the heat—or at least look cool when she wasn't. With a small, frilly chapeau, graced by an osprey feather, and carrying a parasol, she judged the outfit was undoubtedly too dressy for the occasion. But what was she to do? Frowning once more at the half-valley at her bosom, she decided to exchange the parasol for a fan. It could be used as a screen and would help keep her cool.

Stephanie had met Rawlings but had no memory of him. She was greeted by a tall, heavily built man, ham-handed with reddish-blond hair and a florid face. His size might have been intimidating, except that his voice was high-pitched, incongruously so, and his manner toward her courtly and deferential. In his fifties, he struck her as a former worker who had risen to become a manager, which was true. He served her a tall, cool lemonade, which she enjoyed, while he rendered a lengthy, statistic-filled description of the plant and its products. She tried to follow what he was saying and learn about the plant, but her mind was on Kincaid and what she now feared would be a most difficult evening. Then she realized Rawlings had stopped talking and was looking at her hesitantly.

"Is something wrong, Mr. Rawlings?"

"No, miss—it's just—well, are you sure you want this tour? The factory doesn't strike me as the proper place for a distinguished lady like yourself."

She smiled. "Do we have any choice, Mr. Rawlings?

I distinctly remember Mr. Kincaid giving us both our marching orders."

"That's true, miss." He smiled, but still studied her apprehensively.

"Now what's wrong, Mr. Rawlings?"

He sighed. "That dress, miss. Real purty it is, but the factory is kinda dirty. I was just wondering if, well, if I had a coat or something for you to put on."

She laughed and took his arm. "Mr. Rawlings, you are a most thoughtful man, but why don't we just get this over with?"

Accompanied by a younger aide, introduced to her as Ralph Andrews, they left the office, strode down a hallway, over a catwalk, down metal stairs, through an open doorway and into the main factory floor.

Nothing had prepared her for the plant. She felt as if she had entered hell. The heat battered her, oppressive, as though she were thrust into an oven, and with the conglomeration of stenches, musty, soiled, acrid, she felt unable to breathe. And the noise! It was a nightmare, making her want to scream for it to stop, all metallic clatter and sharp, irregular bangs, punctuated with the rhythmic hissing of steam. She heard Rawlings shout something in her ear, but couldn't understand him. She wondered if she were going to faint.

The building was rectangular, immense, nearly windowless, and it took a minute or two for her eyes to adjust to the gloom. What she finally saw appalled her, immense machines trailing clouds of steam, a forest of belts reaching up to the ceiling, a large, open space at one end where men seemed to be putting together a locomotive, and everywhere litter and filth, stacks of scrap metal, piles of metal shavings and stinking rags. She even saw rats scurrying across the greasy earthen floor.

The workers stunned her. Even the biggest and strongest seemed thin, haggard, their eyes sunken. All were filthy, their hands black with grease, their faces and bodies stained, and most had cuts and scratches, some ulcerating, others dripping fresh blood. Some of the men were naked to the waist, their bodies dripping sweat. Others wore filthy shirts and trousers that were little more than rags. Not a few were barefoot, despite the greasy floor and metal fragments.

But it was the faces of the workers that affected her, as they ran the infernal machines or banged away with hammers, mauls and other tools. Some were gray-beards, too old for such heavy work, although she could not know they were only in their fifties. She was appalled to see boys, some as young as eight and nine, squirting with oilcans or toting loads that had to weigh more than they did.

Resolutely, fighting vertigo, she followed Rawlings and Andrews down an aisle between some machinery, stopping, seeing them point, hearing them shout descriptions of what the machines did. At least she supposed that's what they were saying. All she wanted to do was scream and run from this hellhole. It took all her will not to. Workers stopped and stared at her with haunted eyes. A few nodded, smiling sheepishly. She read their lips as they said, "How do, ma'am?" Other faces bore surprise, disbelief, lecherous smirks, and over and over open hostility that bordered on hatred. Repeatedly she felt their eyes strip her gown from her. Fear and apprehension rose in her breast. And in her pretty, frivolous gown, fluttering her fan, she felt ridiculously, even obscenely dressed beside these pitiful creatures. What must they think of her? And these men, these children, working here all their lives, day after day, stunted, desperate, so she could live in luxury. She had never dreamed.

She was led deeper and deeper into hell, amid the suffering and surely damned. A man approached, healthier, better dressed, festooned with arrogance. She felt his black eyes consuming her, then he was bowing. Rawlings's shouts were obviously an introduction. She made out the word "foreman." The two men seemed to confer, heads together, shouting. She stood there, waiting, wishing the foreman would turn away, stop looking up and down her body. Oh, why hadn't she worn something else?

Then he did turn, off to the right to where Rawlings pointed. In an open space near the front of the locomotive they were building, she saw a knot of men, perhaps two dozen or thirty, with more joining all the time. A man was gesturing, telling them something. Then the foreman was marching to them, obviously bent on breaking up the group. She couldn't hear, but from gestures she gathered the foreman was ordering a man out of the plant. He kept pointing toward the door, shouting. He shoved the fellow, a youngish man in a scraggly beard and threadbare suit, toward the door. The worker shoved back. The foreman stumbled backward into the arms of some workers who held him by the arms.

Rawlings was seen, and the whole group of men, their numbers now growing rapidly, marched toward him—and her. Angered, Rawlings stood his ground, halting them. He and the man in the suit began to shout at each other. Over the din she could hear only occasional words, "Get out," "union," "organize." The shouting and screaming grew worse, and in his rage the florid face of Gerald Rawlings became the color of raw liver. The huge hand, which had been pointing toward the open door, suddenly became a fist. He struck the union man in the face, a hard, savage blow. Stephanie saw him fall backward, obviously unconscious, into the arms of workers surrounding him.

The reaction was stunned silence, shock. But it lasted only a second, then all the men were shouting, fists raised in the air. Even over the hellish racket she heard, "STRIKE! STRIKE! STRIKE!" A dozen greasy hands seized Rawlings and began to drag him away, kicking, struggling, cursing.

She felt a tug at her arm. "Let's get out of here." It was Andrews, pointing back toward the way they had come. Then he was running, pulling her after him. Past one machine they ran, a second. Then no further. The way was blocked by a half-dozen men, all shouting, "STRIKE!" and thrusting their fists into the air. Andrews tried to turn another way. No use. They were surrounded. She screamed. Her hand came to her mouth in the purest terror she had ever known. Panic gripped her. She ran, shoving her body forward, trying to bolt past the phalanx of workers, screaming.

A futile effort. Rough hands seized her. Arms came around her from behind, pulling her away. She felt one of the capelike sleeves being ripped from her. Her chapeau fell off. Again and again she screamed. Yet somehow she heard against her ear, "Don't fight, ma'am. I'll look after you."

She was being dragged, pulled toward the open place where the half-finished locomotive was. She turned her head, looking back to the man who had spoken. He was filthy, wearing rags, his face smeared with grease, but he was young, beardless, fair-skinned. She caught a glimpse of brilliant blue eyes. He was nodding to her, encouraging her not to resist, trying to reassure her.

Then she could see him no more. She was in the open space, surrounded by men, her wrists held. She looked down at herself. Her dress had black smears on it. One was at her right breast. Someone had touched her there, and she hadn't realized it.

"STRIKE! STRIKE! STRIKE!"

It was a rhythmic roar, as though from a single, massive voice. Across from her she saw Rawlings, still struggling, though uselessly, against the hands that held him. His face was blackened, bloodied, his clothes dirty, torn. Obviously he had been beaten. To her right she saw Andrews, similarly seized, although not beaten. Then she saw the foreman. He lay on the floor, a mass of blood. She screamed, couldn't help it.

"STRIKE! STRIKE! STRIKE! STRIKE!"

The chant continued, and she realized most of the other noise had stopped, the machinery shut down. Only the hiss of steam could be heard above the massed voices.

"STRIKE! STRIKE!"

Then she saw the union man, the one in the threadbare suit, rise above the crowd, standing on something. He was waving his arms, trying to silence the shouting, finally succeeding.

"You want STRIKE? STRIKE you shall have!"

An unearthly din arose from the massed voices, cheers, yells, then once more a prolongation of the deafening chant, "STRIKE! STRIKE! STRIKE! STRIKE!"

The union man again waved his arms for silence. "We, the workers, have seized the American Western works." More cheers. "We will be oppressed no longer." Cheers. "We will not be enslaved." Each utterance produced cheers now. "We will have decent wages, decent working conditions. We will not die here for Winslow Kincaid."

At the mention of the name, a fearful sound, like a massive growl, rose as from a single throat. Stephanie shuddered as a new chant began, "DEATH TO KINCAID! DEATH TO KINCAID!"

Again the arms were waved, a measure of silence achieved. "We have taken over Kincaid's plant. He must deal with us."

This led to another tumult. Once more the union man waved for order. But before he could speak, someone shouted, "Let's get Rawlings!" Across from her she saw hands pulling at the manager's arms, a fist pound into him.

The man in the suit jumped down from his perch and waded into the crowd, stopping the assault. She heard him shout, "No, no, stop it. We need him." Then he was back above the crowd. "He is our hostage; the other one, too. Kincaid will hear our demands or—"

The threat was lost in the roar of raised voices. All were shouting different slogans, curses, threats.

The arms were waved again, the noise subsided. Then came a voice from behind her. "Let the woman go." She recognized it as the voice she had heard in her ear.

For a moment she thought it was going to happen: They would let her go. The pressure on her wrists and arms seemed to lessen. Then the union man was looking at her, smirking. "No," he shouted. "She's Kincaid's doxy. I saw them at the ball game together. He'll give anything to get her back."

Stephanie shook her head violently, screaming that it wasn't so, but her voice was lost in the massed clamor of outrage against her—against *her*. Fear, panic gripped her, and she struggled against the hands that held her. But to no avail. She felt hands on her body, gripping her breasts and, mind reeling, she knew she was sinking toward oblivion.

The wail of sirens saved her.

"POLICE! COPS!"

There came a moment of stunned silence, then an angry roar as men rushed through the open door, toward the street beyond. Many brandished clubs, strips of metal, tools. For a second Stephanie thought she would be forgotten because of the new peril. But no. She was still held inside the building, Rawlings and Andrews, too.

She couldn't really see what was happening out in the street, but the sounds left no doubt, the clatter of police horses and wagons, a gruff voice ordering the workers to disperse, angry shouts of defiance, the strident sounds of scuffling, groans, curses, threats; then, finally, to her horror, cracking, popping sounds, agonized screams, more popping sounds. The police were shooting.

It happened rapidly then, terrified men running back into the building, a glimpse of bloody bodies on the street outside, pure terror, pellmell panic. She heard a shout, "BRING THE HOSTAGES." Then she was being pulled, carried through the building, out the back, up the stairs. Oblivion came to her. Mercifully.

Part III

Aurial

Seventeen

The moment she saw her daughter, Moira Hodges knew the day of reckoning, so long dreaded, had come. Danielle was as beautiful as ever, though perhaps too thin, yet her inner wound showed in her eyes. She was suffering, and Moira was not at all sure how to help her, though she was determined to try.

Moira believed she knew the roots of Danielle's unhappiness. Etched in her mind was a vision of a sunny afternoon thirteen years before. Moira was standing in an upstairs window at Aurial, looking out at the gazebo where Danielle and her husband, Walter Summers, were talking. They were estranged. Walt had come north to Maryland to seek a reconciliation. Moira couldn't hear them, yet she could tell the conversation in the gazebo wasn't going well. When she saw Walt raise his hand to Danielle, barely restraining himself, then stalk away, out of her life, Moira had put her hand to her mouth to stop her own scream of anguish.

Not a day had elapsed since then that Moira did not

worry about her daughter. She knew with certainty what Danielle was going through—and that her actions were the wrong ones.

Like mother, like daughter. For much of her life Moira had suffered from seemingly unquenchable passions. As a girl of eighteen, she had given herself to Brad Kingston, who had ruled her body as no man since. But "King" Kingston was a rake, gambler, womanizer, utterly worthless, and she had had the good sense to choose his brother.

She had loved Ned Kingston with all her heart. He was a tender, even expert lover, but at best he could only bank her internal fires, not quench them. Then, when he was killed at Gettysburg, her true hell began. She wanted a man so badly—and plenty were available —she felt at times her whole body was screaming. She would look at herself, brilliant red hair, sensuous mouth, ripe body, the vivid zone of flame, her risen breasts, and weep for the wanting to be admired and to give and give and give of herself. Memories of her titanic passions with King Kingston were torture. Yet for seven years she did not take a man, knowing that if she once did, there would be no end to it and she would be ruined. Finally she met Larry Hodges and found true happiness; blessed relief came to her at last.

With her red hair and voluptuous body there had never been any doubt of the passions which lay within Moira Hodges. But Danielle's appearance was deceiving. She seemed so cool, yet she was cursed with the same insatiable fires that plagued her mother. Walt Summers, who had set off the holocaust, was equal to the task. But when he walked out of Danielle's life, Moira shook with fear for her daughter.

Danielle's undoing was Benjamin Fairchild. Moira was fond of him, but time and again she wished Ben would disappear from the face of the earth. Without him—decent, thoughtful, desperately loving Danielle —she would have gone back to Walt Summers and worked out their differences. But Benjamin was there. Danielle divorced and planned to marry Ben. Moira didn't approve, but she realized Danielle would probably have a happy life with her new lover. Then disaster struck with Benjamin's death. Danielle was lost, for she had already given herself to a man other than her husband. There came then a succession of men, until it led to this day of reckoning.

Moira felt she alone knew and understood the pain of her daughter, although she felt her own mother, Glenna, would be far more adept at helping her. Glenna and Danielle, looking so much alike, had always responded to each other with a marked empathy. But Glenna was in New York. It would be a hardship for her to come to Aurial. Moira would do the best she could.

She began by expunging from herself any lurking hint of disapproval of Danielle, offering her only unstinting love and acceptance. Wordless, with eyes alone, she got the others at Aurial to do the same. Morgan Kingston, master of the huge estate on the Patuxent River, had always been close to his sister. Morgan's wife, Miriam Hodges Kingston, still so very blonde and beautiful, reacted to Danielle like a loving sister, which of course she was by marriage. Young Ned Kingston, now eleven, was a properly worshipful nephew. But it was Louise Kingston, a budding thirteen, who was perhaps most effective. The seed of Glenna Morgan had sprung to life again in this family, for this beautiful child of Morgan and Miriam had Glenna's Irish coloring, black hair, sapphire eyes, snowy complexion. This was, of course, Danielle's coloring, and the two, despite their ages, looked amazingly alike. There was a bond between them, and Moira believed Louise's adoring affection for her aunt would do more to cure Danielle's melancholy than anything else. Sooner or later Danielle would begin to forget herself and reach out to Louise.

Moira set in motion an atmosphere at Aurial that she

believed would help Danielle recover her self-esteem, but such indirection, learned from Glenna, was really foreign to her nature. Always impetuous, Moira was best in striking directly at the heart of a problem, which she proceeded to do during Danielle's third afternoon back at Aurial. Mother and daughter went for a stroll along the river, down to the old Kingston place, then back to Aurial to sit in the gazebo.

"I wish I knew your secret." Danielle's answer was to look at her mother questioningly. "I just wish I knew how you can eat so little and keep your figure. You are as petite and lovely as ever." Danielle rendered a small smile, but still did not speak. Moira's laugh was full-throated. "I swear, Danny, my hips have become my enemy."

There was no doubt Moira Hodges, despite her valiant efforts, was losing the battle of the bulge. At fifty-seven she was far from unsightly, but her waist had thickened, her hips spread and her breasts, always generous, were threatening to become ponderous.

Again she laughed. "Larry's so thin and trim I think I hate him sometimes. And you? I'm consumed with envy. How do you do it, Danny?"

Moira knew she was being relentless, but she was determined to get Danielle to talk. Finally she succeeded.

"Oh, I don't know, mother. I think growing up in England helped. They simply eat less there, you know."

"Yes."

Danielle sighed, as though weary. "And Pierre Chambeau made me a virtual vegetarian. I guess I don't think much about food."

Moira carried on the discussion of diet a bit longer, but clearly she had lost Danielle again. Moira's daughter had lasped back into silence. Unable to think of anything else, Moira characteristically attacked the problem directly. "Danny, why didn't you marry James Lavelle?" She saw Danielle look at her hands a long time, as though they were a curiosity. "Didn't he love you? Was he mean to you? What happened, Danny?"

A reply finally came. "Yes, he loved me. No, he wasn't mean, just the opposite." She pursed her lips, as though trying to squeeze the life out of them. "I simply couldn't marry him." Her voice was barely audible.

"Why, Danny? Please try to tell me."

The words were a long time coming. When they did, they fell as blows on her mother. Danielle's eyes filled with tears. "There have been too many men, mother. I am too soiled."

"Oh, *Danny*."

"He was a good man, mother. He deserved better."

Moira reached across the table and took her daughter's hands. "Danny, it's just not so."

Danielle finally raised her head, her brilliant sapphire eyes seeing the green-hazel of her mother's. "I've finally stopped lying to myself. Don't you try to lie for me."

"I'm not, Danny."

"I know what I am now—a woman who likes men. Walter knew it. I'm sure you did. Even Stephanie knows it now."

"What about Stephanie?"

"I received a letter from her in London. She's living with Thomas to make sure of their love. She doesn't want to make the mistake I have."

"She didn't say that?"

"Not in so many words, but that's what she meant. And isn't she right?"

Moira took her hands away from Danielle's and sat back, slumped really, against the bench. She had wanted this talk, this confrontation of the problem, but now that she had it, she didn't know what to say. Danielle had spoken the simple truth. There had been too many men. She had surrendered her virtue too many times. Her self-esteem was gone. Moira knew there was no point in denying the truth. And she knew no way to comfort her daughter. "What're you going to do?"

Danielle's sigh was prolonged, then surprisingly followed by a wry smile. "I guess I could become a courtesan, as Pierre always wanted. Only I'm a little old for that now, don't you think?"

Moira made no reply.

Another sigh came from Danielle. "I'm going to try at long last, try as hard as I know how, to be like my mother. I'm going to stay chaste from now on. I'm going to try to find my virtue." Another wry smile. "It must be around here someplace. I seem to have mislaid it."

Moira's eyes filled and she had trouble swallowing. "It's not far away, Danny. I—I know you'll find it."

"I do hope so, mother."

Hands were clasped anew and eyes spoke volumes to each other, more accurately than words ever could.

"Don't worry about me, mother. I know I'm tired, depressed." Danielle smiled again, wanly. "A barrel of monkeys I'm not. But I'll be all right. It's wonderful being with you, Morgan, his family. I just adore Louise. And Aurial has always been the most healing place I know."

Moira smiled radiantly. "Yes, isn't it?"

"And I want to go to Chicago, see Stevie, try to help her."

"Yes, a good idea."

"But I thought I'd wait till Andrew returns first. I think there must be virtue in not neglecting your children."

"So I've heard." Again there were radiant smiles, a meeting of eyes, a squeezing of fingers.

"I'm glad we had this talk, mother—and I'm especially glad you're—you're here for me."

Moira thought of her tears as her cup of happiness running over.

* * *

Andrew Summers had adopted a bad pun. He was having the *summers* of his life. But it was the truth. Andrew's idea of heaven had become his father's Double Bar D Ranch in Colorado.

In only a few short weeks Andrew figured he'd become a pretty good cowboy. He already knew how to ride, of course, but the quick, agile western ponies, with their sharp turns and quick stops, took some getting used to. Then he'd had to learn how to punch those cantankerous longhorns—the new herefords were more docile—and round up the dogies before they wandered off the range. He had worked with the lasso until he didn't miss too often. But it was the sixgun strapped to his hip that gave him the most satisfaction. He knew he wasn't Wyatt Earp or Billy the Kid, but he'd practiced and practiced till his draw was pretty good. And, although he'd never shot at anything but bottles and a couple of rabbits, he knew he was becoming a pretty good shot. He was grateful to his dad for letting him wear the weapon—after not too long a lecture on when and why to use it.

Andrew had taken a fearful ribbing about being a "greenhorn" and "dude," but he knew that was because the cowhands liked and accepted him. Luke Bascomb, the foreman, and Maury Wexler, the wrangler, kept showing him how to do things the right way, the western way, and all the hands, Big Ben Denison, Jesu Gomez, Ace—nobody knew Ace's last name—Tab Eagle, the half-breed Indian who was going to teach him how to track, even Tao Peng, the cook, treated him as one of their own. Sitting around the campfire listening to stories was about the pleasantest thing in Andrew Summers's whole life. And when the boys took him into the Buckshot Saloon in Cold Spring and bought him a beer, he figured his britches would pop from pride.

Yet it was his dad who made this the "summers" to

remember. Andrew had been eager to make the trip West, but he had some misgivings about his father. After all, he hadn't seen much of him lately. But the fears were laid to rest instantly. Walt Summers was just about the nicest person he'd ever met: tall, lank, easygoing, his yellow hair bleached nearly white in the sun. It seemed to Andrew his father just belonged here. He was part of it all. And could he ever sit a horse!

Andrew guessed it was his father's way with him that he liked the most. Walt Summers left no doubt he loved his son, was glad to see him, and took pride in how hard he worked and how quickly he learned. This was a goad to get Andrew to try his hand at everything, not that he needed one. If anything, he was too eager, and his dad had spoken to him a couple times about not getting hurt.

Andrew quickly came to adore his father. More than once he felt cheated that he hadn't known him all these years, yet it was good to get acquainted with him now. There was a lot to learn. He and his father always had a lot to talk about. Just last night they sat on the front porch—the Double Bar D had a big ranch house, sort of Spanish-looking—and had a good talk.

"Dad, can I stay here?"

"I sure hope so, Andy—after you finish your schooling."

"You mean go back? Do I have to?"

"There're fine schools in the East, son." Walt Summers puffed on his pipe, which had been just about to go out. "Someday all this will be yours. It takes brains as well as brawn to run a spread like this."

There was silence for a time, Andrew's mind dwelling on the thought of owning the Double Bar D, being like his father. Of course, he didn't look like him. He was brown-haired, darker, and unfortunately shorter, more heavily built. He supposedly looked more like his

Grandfather Kingston than anyone on the Summers's side.

"Nice night, isn't it, son?"

"Sure is." It was a magical night, full moon, azure sky, a soft breeze bearing the scent of pine from the mountains. Perhaps it was the very romance of the night that made Andrew say, "Why did you and mom break up, dad?"

After a long pause Walt Summers replied, not without sadness in his voice, "A man does foolish things sometimes. And sometimes there's just no way to make 'em right."

"Do you still love her?"

"Yes."

"Is that why you never married again?"

"I suppose." A match was struck, lighting the darkness, brought to the contrary pipe. "I never figured to find a woman as good as your mother. But I never tried to look, either."

"Any chance of you and her . . . ?"

"Getting back together? I don't see how, son. I wouldn't count on it, if I were you."

Andrew sighed. "I suppose not. I guess she's going to marry that English guy. He's a Duke or something."

"Nice fellow?"

"Yeah, he seems all right, I guess."

"Good." Walter Summers turned in his rocker, searching out the face of his son in the darkness. "Believe me, Andy, I hope she does marry him. I only want her to be happy. She'll make an excellent Duchess —or whatever."

"But you still love her. Doesn't the D in Double Bar D stand for Danielle?"

"The thought may have crossed my mind." To himself he thought—or *darling*. The conversation was suddenly unbearable to him. "Well, son, what say we hit the hay? Big day with the ponies tomorrow."

* * *

It certainly was a big day. There had been a roundup of wild horses a few days before. Now they were being broken to the saddle. Andrew sat on the corral fence, whooping and hollering, as Ace, Jesu, Big Ben, all the boys, took turns on the backs of the bucking mustangs. Andrew itched to try it and he begged and begged Luke Bascomb to let him. Finally Luke turned his black face up to the boy and said, "I suppose there'll be no peace 'round here till you's throwed by one o' them critters."

"I can do it, Luke, I know I can."

"Land on yer butt, y'mean?" But Luke went over to Maury Wexler, the wrangler, and told him to find a nice docile pony for the boy.

A few minutes later Andrew was sliding his legs around a black and white mustang. He could feel the animal quivering with fright as he gripped the reins tight in his right hand, hit hat in his left. "Let 'er go!" he hollered. Instantly he was off on the ride of his young life.

Either Maury Wexler had misjudged his horseflesh or the animal realized it had an inexperienced rider, but in any event Andrew was on the worst horse of the day—kicking, turning, humping, bucking savagely to be free of its rider. Walt Summers, who had been in the house, saw Andrew and was appalled. He ran to the corral.

"GET HIM OFF THERE!" he screamed.

Two riders moved quickly to intercept the bronco, but not quickly enough. The mustang gave a savage leap straight up in the air, and Andrew went flying. He hit the ground hard. He did not get up, nor was he conscious as his frantic father bent over him—nor when he was carried into the house and a rider dispatched to Cold Spring for Doc Slater.

Danielle held the telegram in her trembling fingers. It had been sent to Moira.

ANDREW HURT IN FALL FROM HORSE STOP REMAINS
UNCONSCIOUS STOP AM DOING EVERYTHING I KNOW
STOP TELL DANIELLE IF YOU CAN STOP

WALTER

It took all Danielle's will to remain calm as she
quickly packed and headed for Colorado and the
bedside of her son.

Eighteen

When Stephanie came to, she was disoriented. She didn't know where she was or what had happened to her. Then memories came to her in a rush: touring the locomotive plant, the fight, enraged workers, screams for strike, being seized, the police, shooting, bloody bodies. She closed her eyes then, covering her face with her hands in a vain effort to blot out the visions.

Other memories came to her, and with them terror, rough hands grabbing her, being carried by running men. She had been abducted! Her hands came away from her face. They were filthy, smudged with grease. She looked down. Her dress was streaked with black. Whole handprints were visible. Then she gasped, nearly screamed. Her dress was ripped down the seam, her right breast exposed, smeared with black. Someone had—*God, no!* She jumped to her feet, looked down. Had they . . . ? Panic, revulsion took hold of her. She gagged. Then she realized her undergarments were still in place. They had not. But would they? Where was she? She had to get away.

A moment longer terror reigned within her, then she began to fight it, gradually willing it away while she took stock of her predicament. She was in a small room, not much bigger than a closet really. Light came from a small window high above her head. She judged it to be late afternoon or early evening. She saw a bed of straw on which she had lain, a bare wooden table in the corner. On the opposite wall were shelves of foodstuffs, tins, sacks. It was a pantry.

Her other senses began to function. The room was fearfully hot, stifling, and she could feel sweat clinging to her body. She heard the buzz of flies, then saw them winging in lazy circles near the center of the room. And the stench. Ghastly. She recognized sour urine, feces and, faintly, the odors of cooking.

Fear gripped her again. She heard male voices outside the door, the slide of a bolt. Just in time she remembered to clasp the torn bodice over herself. She shrank back against a cracked, dirty wall, as several men forced their way into the room. In the forefront was the union man, the one with the scraggly beard and threadbare suit. He leered at her. All the faces did.

"So the fat pig's doxy is awake, is she." He gave an exaggerated bow. It was pure mockery. "Did you have a nice nap, Miss Summers?"

Somehow she found voice. "You know me?"

"We may be members of the proletariat, Miss Summers, but I assure you we read the papers." Again he mocked her, grinning this time. "Let me see. The words used to describe you are 'stunning, glamorous, elegantly gowned.'" His laugh was now his weapon. "I wonder if that fat pig Kincaid, that callous oppressor, that enemy of the workers, would find his doxy so *glamorous* now." Again the laugh. "Your tour of the factory seems to have left you looking like the rest of us." His laughter was joined by that of the others.

Stephanie knew pure fear but, from somewhere deep within her, spunk, the desire to fight, arose. It was

perhaps her Irish heritage from her great-grandmother.
"I am not Mr. Kincaid's doxy, as you call me."

"I saw you at the ball game with him. Do not deny
it."

"I was there as his guest—against my will, I might
say. I am engaged to marry Mr. Thomas Hodges."

"Another pig." The union man turned, speaking to
the men next to him. "Hodges is hatchet man for
Kincaid. He does the dirty work. She will serve as well,
whoever she sleeps with."

"I demand you release me." She tried to say it
forcefully, but her fear overrode the Irish in her.

"Demand? You will demand nothing here." He was
puffed up, full of himself, looking at her directly. "Your
wealth means nothing here. You have no privilege.
Your capitalist greed is meaningless among us. You are
with the downtrodden now, the oppressed masses.
Your fine clothes, your jewels and furs, your loose
morals, will be of no help to you now."

His words lashed at her, but still she fought. "The
police will come. You will be arrested."

"Probably. Indeed, most likely. Only I will not be
arrested. I'll be shot down as a dog, like poor Tim
Gossage and the others. But I assure you, my now-less-
than-glamorous Miss Summers, I will not die alone.
You will be in the forefront, feeling the bitter sting of
the oppressors' bullets."

His words were like flagellation to her.

"Lord o' mercy, Gunter, ya do carry on." The voice,
a woman's, came from the rear of the knot of men,
actually from outside the room. "Youse scarin' the poor
chil' half t'death."

"And so she should be scared—the whore of Kincaid."

"An' when did ya become such a high and mighty
judge o' morals—sleepin' with Thad Bishop's daughter
as youse are."

The face of the man called Gunter reddened, but he
persisted. "Shut your mouth, Rosie. I'll have my say."

"An' sayin' is all it'll be, mos' likely. I see ya s'vived the killins at the plant. Who was ya hidin' behind? Jer Bryne or Homer Kitzmiller, mos' likely."

Angered, the union man turned toward his tormentor, who was even now pushing her way to the front.

"Ya jus' leave this poor chil' be, ya hear?"

"She's our hostage. Kincaid'll recognize the union just to get her back."

"So she's your hostage. Tha' don't mean ya have t'scare her out o' her wits." The woman began to shove at Gunter and the others. "Now ya scallywags scat out o' here, leave this chil' be."

In a moment all were gone, the door closed. Stephanie saw her benefactress as a shortish woman of ample figure, large in breast and thigh, with graying hair, a round, pudgy face. She wore a faded black cotton dress, a smudged white apron.

"Who're you?"

"I'm Rosie, miss, Rosie Cook. I run this boardin' house." She looked at Stephanie and grinned. "My, youse sure a purty one—or would be if ya was cleaned up some. Such hair, and them eyes."

"What's going to happen to me?"

"Have no fear, hon. It's mos'ly jus' jabberin' o' the menfolks." Rosie's interests lay elsewhere. "Tha's a right purty dress. Can't say I ever see one s'nice." She came to Stephanie, inspecting the rip. "I can fix that real easy. Tell ya what. Ya take off the dress. I'll wash it real good, get out m'needle and you'll be as good as new."

"No." Stephanie clutched the bodice tighter.

"Now, now, dearie. I got some water heatin' on the stove. I'll bring a basin. A good wash'll make ya feel better." Then she understood. "Don' ya worry none 'bout them critters, hon. They'll come in here over m'dead body. An' I'll bring ya a dress t'wear." She seemed to size Stephanie up. "It'll be miles too big, ya bein' so tiny'n all, but at leas' it'll perteck yer virtue."

As she turned to leave, Stephanie said, "Where am I?"

Rosie gave her a pensive look and hesitated. "I bes' not tell ya that, sweetie. But you'll be all right. I'll look after ya."

"Is this . . . your home?"

"Not much o' one, I'll tell ya. But it's all I got. I take in boarders. M'son lives with me. Earl's his name. A fine lad he is, too."

Rosie left her, returning soon with a basin of steaming water, setting it on the table in the corner with a rag and a bit of soap. "Now ya have a good wash. Here, I'll help ya with your dress." Stephanie turned her back hesitantly, then moments later heard, "My land, chil', I never seen such a figger. Youse sure a rip'n."

Alone at last Stephanie bent to her ablutions, truly grateful to cleanse the grime and sweat from her body, the telltale smears from her breast. Which one had done that? Rosie had even produced a small, cracked mirror for her to use, and a broken comb to run through her hair. As she looked at herself, memories of the dilapidated mirror in Glenna's attic flooded her. All this had begun with that.

The door opened and Stephanie turned in fright. But it was only Rosie, bearing a faded dress of cheap cotton. At one time it had been pink in color.

"Found this with m'things. I outgrew it years ago. Maybe it won' be too big for ya."

It *was* too big. But as Stephanie swept the dress over her head, she was grateful for any covering. With the belt cinched to her waist she felt the garment was not too bad.

Rosie laughed. "It never looked that good on me, dearie."

"Ma! When's supper?"

Rosie turned toward the door. "I'm in here, son."

The face which came to the door matched the voice she'd heard in the factory, and Stephanie recognized the young man who had protected her and tried to gain her release. He had cleaned up, washing away the grease, and put on a clean white shirt and trousers. Both were of the poorest quality. He was rail-thin, very young, probably not much older than herself. He had dark hair, a sensitive mouth, vivid blue eyes. It was a face of innocence that stared at her.

"We'll eat real soon, Earl. An' I wan' ya t'tell Gunter an' the others this chil' is gonna sit an' eat with us, proper like. I ain't runnin' no jail here."

Rosie pushed by her son. Through the open door Stephanie saw a kitchen, Rosie going to a stove, lifting a lid on a large pot, stirring with a wooden spoon. Her gaze came back to the youth who still stood in the doorway staring at her.

"You're Earl Cook?"

"Yes, ma'am."

His gaze was so intent it made her nervous. "I—I want to thank you . . . for trying to . . . help me."

Her words stopped his gaping and he looked down at his feet. "I jus' wish I coulda done more, ma'am."

She realized how very shy he was. Smiling, she said, "I'm not a ma'am, Earl. I'm a miss."

"Yes, ma'am—I mean, miss."

She recognized him as hope. "Can you help me escape?"

Now he looked at her. "I'd like to, miss—but it ain't easy."

"Why am I being held?"

"Gunter, the others, figger Kincaid'll at leas' talk to us—t'get you back."

"Don't they have Mr. Rawlings, the other man?"

"Yes, but not here, 'nother place." His expression turned even more earnest. "But don' ya worry, miss. I'll look after ya."

She shuddered. "I do hope so, Earl." Another thought came to her. "Who is this man Gunter?"

"Gunter, he's a—I don' remember the word, sosha—something or other."

"Socialist."

"That's it. But don't pay him no mind, miss. Gunter's mos'ly jus' talk."

She remembered Gunter's flaming oratory at the plant, his scathing mockery of her a few minutes ago. Neither thought reassured her.

At dinner she sat next to Earl, who gave her a sense of protection. The table was long, really just rough boards hammered together, with benches instead of chairs. The food, served on tin trays and cracked china plates, was a thin stew, mostly broth with potatoes and onions, very little meat. The men, including Gunter, ate in silence, wielding their spoons ravenously. Stephanie tried to be more dainty, but she was hungry, too.

"So how do you like a proletarian supper, Miss Summers? Hardly measures up to the Palmer House, does it?"

Gunter sat across from her in the middle of the table. The food seemed to have energized him. Mockery was in his eyes. "How would you know? You didn't cook this meal, Mr. Gunter."

"And precious little cooking you do, either, Miss Summers."

"I'll have you know I do all our cooking." It wasn't true, but at least she had no servants.

His laughter flooded over her. "How like the rich and pampered to presume the common touch. But you don't fool me, Miss Summers. You are Kincaid's doxy. Your talents lie elsewhere."

Her face reddened and she couldn't help it. "I am no one's doxy. I am engaged to Thomas Hodges."

"Same thing. He's Kincaid's toady."

She opened her mouth to protest, but got no chance.

"Hodges, Kincaid, it's all the same. Either will be eager for the return of a—"

"Why not let her go, Gunter?" It was the voice of Earl beside her. "We've got Rawlings and Andrews."

Gunter laughed. "But they are expendable, my dear Earl. They lack the . . . the, shall we say, physical attributes of our lovely, loose-moraled Miss Summers."

The words scalded her, but she was saved by the appearance of Rosie, carrying the kettle, ladling out more stew into the plates. As the devouring resumed, Stephanie glanced at Gunter. A strange man. Obviously he was educated; his accent, his vocabulary suggesting he had attended a university somewhere. He glanced up, saw her looking at him. To her surprise she did not evade his mocking gaze.

"I understand you are a socialist, Mr. Gunter."

"Proudly so."

"And what, pray tell, is a socialist, Mr. Gunter?"

"A socialist is one who opposes the capitalist usurpers whose days are numbered. The workers of the world are uniting. This very day, with our blood and lives, we have broken the chains of bondage. We will take the fruits of production from the evil, grasping Kincaid and distribute it among those who perform the labor and deserve the fruits."

"You sound like Robin Hood."

"Exactly. We will kill, bomb, plunder and attack, attack, attack, until the monster of capitalism is destroyed and the workers of the world have what they have rightfully earned."

"Your program also includes kidnapping?"

"Rawlings and Andrews are the lackeys of Kincaid. They do the actual oppression, while he wallows in his gold bathtub sipping champagne."

"And exactly how have I oppressed you, Mr. Gunter?"

The question unnerved him, but he was equal to the answer. "You, Miss Summers, are a symbol of capitalist decadence. You are rich, idle, pampered. The very clothes by which you express you ostentation represent the blood and sweat of the proletariat."

Stephanie's face reddened. But she had no need to reply, for Rosie Cook, having emptied the pot of stew, spoke from near the head of the table. "Shush your mouth, Gunter. No sense in badgerin' this poor chil', especially when you ain't never sweated none, or even got your han's dirty in that infernal fact'ry." She saw Gunter redden, then turned to Stephanie. "Come, chil', les' go in the kitchen and leave these savers o' the workers to their blood and sweat."

Stephanie followed her into the kitchen, grateful to be away from the table and her confrontation with Gunter. She sat for a time at a table, then began to help with the dishes.

"No need, dearie. Ya'll jus' ruin those purty han's o' yours."

Annoyed by these constant references to her uselessness, Stephanie said, "I'm not fragile, Mrs. Cook. I want to help." She picked up a less-than-clean towel and began to dry plates and cups. In a moment she asked, "Do you have a husband?"

"I did. He was killed in that infernal fact'ry."

"I'm sorry." Stephanie looked at Rosie, her hands deep in suds. She seemed to show no reaction. "How was he killed?"

"Steam line busted. It was old, worn out. Nobody'd fix it. Scalded Adam t'death."

"That's awful, Mrs. Cook."

"Can't be helped, I guess. Los' a boy there, too. Stack o' metal fell on him, crushed him t'death. Earl's all I got lef'."

Stephanie could feel her eyes smarting. "That's terrible, Mrs. Cook. How have you stood it?"

Shoulders were shrugged. "It's jus' life—or part o' it. Ya bring the youngins into the worl'. Mos' of them die as babes. Los' three that way. Them what lives—well, there's always somethin', ain't there?" She turned to Stephanie and smiled. "I do all right. This boardin' house, such as it is, keeps me busy. I get by. Got no complaints. Wouldn't do no good if I did."

Stephanie felt consumed with compassion for this woman. Her eyes filled with unwanted tears. To curb her emotions she asked, "Isn't there anything you want, Rosie?"

"Oh, yes, dearie, yes indeedy. If I had m' druthers, I'd take a place out in the country, with lotsa green grass and trees and fresh air. Lord o' Mighty, would I love t'be able t'breathe once—without all this. . . . Ya know what I mean? Ya prob'bly smell it more'n I do." She took the wet towel from Stephanie. "No need t'do the pans, dearie. They'll dry theirselves. Ya jus' take a rest."

Greatly upset, Stephanie obeyed, walking away from the sink to look out a window, seeing only her own reflection.

"I wouldn't think 'bout goin' out that door, dearie. These streets ain't no place for a proper lady at night."

Stephanie saw then that it was a window in a door she was looking at. "Yes, Rosie, I'll stay here. I have no choice." She turned at a sound, and saw Earl Cook enter the kitchen from the dining room.

"Gunter says I should lock ya back in the pantry now, miss."

Stephanie nodded and sighed, said goodnight to Rosie and entered her cell. As Earl followed her to the doorway she said, "Earl, how many were killed today?"

"Seven dead, nine hurt bad. Some o' them is likely t'die."

The numbers appalled her. "But why?"

He shrugged. "Can't really say, miss. Seems like it's always that way in a strike. The men go out. The cops come, or the Pinkertons, sometimes soldiers. Men jus' have t'die, I guess."

"What's going to happen now, in the strike, I mean?"

"Oh, scabs mos' likely. Kincaid's a'ready got goon squads—the ones that's derailin' the trains out West. Likely as no, he'll bring 'em in and try to run the plant."

"There'll be fighting?"

"'Magine so, miss. Can't be helped, I guess."

"Can nothing be done?"

"Hope so, miss. The strike's 'tractin' lotsa 'tention. Mr. Debs is comin' Monday."

"Who is Debs?"

"Eugene V. Debs, Miss. He's—well, I dunno exactly what he does, but he's a big labor leader. S'posed to be a good man. Mr. Gompers, Samuel Gompers, is comin', too. He's head o' the 'merican Fed'ration o' Labor. Men like that gotta help, I reckon."

"Yes, I hope so."

He looked at her shyly. "I bes' say g'night now, miss. I'm lockin' you in. You sleep good."

"Yes, I will. Goodnight, Earl."

The airless pantry was stifling to her, and she feared for a moment she might suffocate. But she told herself she wouldn't. More, she managed to convince herself she really wasn't afraid. Rosie and Earl certainly intended her no harm. And sooner or later Thomas would rescue her. A ransom would be paid, demands met, something.

She tried then to think of Thomas and their love, but her mind repeatedly returned to Rosie. A husband and son killed in that hellish factory, a remaining son doomed to work there forever. Rosie was a good woman, who deserved more. But she could only eke out a meager existence working herself to death in this decrepit boarding house—while longing for sunshine. It wasn't fair. It wasn't right. Stephanie had so much, and this poor woman so little.

To her surprise, she fell asleep, so soundly she did not hear the rasp of the bolt outside the door or the turning of the latch. Probably it was the change in the fetid air in the room that awakened her. She saw the open door and in the dim light from the kitchen the outline of a figure against it.

"Who's there?"

The figure stepped forward. The door closed quickly, plunging the cell into blackness. Terror seized her, but she had no time to scream or even react before a body fell on her and a hand came over her mouth.

"I want what he gets."

In her panic she recognized Gunter's voice just before she felt another hand at her breast. She struggled, twisted, tried to bite, but to no avail. His weight was atop her. She could barely move.

"Come on. Share the wealth."

She struggled with all her might. But at best she could only pummel his back with her fists, kick with a free leg and make squealing sounds through her nose.

"You know you'll love it."

She knew she was losing, for he had her pinioned and her legs were already separated when he fell on her. She felt her skirt being pulled up.

Then there was light, a growling sound and the weight was pulled off her. Earl. He had Gunter by the collar of his nightdress. His hand was raised to hit him.

Gunter, quite amazingly, seemed unimpressed. "Just checking on our prisoner, Earl—seeing if she was still here."

"You leave her be, Gunter." The young man's voice was quivering with rage. "I'm warnin' ya."

"Sure, Earl, sure. You keep a good eye on Kincaid's doxy, hear?" He shook himself free of Earl's grasp, turned to Stephanie, smiled, bowed. "Goodnight, Miss Summers, pleasant dreams." He strode out as though nothing had occurred.

Stephanie lay there in bed, still shaking from fright.

"You all right, miss?"

She managed to nod, then saw Earl leave for the kitchen. In a moment he returned with a key, handed it to her.

"You can lock yerself in now. I shoulda done it b'fore." He hesitated, pursing his lips. "An' I'll sleep in the kitchen, too."

Nineteen

Thomas Hodges learned of the strike and Stephanie's abduction Saturday evening—by reading the newspaper in San Francisco, not by receiving a telegram from Kincaid. STRIKERS HOLD SOCIALITE was the banner headline. Below was a photogravure of Stephanie in the revealing golden gown she had worn to the Palmer House.

Sick with apprehension, Thomas left at once for Chicago, traveling two nights and a whole day on the train to arrive Monday morning. Dodging reporters, he went at once to Kincaid's office.

"I'm sorry I didn't let you know, but I didn't know where to wire you. There was nothing for you to do anyway."

"What's being done?"

"Everything. Police, our own people, are looking everywhere for her, Rawlings and Andrews, too. Every lead is being followed. We'll find them—and those socialist bastards will hang."

"You haven't found her yet?"

"No, but we will—any minute now."

"Have you heard from the kidnappers?"

"Yes. The bloody anarchists demand union recognition in exchange for the hostages."

"You'll give it, of course."

Kincaid looked at him sharply. "Over my dead body, Hodges."

"But—"

"No buts," he thundered. "I'll not let some long-haired, wild-eyed radicals tell me how to run my business." He looked at Thomas, obviously distraught, and his voice softened. "I know how you feel, Thomas, but we'll get her back all right and in one lovely piece. But giving in is not the way. Give in once and you give in forever. I'm going to fight these lawless scum with everything I've got. I've men on the way now. This strike is as good as over."

Thomas could do nothing but nod agreement; still, his apprehension remained, roiling his stomach. If anything happened to Stevie, he didn't know what he'd do.

Stephanie knew that thanks to Rosie and Earl Cook, her captivity was a great deal easier than it might have been. She was permitted freedom of the kitchen and access to the dining room. Someone was with her at all times, yet she knew escape, at least into the street, was probably possible. She didn't try and wasn't at all sure of her reasons. Fear of being locked in the pantry all day if caught was no doubt one reason. Still, there was something else, which she didn't understand. She served some purpose by being here, although she had no idea what.

She realized she had been profoundly affected by this sudden turn of events: the visit to the factory, the violence and death she had witnessed, the lives of these people who held her captive. But it had all happened so fast. Her mind couldn't cope with it. She knew only that she, Stephanie Summers, had led a very sheltered life. Things happened in the world that she knew nothing about. Indeed, it was like a whole other world, utterly foreign to Aurial, the grand homes of her grandmother and great-grandmother. It was a dark, forbidding world, full of danger and death, filth, hunger and disease, all in return for backbreaking labor in unwholesome places. Gunter, for all his hateful arrogance, mockery and lust, was right in one thing. She was a symbol of decadence. She now knew there was more to life than gowns, balls and frivolous good times.

Stephanie spent a lot of time with Rosie, helping her in the kitchen, serving the food, glad to be away from the mocking, smirking eyes of Gunter. She found herself liking Rosie. She hadn't realized how much she'd missed having a woman to talk to. In her conversations with Rosie, Stephanie learned that most of the men earned twelve to fifteen dollars a week at the factory, the skilled boilermakers and machinists perhaps twice that or a little more. Simply to survive, wives and all but the youngest children had to work at what they could find. In this environment a penny was a prize. Rosie charged fifty cents a day for room and board. That's what Kincaid had paid for Stephanie's box seat at the ball game.

"How do you manage, Rosie?"

"I just do, that's all." She laughed. "You'll be s'prised how many times a body can boil a chicken neck or back."

"But what if you become ill?"

"God willin', it'll be m'time then, chil'."

Stephanie also had opportunities to talk to Earl. Following Gunter's attempted rape, Earl had assumed the role of her bodyguard, for which Stephanie was grateful. Beneath his shyness, she saw him as a sensitive, intelligent person.

"Did you go to school, Earl?"

"Yes, miss, grammar school, three years. Then I had to—"

"Go to work?"

"Yes. M'dad was killed."

She pursed her lips, the whole scene suddenly before her, a young boy dropping out of school, entering the American Western locomotive works. "Couldn't you go back to school, maybe study at night or something? If you did, perhaps you could improve yourself, get a better job."

He shrugged. "I s'pose. Maybe I can one day."

She smiled. "I hope so, Earl." At least he was looking at her, meeting her eyes. But only for a moment. His head went down again. She brightened her voice. "Have you a girlfriend, Earl?"

He looked at her, his face reddening. "Me? Naw."

She smiled. "I can't imagine why not. You're very good looking."

His flush deepened. "I got no money for girls." He hesitated, seeming to waver, then blurted, " 'Sides, there ain't no girl as purty as you." His face turned deep red. "I—I'm s-sorry. I—I shouldn't ha' said that."

"Yes, you should." She smiled. "I think it's the nicest compliment I've ever had."

He stared at her a moment, greatly distressed, then looked down. She waited, trying to imagine what it would be like to be married to a man like this. He would be loving, adoring really. She would cook for him, sew, send him off to work each day with his lunch pail. But in her mind it was all happening in the flat she shared with Thomas. Incongruous. Utterly impossible. "Earl, would you do me a favor? Could I see some of the rooms upstairs?"

He looked shocked. "The men's?"

"No, I was thinking of some of the homes, the apartments where the people live, couples, families."

"They ain't homes—hardly even 'partments." He shook his head. "I don't think you wanna see 'em, miss."

"My name is Stephanie, Earl." She smiled. "My friends call me Stevie."

"Stephanie. It's a purty name. Stevie is. . . ." Again he blushed.

She laughed. "I know, a boy's name, and I don't look like a boy." He shook his head. "Will you take me, Earl?"

He sighed. "I can't let ya out inna street."

"I'll give my word not to run away."

He pondered her a moment. "There's another way. Come on."

He led her through the dining room and up the creaking stairs of the boarding house, all the way to the roof. The sun was blinding at first, blisteringly hot, but she welcomed the smell of less fetid air. She figured they were up four stories. In the distance she saw Lake Michigan, so blue, sun sparkling on it, the high-rise buildings of the Loop. It was a whole other world, the one to which she belonged.

Stephanie followed Earl across the roof. He helped her over the balustrade; lifting her by the waist, setting her down. Blushing again, he said, "You sure is tiny, miss."

She smiled, looking up at him. "Stephanie. And you are very strong, Earl." For the merest of instances she thought he might try to kiss her. But his shyness won out. He walked across the roof, unbolting a door. She followed.

For a half-hour on that hot Saturday afternoon, Stephanie toured the nether world of Chicago. She felt assaulted by the heat, the stench, the filth. The stairs were littered with garbage, among which little children, some naked, distended bellies protruding, sat listlessly, staring up at her, all eyes, as she stepped by them. More than once she saw rats, so big and bold they didn't even run till she was almost upon them. Then they scurried only a short distance.

The whole building seemed open, every door, all the

windows, even the broken ones, as the inhabitants tried vainly to combat the heat. But the flies! Hordes of them. Stephanie swatted constantly. Each floor consisted of a hallway, with rooms off to the side, and she remembered someone speaking of "railroad flats." This must be what they meant. And the people! Through each doorway she saw a half-dozen or more people, sitting listlessly, fanning themselves with a paper or just their hands. Many of the men were naked to the waist. They were of all ages, from graybeards and wizened old women, all the way down to babes suckling at breasts. And the eyes! Curiosity, hostility, ennui was in them, defeat. No one spoke to her.

On the second floor Earl took her inside an apartment. She counted. Seven people were in the room, sitting around a table or on a battered couch, in the window wells. A wood stove obviously served both for heat in winter and for cooking. There was a sink, but no running water. The chamberpot had lost its lid. It was unemptied.

"How's Mary today?"

Earl earned no response, just a motion of a woman's head, a woman who did not take her eyes off Stephanie. Earl entered a room to the right. Stephanie followed, if only to get away from the eyes. What she saw made her shudder. There was a narrow straw bed, covered with a filthy sheet. On it lay a woman, naked to the waist, halfway on her side, a baby at a shrunken breast. Two other children, the oldest perhaps two, were asleep next to her. Both had vomited, run at the bowels. Nothing had been done to clean them up. All were covered with flies.

"Feelin' better t'day, Mary?"

Stephanie forced herself to look at the woman. Her body was so emaciated that the ribs were showing. Her hair was matted to her head. Shrunken eyes opened above dark rings. They were dark, uncaring, defeated eyes, then they brightened in recognition. "Some, Earl, thankee." The eyes closed. The woman didn't move. Stephanie could only stare. Why, Mary wasn't much older than herself!

Earl touched her arm. "We bes' go now."

Outside in the hallway Stephanie said, "Take me back. I think I'm going to be sick." Indeed, all her will was required not to gag and retch.

Back in the dining room of Rosie Cook's boarding house—and it was a haven of cleanliness compared to what she had just seen—Stephanie was greeted by a smirking Gunter. "I see you got your picture in the paper, Miss Summers."

He shoved it toward her and she took it, gasping in shock. Under a banner headline was a photogravure of her. The artist had drawn from the photograph taken at the Palmer House, she in her gold gown, Kincaid beside her. The engraving was frontal. Her breasts were obscenely, lewdly exposed.

"Hardly does you justice, Miss Summers, I'd say."

Embarrassed, blushing and unable to help it, she glared at Gunter and handed it back to him.

"Don't you want to read about yourself? You're a heroine of the capitalists."

She saw his mockery. "Yes, thank you, I will."

She carried the paper into the kitchen and sat at the table to read. It was appalling. The story was mostly about her, her abduction, the search for her. She was a socialite with a capital S, daughter of, granddaughter and great-granddaughter of, betrothed to. She had been in Chicago about six weeks, creating a sensation with her beauty and her gowns designed by Pierre Chambeau of New York and Paris. There were a few paragraphs about Rawlings and Andrews, blustery quotes from Kincaid, but the barest mention of the massacre at the plant entrance—and not a word about the appalling working conditions that had led to the strike. When she finished reading, Stephanie could only stare at the *Tribune* in disbelief. She was full of shame. Somehow she felt dirty.

"Why, darlin', what a bootiful piksure o' you. Ya look jus' lovely."

Stephanie hadn't realized Rosie was standing beside her. She looked up, misery on her face.

"Jus' wish I had the figger for a dress like that."

Abruptly, savagely, Stephanie folded the paper to hide the photogravure. She was trembling, couldn't help it.

"Yer purty dress is finished, Miss Stephanie. The stains all come out and the seam sewed up real good." Rosie held up the dress pridefully. "One of the purty sleeves was missin', so I took t'other off, too. Hope ya don't min' none."

Stephanie's swallow came hard. Her voice sounded strained. "No, it's all right. Thank you."

"Sure is a lovely dress. Why don't ya put it on for supper?"

"No." She was shaking. "M-maybe tomorrow."

Danielle could think only that her son might be dying, if he were not already dead. As she alighted from the train at Cold Spring, she was unmindful of her extreme fatigue from the long train ride or her raw nerves. Nor did she recognize where she was. She should have. She had been in Cold Spring before, after her rescue from the retarded giant "Shorty" in 1871. She stood on the platform, suitcase beside her, searching out some conveyance.

"Miz Summers?"

She turned, saw a youngish man with long black hair under a straight brimmed hat. He was swarthy-skinned and wore beads. Obviously he was Indian.

"Mister Summers sent me, ma'am. My name's Eagle."

She followed him to a two-wheel gig. On the ride to Double Bar D not a word was exchanged. Danielle tried to keep her mind on Andrew and her worries, but she was not entirely successful. So she was to see Walt again. How many years had it been? Her mind would not function enough to figure it out. She noticed the terrain. A wide valley, hot, the grass yellowing in the summer sun; mountains, a few snow-capped, in the distance. Beautiful. As they drove through the gate, she observed the name burned into a slab of wood, corrals with horses, a barn, other buildings, cattle in the distance. The house seemed low, rambling, made of stone, wide porch. It was all incongruous. She still thought of Walt at Seasons, the grand plantation house, the drive lined with live oaks, all green, smelling of magnolia and honeysuckle.

As soon as the gig stopped, Danielle jumped down unaided and marched for the house, up stone steps, across the porch, opened the door, entered. It felt cool, dark, till her eyes adjusted. She saw a man approach, short, squat, wearing a long white apron. He was Oriental.

" 'Day, missy."

She nodded in greeting, but did not smile. "Where's my son?"

He pointed. "Up steps, missy, on left."

She mounted the wide staircase made of dark wood, turned left along a balcony, peered in the first doorway, then ran inside to Andrew. He lay on his back under a light cover, eyes closed, so very still, as though sleeping. She went to the left side of the bed, bent over him, touched his face, her eyes filling with tears. "Oh, Andy, Andy, my darling." There was no reaction.

She was aware of another presence in the room, just before she heard, "Thank you for coming, Danny."

She stood up, turned, startled. He stood in the doorway, so tall, trim, a serious expression on his face, his brown eyes intent on her. He wore a blue shirt, jeans, cowboy boots, a kerchief at his throat, a Western hat. When he removed the hat, she saw his hair was still bright yellow, without a trace of gray. His complexion seemed deeply tanned, dry.

To him she was as lovely as ever, all blue eyes, snowy skin, soft lips. She seemed thin, tired, but she was still the most beautiful person he had ever known. Beneath her travel suit he saw the sharp rise of her bosom.

"How could you let this happen, Walt? I trusted you." Her voice was higher pitched, edging on stridency, revealing her nerves.

As calmly as he could he said, "He wanted to break a horse, begged to. Men do it all the time—with nothing more than a sore backside." He twisted the hat in his hand. "It just happened, Danny. I'm sorry."

"You're sorry." She stopped, breathing heavily, trying to control herself. "And he's not a man, he's a boy."

"He's a man—and a very fine one. He had a splendid summer, said so himself." He saw the anger in her eyes. Softly he said, "Danny, there's no point in quarreling over what has been. It won't help Andy."

She sighed, visibly wrestling with her anger, her nerves. "Yes, you're right. I'm sorry." She looked down at the bed. "What's wrong with him?"

"That's just it, nobody knows, not even the doc. He has no broken bones, at least none to be found. He seems all right physically. He just—he just won't wake up."

"Oh, God, Walt." It came as a wail, and her face began to crumble into tears. Both hands came to her mouth, as though she were trying to hold her face together. She looked at her former husband, her eyes full of anguish. "I—I knew . . . we shouldn't . . . have named him . . . Andrew . . . Morgan."

He came to her and put his arm around her shoulder. "You're being silly, Danny. The fact that Andrew Morgan, your mother's brother, took a knife and died young in the gold fields of California forty years ago has nothing to do with our son."

She felt his arm, liked the comfort in it. "Yes, I—I know you're right." She wiped her cheeks with her fingertips, struggling for self-control. "Wh-what did the d-doctor say? What's going t-to h-happen to him?"

Walt hesitated, then shrugged. There was no point in

lying. "Doc says he may come out of it in a few days, a few weeks. Then again—" he sighed, "—he may—never."

"Oh, God!" She turned in his arm, pushing it aside, looking up at him, anger surfacing again. "Who is this doctor?"

"His name's Slater. He's from Cold Spring."

"A country quack? What does he know? How come you haven't gotten a better doctor? Andrew is my *son*."

Again he endured her anger, remaining calm. "Andy can't make a trip. I thought about bringing in a doc from Chicago or New York, but—" He pursed his lips. "Slater's a good man, Danny, a lot better than we had in the war. He says a city doc will just come out here, look at Andy and say the same thing. I believe him." He tried to be as reassuring as possible and was rewarded with signs of her wavering. "I know it's hard, Danny, but all we can do is wait, hope and pray."

"There's nothing to do?"

"He takes care, Danny. We keep giving him water, broth and such. You open his mouth and spoon it in. He swallows all right. Then he has to be bathed, the bed changed. Doc says it's important to move him often to keep him from getting sores."

"I'll do it all. I'll do everything." At once she turned to bend over her son. "Oh, Andy, Andy, get well. Please get well."

For the next hour Danielle badgered Tao Peng for broth, soap and water, fresh linens. She fed her son, bathed and changed him, insisting on doing it all herself.

Walt let her be, even going outside for a while. Then he came to the doorway of the sickroom, looking at his ex-wife as she stood over the bed looking down at her motionless son. "Danny, I know you're upset, worried. But you've had a long trip. You're exhausted. You're not going to help Andy one bit if you collapse." He saw her look at him. "I've put you in the next room. There's an adjoining door. Why don't you lie down and rest for a while? I'm nearby. So is Tao Peng."

She heard the authority in his voice and wavered. "Yes, you're right. I will try to rest."

To her surprise she fell asleep at once, on top of the bed, removing only her shoes. Two hours later she arose, unpacked her suitcase, then sponged herself with water from a basin. Attired in a cool dress of blue cotton, she checked Andy, moving him to his other side, then made her way downstairs. She saw the Chinese cook setting the table for supper. She went to him and smiled. "Please forgive me for . . . being so irritable."

"Is okay, missy." His smile showed yellow broken teeth. "Boy get well soon, missy."

"Yes, I hope so. Should I feed him now?"

"Just did, missy."

"Where's Mr. Summers?" The cook motioned toward the door and Danielle went outside to the porch. The sun had just set. In the early twilight she saw Walt standing at the foot of the steps, deep in conversation with a black-skinned man. The Negro saw her and doffed his hat, approaching her.

"Miz Summers, it was my fault that boy was hurt. I shouldn'a let him ride." He looked down at his feet. "I loved that boy, Miz Summers. Can't tell you how sorry I is."

She looked at him, a big, burly man, complexion so dark it was almost black. The whites of his eyes were a sharp contrast. "It's not your fault. It couldn't be helped." He looked at her a moment longer, as though wanting to say something more, then he turned and walked away.

"Thank you for saying that, Danny. He feels terrible."

For some reason, unfathomable to her at the time, her irritation rose. Words fled to her mouth, uncensored. "I didn't know you had slaves here!" At once she saw the glint of anger in his eyes, the hurt, the telltale twitch near his mouth as he wrestled with his own tongue. He won.

"That's Luke Bascomb, my foreman."

She appealed to him with her eyes. "I'm sorry. Forgive me. I—I don't know . . . why I said that."

"Probably because I had it coming."

Twenty

Stephanie was released at mid-afternoon on Monday. It happened abruptly. She was serving lunch when there was a commotion in the front hall, then a group of men burst into the dining room. The men at the table looked shocked. One rose, said, "Mr. Debs!" The others also stood up.

Eugene V. Debs was a slender man of medium height. To Stephanie he had an almost clerkish or professorial look. But at the moment he was terribly angry, and there was an intensity in his eyes. He would brook no opposition.

He studied her a moment. "I want that young woman released at once. I want the others let go, too."

The men at the table looked stunned, cowed—all but Gunter. "Not until our demands are met."

Debs turned a withering eye on him. "Who are you?"

"I am Gunter Hopmeister, organizer of this strike."

Again the withering look. It was held for several

moments, as though the labor leader were forced to look upon a disgusting object. "Mr. Hopmeister, you are a pipsqueak—either that or a fool!"

"Call me what you will, Mr. Debs. I give the orders here. We will not release our prisoners until our demands are met."

"Prisoners? Demands?" He eyed Gunter a moment, then looked at the others at the table, one by one. Then he addressed them. "You are workingmen—as I am. Your cause is my cause, the cause of workers all over the country. You are striking for fair pay, shorter hours, better working conditions, safety on the job, union recognition, justice, decency, a better life for yourselves and your families. You are honest, God-fearing men. You are *workers!* You are not *kidnappers!*" He stared at the men, who now stood around the table, downcast, utterly defeated.

Then Debs returned to Gunter. "You—you *guttersnipe!* You have done a gross disservice to these men, to those who died at the plant gates, to the whole labor movement of this country."

"I have not." There was a certain lack of conviction in Gunter's protest, however.

"You have made us all look like common criminals, not decent men fighting for justice." Debs pointed his finger directly at Gunter. "If you say one more word, if you are not gone from my sight by the time I count to three, I will turn you over to the police as the kidnapper and woman-abuser you are. ONE!"

By the second number Gunter Hopmeister was gone from the room and house.

Debs turned to Stephanie. "Miss Summers, if you will make yourself ready, please. I am to have you at the offices of American Western within the hour. I gave my word."

She nodded, turned and followed Rosie into the kitchen. The older woman threw her arms around her. "Thank God."

"Yes." Freed from Rosie's hug, she went to the

pantry and began to change into the blue cotton she had come in. It seemed so lavish and elegant now, and minus the sleeves much too décolleté. Rosie fastened the back, then combed her hair. "You look jus' lovely, dearie, a reg'lar lady o' fashion." She hesitated. "An' none the worse for wear?"

Stephanie turned, looked at her, feeling strangely sad. "None the worse for wear."

"I'm awful sorry—for all this, Stephanie."

"It wasn't your fault, Rosie." She managed a weak smile. "Without you it might have been much worse." They stood there a moment, looking at each other. Suddenly, impulsively, Stephanie hugged the older woman, kissing her cheek. "I love you, Rosie. I'll miss you." Rosie held her away, tears in her eyes, obviously finding it difficult to control her emotions. "I owe you a lot, Rosie."

Mrs. Cook just shook her head. "Dear chil', dear chil'."

Stephanie turned and picked up the faded pink dress from the bed. "May I have this, Rosie? I'll pay you for it."

"It ain't worth nothin', chil', 'Course you can have it. But why?"

"My great-grandmother has a trunk in her attic. She keeps special gowns in it." Stephanie smiled. "I think this belongs there."

Rosie was about to say she didn't understand when Earl appeared at the door. "I'm to fetch you now, miss."

"Stephanie, remember?" She walked around Rosie to face Earl. "Thank you for protecting me."

He looked extremely unhappy, but couldn't take his eyes from her. "I feel ter'ble it happened. I deserve all that happens to me."

"Nothing will happen to you. I'll not tell anyone about you—any of you." She smiled. "Not even Gunter."

He nodded. "God bless you, Stephanie."

She gave Earl a most dazzling smile. "So you do know my name." Looking at him, she said, "Rosie, you have a bright son. See that he gets some schooling. He can do better with his life."

"I tol' you I would." He looked at her a moment, glancing down, obviously wanting so much more. "We—we bes' go now."

Still she held him with her eyes, smiling. "Yes." Then she stepped forward, hugged him, gave him a quick kiss before she left the room.

There was a significant crowd outside American Western when Stephanie drove up. She was surprised, perplexed, a little frightened, then she saw Thomas, opening the carriage door, leaping inside, sweeping her into his arms.

"Oh, Stevie, Stevie, thank God."

He felt so good. "Yes, yes."

He kissed her quickly, then held her away, looking at her intently. "Are you all right?"

"Yes, I'm fine."

"You sure? They didn't . . . ?"

"No, I'm fine. Really I am. I wasn't mistreated."

"The bastards! They'll pay for this."

Then she was out of the carriage, standing beside Thomas. She was aware of cameras, exploding flash powder, milling reporters being restrained by police, a barrage of questions. Suddenly she saw Kincaid, smiling, puffed up, coming toward her. Oh, how she hated him!

He reached her, his arms outstretched to embrace her. With all her might Stephanie pushed him away. "Get away from me. It's all your fault." Fortunately few heard her amid the general uproar. But Kincaid did and glared, then turned on his heel and stalked away into the building.

She turned to Thomas. "Can we go home now?"

"Yes, darling, of course."

But the press was not to be denied, hurling questions with even greater velocity and volume. One reporter broke through the police restraint. "Please, Miss Summers, you must tell us—"

Thomas pushed him away. "Leave her be. Can't you see she's been through hell?"

She had raised a foot to step into the carriage. Now she stopped and turned, looking at the reporters. "It's all right, Thomas. I'll answer their questions."

"No, darling. You're tired."

"I'm all right." She turned to the reporter. A card with *Tribune* written on it was stuck in his boater. "What do you want to ask me?" This led to a deluge of questions. She raised her hand for silence. "If you ask me one at a time, I'll try to answer."

"What happened to you, Miss Summers?"

"I was touring the plant when the strike broke out."

"We know that, what happened afterward?" The voice came from the rear of the crowd.

"I—I fainted. When I came to I was . . . locked in a pantry."

"Where was that, miss?"

"In a home, here in Chicago. I really don't know where."

"What d'you mean, you don't know where?"

She looked around for a face to go with the question, but could pick out none in particular. "Just what I said. I don't know where I was. And if I knew, I wouldn't say."

"You won't say? Are you—"

"I was treated with kindness. I was not harmed. I don't wish to harm them."

"Are you protecting your kidnappers?" Before she could answer, another question was shouted. "Were you physically abused, Miss Summers?"

"No, not in any way."

"Surely, Miss Summers, some attempt was made—a beautiful woman like you."

She caught the smirking face that went with the voice and bristled. "Think what you will, sir. I'm telling you I was not . . . not dishonored."

"Then why are you protecting them?"

It was the same voice, same face, leering, excited. She glared at the man. Forcing away her annoyance, she said, her voice surprisingly firm, "The workers who held me are basically decent, law-abiding. They made a mistake in holding me, the other hostages. I see no reason for punishing a mistake. We all make mistakes—except you, perhaps."

Laughter defused the exchange and Stephanie felt she had done well.

"Did you wear that dress the whole time, Miss Summers?"

"No, it became dirty, torn. I wore another garment most of the time—a dress." She held it up. "This one." Then, on shouted commands, she held the pink dress a moment longer for photographs.

"Were you kept locked in the—" he looked down at his notes, "—pantry, wasn't it?"

"Yes, a pantry. No, I was locked up only at night. I was given considerable freedom."

"What did you do?"

"I helped serve meals, did dishes, that sort of thing."

"Were you frightened?"

"No, I had no feeling they wished to harm me. They were, in fact, very pleasant to me."

This brought a hubbub of questions. Thomas raised his hands. "That's enough for now. Miss Summers has had an ordeal."

But when he tried to turn her into the carriage, she twisted away. "I want to say something to you all." She waited, hearing reporters mumble that she had a statement. There was a shushing sound. Suddenly she had relative silence, a score of men listening, pencils poised to take notes.

"When I visited Mr. Kincaid's factory, I was appalled. It is a hellish place, badly lighted, filthy, full of steam and dangerous machinery, and so hot and evil-smelling I could hardly bear it. I don't blame those men for striking. It is no place for a person to work. And they are paid wages so low they can't support their families. There were children working there, some as young as eight. What life is that for a child?"

She saw the reporter with the smirking face. He had stopped taking notes.

"When I was being held . . . hostage, I had a chance to see how the workers and their families must live—ten and twelve people in two rooms, babies sick and dying, flies everywhere, stench and filth and rats all around, no medical help, not enough food."

There was open laughter now, wounding her. But she pressed on. "I—I don't see how we can claim to be the richest country in the world when . . . when there is so much . . . so much suffering among the people." She realized in consternation that tears were running down her cheeks. "Mr. Kincaid employs these . . . these people. They . . . die for him. They live . . . stunted lives. They are brutalized. Their families . . . their wives . . . and children . . . suffer for him." She was nearly sobbing now. Thomas tried to turn her away, but she pushed against him. "I—I don't see . . . why Kincaid . . . has to make so many . . . suffer. Why . . . can't he pay . . . a decent wage . . . make the factory . . . safe?"

There was still a few chuckles, but they died into an embarrassed silence.

Thomas put his arm around her. "Miss Summers is obviously very upset. She has had a trying time. I'm taking her home."

Stephanie let herself be turned away. She mounted the step of the carriage, then half-turned back. "I—I know I'm just . . . a girl, silly . . . and frivolous. But . . . I can only . . . tell you what I saw and . . . what I feel. I didn't know . . . before. I don't think . . . any of you do, either."

She cried all the way home. But she realized it was mostly in anger for having wept in front of the reporters, for failing to communicate what she felt.

Her own apartment came as a shock to her. She saw

the gilded settee, velvet couch, Chinese screen, walnut dining room set, elegant china closet displaying her service for twelve, silver tea set, all newly purchased, paid for by Kincaid's high salary, the labor of. . . .

"We have so much. They have almost nothing," she murmured.

Thomas embraced her. "I was sick with worry that I might lose you." He smiled. "But you're here, home. Thank God."

She saw his tailored suit of fine, light worsted, his monogrammed shirt, silk tie. Images of nakedness and rags flitted across her mind. Then she saw him, brown eyes soft, caring, full of love, and knew this was the man she loved. She smiled and he kissed her, passion welling within him. She accepted the kiss but felt nothing. When it ended, she turned from him, walking slowly through the living-dining room, running her hand over a chair back, across the waxed surface of a table.

Thomas Hodges was surely a sensitive, perceptive man. He recognized Stephanie's lack of ardor. Although disappointed, he was not puzzled. She had been through an ordeal. She needed time, tender handling, to come around. In his love he set himself on this course. "Do you want to talk about it, Stevie?"

She seemed not to have heard. "Do you realize they could live weeks, maybe a year, on what this dining room furniture cost?"

"Who, dear?"

She heard him now and turned to face him. She saw compassion, tenderness in his eyes. "The woman I stayed with." She hesitated, looking at him. Yes, she loved this man. "Mrs. Cook, Rosie. She's a kind, lovely woman. And she was good to me." Again she felt the surge of tears in her eyes. "Her husband and one son were killed at the plant, Thomas. Her husband was scalded to death from a steam line Kincaid wouldn't bother to repair."

"I'm sorry, Stevie." He knew nothing else to say.

"She has one son left, Earl, a nice young man. He works at the plant, too. But he could be much more. Rosie runs a boarding house to survive." She saw Thomas nod. He was listening. "Rosie and Earl protected me. There might have been trouble, otherwise— almost was."

"I'm glad they did." He came to her, putting his arm around her shoulder, bending to kiss her hair. At once he detected sour, fetid odors. "Do you know what you need?" He smiled. "A bath. It's just what the doctor ordered."

"I thought you wanted to know what happened."

"I do. You can tell me everything as you luxuriate in a hot tub." He led her into the bedroom, then went to the bathroom to turn on the water. When he came back to her, he said, "This Earl fellow protected you, you say?" He began unfastening her dress.

For the next hour Thomas fussed over her as though she were a child, keeping the water hot and sudsy, washing her all over repeatedly, shampooing her hair, reaching into the water to massage her feet and legs. All the while she poured out her tale of everything that had happened: Rosie and Earl, Gunter Hopmeister— omitting only his nocturnal visit, for she felt that would enrage Thomas—the tour of the tenement with its filth and disease, the sick babies covered with flies.

Thomas encouraged her, asking questions, for he understood she needed to tell all this. But, in truth, he heard little and cared not at all. His concern was only for her, helping her recover, bringing back the woman he loved. At the same time, however, he was in a sexual turmoil. Seeing her unclothed, touching her, sliding his hands over her body aroused him to the point where it took all his will to restrain his passion.

"When I saw my picture in the paper, I couldn't stand it, Tommy."

"Why was that?"

"I was practically naked."

"You were lovely."

"Not in that dress. Not anymore. Do you realize that what that dress cost would feed one of those families for a week, maybe a month?"

"Perhaps so, darling."

"Tommy, I want to send some money to Rosie, Earl. Some of my clothes, too. They need everything. Can I?"

"Of course, dear, if you want to."

He had her out of the tub now, drying her inside a towel. He was painfully aware of his physical reaction to the intimacy of what he was doing.

"Do you really mean it, Tommy?"

He smiled. "I said it, didn't I? We'll look them up. Can't be too hard to find a boarding house run by a Rosie Cook."

He was squeezing the water from her hair into a dry towel. She couldn't turn to look at him, but she knew full well his solicitousness. "I knew you'd understand, Tommy. I knew I could talk to you."

"I should hope so."

She took the towel from him and wrapped it around her head. Now she could see him, the love in his eyes. She saw the passion, too. Aware now of her nakedness, the compounding of their chemistry, she said, "It's good to be home, Tommy—with you."

"It better be." He wanted her so. Still he restrained himself. "Do you want me to powder you?"

She smiled. "If you do." She laughed. "And I suspect you do."

"You know me too well."

As the talcum was sprinkled on her shoulders, and his hands, so smooth now, began to massage it into her breasts, sliding gently over her nipples, she felt as a welcome friend the acceleration of her desire. Closing her eyes, she let the powdering and rubbing continue, waist, hips, thighs, the rounded hillocks of her derriere. She bent over, giving him a flat surface to powder her back, then welcomed his hands to her full breasts, feeling his eagerness, hearing his breath of desire. When she stood up, she opened her eyes, knowing they were full of passion now. With true joy, in the relief of a homecoming at last, she could say, "You've too many clothes on, Tommy."

Twenty-one

Stephanie read the newspapers the next day in consternation, then anger. They had it all wrong. It was horrid. She was front-page news again. Her photogravure in the revealing ball gown was used, not any of those taken at her actual release, thus suggesting she was so attired during her captivity. The story described her "tearful embrace of her fiancé." Words such as "harrowing," "ordeal" and "brutal" colored the story. The *Tribune* managed to imply, without actually saying it, that she had been raped.

The papers used not one word of her statement about conditions at the factory or how the workers lived. In truth, she was liberally quoted in the *Chicagoer Arbeiter-Zeitung*, a radical newspaper, but it was in German.

She was still fuming when Thomas came home from work. "How can they do this to me?"

"Do what, dear? It's a marvelous picture of you."

She gaped at him, disbelieving. "You think so, do

you? And I suppose you like this line." She picked up the *Tribune* and read, "Miss Summers was kept bound and gagged for three torturous days while her tormentors had their way with her."

He laughed. "You know the *Trib*, Stevie."

"I said I wasn't mistreated. Didn't they *listen?*"

He put his hands on her upper arms. "The press always sensationalizes everything. Pay it no mind, honey."

"But they didn't use a word of what I said about the factory, the homes."

He turned away, going to the buffet and the liquor bottles. "That's just as well, Stevie."

She stared at him in dismay. "What d'you mean, it's just as well?"

Apparently calm, he poured a generous whiskey, sipped. "Surely you must see it, Stevie. We are engaged in a strike, a serious strike. This sort of propaganda about unsafe working conditions, suffering workers— well, it doesn't help us a bit."

"*Propaganda?* It was the truth! I saw it with my own eyes."

"You went through hell, Stevie. You were upset. Fortunately I was able to make Mr. Kincaid understand that. He was angry at first over what you said."

"He was, was he?"

"Yes, but it's all right now. He hopes you'll feel up to attending a party at his house tonight."

She stared at him, unable to believe her ears. Then she turned away, stalking toward the kitchen. "Over my dead body," she spat.

Another time he would have ignored such a remark, attributing her upset to the aftereffects of her captivity, offering her sympathy and understanding. But this time, perhaps because of a hard day at work or perhaps because of the whiskey, he did not. In three strides he caught up with her and grabbed her wrist, halting her. "What the hell's the matter with you, Stevie?"

"Me? The question is what's wrong with *you?"* Fury made her eyes icy blue. There was acid in her voice. "Do you *want* to go to jail?"

"What're you talking about? That's stupid."

"It is, is it?" She wrestled her arm free of him and retreated around the dining room table, in front of the china closet. "Your father was here while you were gone." There was a dry coldness in her voice. "He came to warn you about Kincaid, what he's doing."

"Dad?"

"He's terribly worried about your involvement in Kincaid's railway car deal. He's afraid you'll be ruined for life, maybe even go to prison. He asked me to persuade you to quit Kincaid, while there's still time."

"What *are* you talking about?"

Her anger flared, making the pitch of her voice rise. "Your father. That's who I'm talking about. You do remember Lawrence Hodges, don't you?"

"Don't be sarcastic with me, Stevie."

"Or are you so enamored of Winslow Kincaid you've lost your memory along with your decency and integrity?" Her anger was at the flood level now. "I thought you had good sense, at least. But no. You've become just as power-mad and corrupt as he is."

"STOP IT!" He was visibly shaking now, both from his anger and his effort to control it short of an explosion. "I'll not be talked to this way." He was no longer shouting, though he still seethed with fury. "And I'll not talk to you as long as you're hysterical."

She wanted to scream at him that she wasn't hysterical. She wanted to tell him how stupid he was being, how she was ashamed of him. But, also wrestling for control, she managed to calm herself, gripping the back of a chair, breathing heavily. At last she could say, "You're right. Being angry is not helping."

He turned from her and went back to the buffet, replenishing his whiskey. When he looked at her again, he was calmer and saw she was, too. "What did dad say?"

"He said Kincaid is trying to corner the railroad cars of the whole country."

"That's true."

"He said it's illegal and he's—"

"It's not illegal, Stevie. There are no laws against it. I'm a lawyer and I know what I'm talking about."

She nodded. "Yes, you're right. I got confused. Grandfather said there are no laws yet, but some senators in Washington—one of them was named Sherman, I think—are trying to pass laws."

"We know that. It'll never happen, Stevie, believe me."

She sighed. "Grandfather had just been to Springfield. The state legislature wants to stop Kincaid."

"That'll never happen, either."

She looked at him, so outwardly calm, raising his whiskey, swallowing. "Don't be so smug, Thomas. Kincaid doesn't know everything. He's not all-powerful. He's not God." She saw the glint of anger in her fiancé's eyes. "Grandfather says Kincaid cannot be permitted to hold the American people ransom to his greed. He will be stopped, one way or another." She saw Thomas's deprecatory smile, heard the scorn in his laugh. "Patronize me if you wish, Thomas, but your father is personally investigating Kincaid. He's preparing a dossier of criminal charges."

"Really, Stevie, you have to be kidding."

"I'm not, Thomas. Grandfather suspects Kincaid is derailing trains to create an artificial shortage of freight cars. He won't get away with it."

"I don't believe it, Stevie."

"Earl Cook told me Kincaid has a goon squad wrecking trains. These are the men he's bringing in as scabs during the strike."

"A socialist, a wild-eyed anarchist said that, did he? I'm not going to believe it, Stevie."

"Is it possible for you to believe anything bad about Kincaid? Or are you so enraptured of him, so deeply involved yourself, that you're blind?"

Again the glint. "Stevie, you better stop it."

"Winslow Kincaid propositioned me, Thomas." She saw his anger give way to shock. But shock at what? The proposition or her accusation? "Tell me what you think of him now."

He wheeled, poured out more whiskey, but the glass was shaking. For the merest moment he realized he was being foolishly defensive, but his anger overrode his reason. "What I think is that you're imagining things."

"No, Thomas. While you were away, Kincaid phoned, asked me to go to a party at the Philip Armours'. I didn't want to, but he said it was mostly business and you'd want me to do my part. Then he asked me to wear my gold dress. I didn't want to do that either, but he gave me no choice. He managed to get past the doorman and came directly up here. He wanted a drink."

"So what's so terrible about that?"

"He gave me a very expensive necklace, heavy gold set with star sapphires." She made a snorting sound. "To match my eyes, he said. I refused it, but he insisted it was a bonus to you for my *many* contributions to the company's success."

"So? It probably was. What'd you do with it?"

"It's in the bedroom. You can have it. I certainly don't want it." She eyed him closely. "He would have raped me, Thomas."

"Listen, Stevie, I—"

"He said if I wanted to insure your *brilliant* future with the company, I knew what I had to do."

"He didn't say that."

"Not in so many words, but that's what he meant." She watched his distress. "Really, Thomas, I'm not making it up."

"Did he touch you?"

"Yes. He put his hands on my shoulders and tried to kiss me. I turned my cheek."

"Stephanie, you're imagining things. He likes you,

thinks of you as the daughter he never had. I've heard him say so himself. A fatherly peck on the cheek hardly constitutes rape."

"It wasn't fatherly, Thomas. And it wasn't all he was going to do. He knew there was no party that night—he'd made it up. Fortunately your father rang from downstairs at that moment and I was saved."

"You weren't saved from anything, Stevie."

"He called up last Friday. I was to go out with him that night. Fortunately I had the plant tour that afternoon. I was saved from him by wild-eyed radicals and anarchists, as you choose to call them." She looked at him. Distress was written all over his face. "You don't believe me, do you, Thomas?"

His sigh was deep, prolonged. "I believe you've had a harrowing experience. You are tired, upset, confused —understandably so. Your mind is . . . playing tricks on you. I think I should call a doctor."

"You think I'm *crazy?*" The words came out with a choking sound, like a sob.

"Of course not."

"You're the one who's crazy—crazy stupid." Tears came abruptly then, spilling out of her eyes. "No matter what . . . that man does . . . you—you *adore* it." A heavy sob came. As a wail she said, "God, Tommy—I'm so . . . *ashamed* of you."

"Stop it, Stevie, just stop it." He said it calmly, looking at her, feeling helpless. "Darling, why does it matter? Why does any of it matter? The only thing that counts is that we love each other."

She looked at him through streaming eyes, her hands at her mouth. "I don't know . . . anything . . . anymore."

"Yes, you do, Stevie. We were going to be married as soon as I returned, remember?" She was staring at him, as though he were an apparition, slowly shaking her head. "I love you, Stevie. That's all that matters."

He came to her and tried to put his arm around her,

but she lurched away from him, her eyes wide, as though in terror. "Don't touch me. Please, don't touch me." Then she ran into the bedroom, closing the door.

For the next three days there was tension between them. They did not quarrel again, but their conversation remained strangely formal and certainly minimal. They shared the same bed, but all forms of intimacy were discontinued. Her matter-of-fact "goodnight" wounded him. On Thursday evening he tried to take her in his arms, hoping to kiss her, make love to her and thus break down this barrier between them. But the expression in her eyes told him it was not yet time.

"Stevie, have you found the fatal flaw in me, in my character, you were seeking?"

"I wasn't seeking it."

"I know. I'm sorry. Shouldn't have said that. But have you anyway?"

She looked at him levelly. "I don't know. I hope not."

He nodded his head slowly. "That's something anyway."

"Thomas—" She studied him a long moment, as though searching for something in his eyes. "—I'm trying to understand you, what you're doing. I want to believe in you, trust and respect you."

"How about love?"

"I do love you. But my mother also loved my father, and—"

"I know. You needn't explain." He looked away, pulling down the corners of his mouth into a frown, then returned to meet her gaze. "Stevie, I know you don't like Kincaid. Maybe you're right about him. Maybe I'm wrong. But a man has to work. If he takes a man's money, he should be loyal to him."

She thought: How can Thomas distort a principle so to justify himself? She said: "You don't need his money, Thomas. Your own father said you are a good attorney. You can go with his firm or start your own."

"And make the kind of money I do now?"

"We don't need all this money—" she gestured toward the room, "—all these things. I'd live happily in a shack as long as there was love and honesty there."

"I am honest, Stevie."

She looked at him with as much earnestness as she possessed. "I believe you are, too, Thomas. Then leave Kincaid—at once."

He sighed. "Stevie, a man must do what he must. You have no right to ask me not to."

She nodded. "And a woman must do what *she* must."

He threw his arms around her. "God, Stevie, don't leave me! I couldn't bear to lose you."

She stood woodenly, unresponsive to him. "I'm still here. I want things to work out."

"They will, darling, they will."

They didn't. The next morning, Friday, as she was reading the *Tribune,* a news item leaped from the pages:

> On information received from Attorney Thomas Hodges, Chicago Police yesterday issued a warrant for the arrest of Rose and Earl Cook, mother and son, on charges of kidnapping Miss Stephanie Summers, fiancée to Mr. Hodges.
>
> Officers went to the Cook home, a boarding house, at 4386 Poplar Street, but discovered the suspects had fled. Their whereabouts are still unknown.

There was more to the article, mostly a recapitulation of the circumstances of her kidnapping, but Stephanie could read no more. Her eyes filled with tears. Slowly, sadly, she rose and walked into the bedroom.

An hour later she was standing before the desk of

Thomas Hodges at his office. She wore a travel suit and carried her suitcase.

"You saw it?"

"Yes."

"I asked them to keep it out of the papers, but—" He shrugged. "My luck hasn't been too good lately."

"Why did you do it? I said they were kind to me. I wanted to help them. You even said you were arranging to send them some money." She saw the distress on his face, but was unmoved. "It was all a lie. Why, Thomas? What did those two poor people ever do to you? Why did you have to drive them from their home, make them fugitives?"

"They're kidnappers, Stevie, pure and simple. They broke the law. They threatened you, locked you up in a pantry. They must be punished. If you weren't so—I don't know, so—"

"Compassionate? Forgiving?"

"Use whatever words you want, but someday you'll thank me."

She merely looked at him, nodding slowly. "Yes, I'll thank you for saving me from a marriage that would have destroyed us both." She removed the engagement ring he had given her and placed it on his desk.

"Don't leave, Stevie. I love you."

"I'm sorry for that." She picked up her suitcase and turned toward the door.

"Where will you go?"

She never replied.

Twenty-two

Andrew Morgan Summers remained unchanged. He lay unmoving, as though in sleep, despite the attention lavished upon him by Danielle. She spent hours with him, doing all that seemed required—and more, for she talked to him as though he were awake and hearing her. And she prayed, almost constantly. She refused to believe her son would not recover, no matter how unlikely it seemed with each passing day.

Despite her worry Danielle knew her vigil must not be constant. She had to get out of the sickroom, if only to be rested and mentally prepared for her return to Andrew's side. And so she toured the ranch with Walt, even went horseback riding for short periods. Coming from Aurial, she was an accomplished horsewoman. The fresh air, the splendid panorama of the mountains always exhilarated her.

It was strangely difficult for Walt Summers to have her there. Danielle's beauty wounded him. Her femininity, her perfume, even simply having a woman in the house brought him pain. He ached for this woman he had married and still loved. He wanted her there always. Yet he refused to hope, protecting himself from the pain it would bring when she left him again. His problem was to find some middle ground between enjoyment of her presence and hopelessness.

They sat rocking on the porch in the waning twilight, amid soft breezes smelling of hay, looking at a velvet sky giving birth to stars. "It's so lovely, Walt. No wonder you like it."

"Yes, isn't it."

"See the mountains, so stark now with the sun gone. Yet they still don't look forbidding, do they?"

"No. It's my favorite time here, Danny. I'm glad you can see it."

There was silence for a time, then Danielle spoke. "I may understand why you like it here, but I'm still surprised. I thought you a confirmed southerner."

He languished in silence for a time, also. Finally, "Places change, Danny. People do, too."

"What does that mean?"

"Oh, I don't know. At least I'm not sure I can express it. The South I knew and loved and fought for died. I'm not even sure now it ever existed. Certainly it's gone now, finished in a war which never should have been fought and which nobody won." He puffed on his pipe a couple of times. "I wearied of the endless search for the past, the hope for return to something lost, something I'm not sure ever was so great. I regained Seasons, built it up to something of value, then I sold it and came out here. I wanted a fresh start, a new beginning. And it's here. There's hope out here, promise. There are no yesterdays, only tomorrows."

"Yes, I sense that." She rocked in the chair a few times. "You said people change, too."

"Yes, though probably never enough. Certainly not quickly enough. But I try. I have black memories of a certain night. I cannot believe it was myself. Yet I know it was." He paused for a time, puffing through a cloud of smoke that drifted lazily off the porch on the breeze. "I keep telling myself there may be enough regrets in the world to assuage my guilt."

She felt a wrench from his confession, yet was determined to keep this as light as possible. Smiling, she said, "Is that why you have a Negro foreman and a Chinese cook? And I see an Indian and a Mexican."

"No. I hired them because they're good men. Luke Bascomb is the best cattleman I know. He taught me what I had to know to keep this place going." He smiled. "I guess the real truth is we all ended up here because we were losers. As a colored man Luke couldn't get a job. Tab Eagle was a drunken, no-account half-breed. Gomez was a Mexican and a thief to boot. Ace was a gunfighter, a murderer and ex-con. We all came here hoping for a second chance." He laughed now. "I should have named this ranch the Second Chance, I guess."

She was not oblivious to what second chance he meant, but she turned it away. "I think you've done well with your second chance, Walt. Your home is just lovely."

"Yes. Most of it was here before. It's one reason I bought this ranch. I've enlarged it some, bought some furniture, that's all."

She rose from the rocker and went to the porch steps, leaning against the pillar, looking up at the sky. "You've made a home for yourself and I never have. Isn't that surprising?"

"Oh, I don't know. Just the way things work out, I guess. I left off being surprised long ago." He looked at her, sadly watching her figure in profile against the waning sky. "Have you been happy, Danny?"

He saw her smile, her teeth picking up the little remaining light. "Like you, I left off trying to figure what happiness is a long time ago."

"I know." He rendered the smallest of chuckles. "Andy told me you were going to marry an Englishman, a duke or something."

"A mere earl. I didn't. And I don't want to say anything more than that."

"Sure." He relit his pipe, lavishing generous time on the process. "It's good to have you here, Danny. I'm glad we're able to talk after all this time."

"Yes." She turned, looked at him, but was not really able to see his face. "But there can be nothing more, Walt."

"I know."

In ensuing days she gave herself wholly to the nursing of Andrew, yet she knew she was infected by Walter Summers. He had changed—and for the better. Patience and resignation seemed to have bred a tolerance in him he had never had before. Yet he remained the most quietly authoritative and the most genuinely masculine man she had ever encountered. His love and concern for Andrew were no less than her own. He seemed to have an instinctive understanding of Stephanie, sharing Danielle's worry that she was living with Thomas Hodges without marrying him. He promised to write to her, stating his views.

"Danny, I'd like to say something. And I'd like to ask you to believe me."

They were enjoying the evening air again. It was later this time, darker. Neither one of them could really see the other in their rockers, although she had a powerful sense of his presence. "Yes?"

"One of these days Andy's going to get well and—"

"Is he?"

He heard her anguish. "Yes. We have to believe that, both of us."

"Yes, I know."

"One of these day's Andy'll recover and you'll leave. I may never see you again. I won't be able to live with myself if I don't say something—right now, while I have the chance."

She sucked in her breath, waiting.

"Because of me, my mistakes, my folly, my—my bigotry, you haven't had a very happy life. And I wanted that for you. More than anything, I wanted that. I don't know what good it's going to do to say I'm sorry, sorrier than I can ever express. Maybe it'll make me able to live . . . maybe it'll help somehow to have at least said I'm sorry."

She was moved to the point of tears. She wanted to reach out and touch him, but made no effort. "No, Walt, it's not your fault. You have nothing to regret. I lived this life. I committed my own follies." She looked toward him. In the darkness she couldn't see, but sensed he was looking at her. "I—I lost my own . . . virtue, Walt. You did not take it from me."

Silence lay between them then. Both could almost reach out and touch it.

"Danny?"

"Yes?"

He sighed. "The night before his . . . his accident, Andy asked me if there was any chance of you and I . . . getting back together."

"You told him no, I hope."

"Yes, I guess so." He sat forward then, turning toward her. "Danny, everybody gets a second chance. I have to believe that."

She was silent so long he was about to ask if she'd heard him. Finally she said, "Walt, I won't deny you attract me. You've done so much with yourself. You are a good and decent man—who deserves better."

"What are you saying?"

"There have been too many men, Walt. I loved Benjamin, truly I did. When he died—oh, God, Walt, need I say it?"

"No. I never asked."

"Again and again, Walt, so many times. I am soiled —beyond conception."

Her confession hurt him. Images of his wife in the arms of other men were whiplashes to his mind. He stood up. "Like I say, I'm going to change the name of this ranch." Then he went into the house.

She sat in the darkness for a time, rocking, mind

seemingly numb, unthinking, unfeeling. Then she slowly rose and also entered the house. He was standing not far away, at the buffet, having just poured himself a whiskey. They looked at each other, all eyes, all questions.

"Oh, Walt!"

She ran to him, into his open arms, holding him close, clutching, her head against his shoulder. It felt so good, so familiar. She raised her head. The kiss which came to her, so tender, so deep, had the quality of blessedness.

"I will, Walt, I need it so."

"No. Not it. Me, you, us."

She stared at him, eyebrows raised, eyes wide. "Oh, Walt, I don't know that."

"Then we'll wait until you do."

She looked at him. "Yes. Thank you."

She meant it. She lay alone in bed that night next to Andrew's room, feeling grateful. She had known her ex-husband's desire for her, yet he had refused. And she? In shame she admitted she would have gone to bed with him—willingly. But he wanted more than just her body. He wanted her. She was fortunate in that. Virtue was so hard, so very hard for her to find.

The next day, as they sat on either side of Andy's bed, watching for signs that never came, she said, her voice barely audible, "I would have last night, Walt—and hated myself for it."

"I know. That's why I didn't—and I wanted to. Believe that."

"Yes." She looked at him, agony in her eyes. "Oh, God, Walt, why am I so . . . so easy?"

He looked away from her, down at his hands, as though they were a great curiosity. "If you are—and I don't admit you are—then it is my fault. Way back, in the garret, I started something, didn't I?"

"Yes."

"I used a drug, the aphrodisiac."

"I didn't need it."

"Only later did you know that—either of us know it." He shook his head. "I made it hard for you to . . . to live with yourself. You've been. . . ." He could not find the word.

"Searching?"

He looked at her, his lips pressed into a hard line. Then he stood up. "I better find Luke. Got to keep this ranch running."

The following day he asked her to go riding, up into the mountains. "It's so far. It'll take hours."

"Probably." He looked down at Andy. "Tao Peng was perfectly good at looking after him before you came. It'll do you good to get away. There's something I thought you might like to see—although I'm far from sure."

She wavered, then nodded. "All right, I'll go."

It was further than she thought, and by the time they reached the pine forest with the sharply rising terrain, she was tired. They stopped to rest.

"How much further, Walt?"

"We're almost there now."

"And where is it you're taking me?"

He stared at her, genuinely surprised. "You don't know?"

"Should I?"

"Don't you remember?"

She smiled. "I enjoy games, Walt, but I like to have a clue."

One more time. "I thought you remembered, but you don't, do you?"

She sighed. "Remember what?"

"A fellow named Walt Patten."

Memories flooded her and she looked at him in shock. As Walt Patten he had rescued her from the demented giant in a cabin in the mountains. "You—you don't mean . . . ?"

"I thought you knew. The town of Cold Spring, where—"

"It never occurred to me."

"God, I thought you knew. That's why I came out here. I felt . . . part of it all." She was staring at him, surprise, disbelief on her face. "I was going to show you the cabin where we—. Maybe it's a mistake. Maybe we should go back."

"No, I want to see it." But she, too, was far from sure of that.

After twenty years the cabin was little like she remembered, rebuilt, larger, real beds, a better stove. But the location was the same, the cabin hidden under overhanging rocks, a defile sloping toward a valley below.

"We still use it as a line cabin in the winter."

Memories swept her, the pathetic Shorty, a childlike giant, keeping her naked, playing with her as a doll, her desperation to escape, sickness, Ears Dugan, the fight which took his life, Shorty wounded, her own surrender to death, waking, finding Walt, his nursing her back to health.

Walt Summers smiled. "I can't conjure up a storm, Danny."

She remembered, a violent storm, full of thunder and lightning. A tree had caught fire out in front. Frightened, she got up in the middle of the night, screamed, leaping into Walt's arms. They had made love.

She smiled. "I remember you didn't kiss me."

"I was afraid you'd remember me from London."

"I would have, too." They looked at each other, hesitant, expectant. "Is that why you brought me here?"

"God, Danny, I want you so. I've wanted you every night for thirteen years. And I have no right to hope—none at all."

"Walt, I'm so soiled."

"Aren't we both? Haven't we suffered enough, Danny?"

He cleansed her. With his hands, his lips, his body, his passion, his love, he washed away folly, shame. He tamed the beast of self-loathing within her. His lips fit her mouth so perfectly. His hands knew, unforgetting, how to cup her breasts, extend her nipples, soothe her aching thighs. And in his loving restraint, his expert movements, he fulfilled her and fulfilled her and fulfilled her as no other had. She wanted to say there was no other lover like him. Instead she sighed, "I love you, Walt."

Still joined, he looked down on her from extended arms, love, gratitude, awe in his eyes. "Welcome home, Danny."

She knew. He needn't have said it. "Yes."

Consciousness came slowly to Andrew Summers. He had been aware of his mother's voice, her presence, his parents speaking together, though he had not fully understood and had no capacity to open his eyes until the wound in his brain healed, the suffocating clot absorbed. It took time. There was no other remedy than nature's.

But it was no surprise to him when, opening his eyes finally, he saw his mother and father embracing at the foot of the bed. He watched a moment, filled with happiness.

"Tell me I'm not dreaming."

They turned, startled. Then excited, delighted smiles lit their faces.

Twenty-three

"I really am surprised about Thomas—or then, maybe I'm not."

Glenna looked at her great-granddaughter, so lovely, even though pensive, downcast, obviously depressed. Stephanie sat on the bed, her open suitcase behind her, in the room she had left so happily to go off to Chicago.

"When Thomas was here in June, I felt he was too involved with that man Kincaid. Winslow Kincaid. Such a terrible name. I knew his reputation from Franklin. A much too grasping man. I hoped Thomas would see through him."

"Apparently not, GlennaMa."

"You did the right thing in leaving him. It should bring him to his senses."

Stephanie looked up. She had intended to go directly to Aurial, but at the last moment decided to come to New York, see this old woman she loved and get her advice. "That's not why I did it, GlennaMa. I wasn't trying to bring him to his senses. I couldn't anyway. I left because—because I had to. It's over between us."

Glenna smiled. "I can see that you no longer love him."

"Of course I do. You know I do. But—oh, Glenna-Ma, isn't it better to have found out now, before we married? What's that term you used?"

"Irreconcilable differences?"

"Yes. I thought Thomas one sort of person. I know now he's quite another."

"So it seems."

"Do you blame me, GlennaMa?" There was appeal in her voice.

"Not at all, Stevie. Believe me, not at all." She would have risen from her chair and gone to Stephanie to comfort her, but her rheumatism was bad and it required too much effort. "What will you do now?"

"I'm going to Aurial. It's a good place to think about things."

"Yes, it certainly is. But I'm glad you stopped to see me."

Stephanie nodded, even managed a wan smile. She twisted around and lifted the faded pink dress from her suitcase. "This is the dress Mrs. Cook gave me to wear. It's kind of special to me. I thought I'd put it in the trunk in the attic, if you don't mind."

"Of course. It surely is part of our history."

"And may I add a couple of these others, the gold one and the pale blue Pierre Chambeau made first for me?"

"Certainly, but why? There's lots of use in them yet."

"No, I'll not wear anything like this again. They're too ostentatious, too extravagant. What I probably should do is sell them and send the money to Rosie—or give it to the poor." Silence stretched so long that Stephanie finally glanced at her great-grandmother, seeing a most somber expression on the beautiful, wrinkled face. "What's the matter, GlennaMa? Did I say something wrong?"

Glenna did rise then, though with difficulty, for she

was suddenly too agitated to sit. Leaning on her cane, she looked at Stephanie. "I understand, child, that what you saw during your captivity was extremely upsetting to you. But I do believe your reaction is a bit . . . excessive."

"But, GlennaMa, they were so poor. They had nothing—but disease and filth and flies and—"

GlennaMa stopped her with a wave of her hand. "I know full well. I was born poor and I have seen more poverty than you can imagine. I've worked with more organizations trying to help children, orphans, widows, unwed mothers than I can even remember. You needn't tell me."

"But, GlennaMa, how can you bear it? They are so—"

"I can't bear it and I don't. I do all I can. I have my whole life."

"But this house, GlennaMa. It's so large, so luxurious, so—"

"If I gave this house, these furnishings, the clothes off my back, all I would accomplish is to add one more old woman to the ranks of the impoverished."

"Perhaps, GlennaMa. You are just one person. But a man like Kincaid, he—"

"It would be the same if he surrendered his possessions."

"I don't mean that. But would it hurt him to pay a decent wage, provide better working—"

"Indeed it would not. That is exactly what must happen—and will someday." Glenna came to sit on the bed beside Stephanie, taking her young hands within her old ones. "Your great-grandfather, my Daniel Morgan, was an abolitionist all his life. He fought slavery. He ran Aurial as a free plantation, providing decent wages and housing to free men. Always it has been so at Aurial."

"I know that."

"Even today Morgan Kingston runs a great estate. He works hard, he provides employment to many men.

My last husband, Franklin Fairchild, was an extraordinarily wealthy man. His bank was one of the most powerful in the country. Yet he carried on an active policy of loaning funds to small businesses. I can't tell you how many young men he started on the road to success." She studied Stephanie a moment. "Do you understand what I'm saying?"

She shook her head. "I guess I don't."

"I'm saying, Stevie, there is nothing wrong with money per se, earning money, having money. The world would be far worse off without money. It is quite unimaginable, really. It is how the money is obtained and the use to which it is put that makes money good or evil."

"But they have so little, GlennaMa. What justice is there in—"

"There is no justice, none at all. Daniel fought injustice, Franklin, too. I hope you will fight greed and unfairness your whole life. This country will prosper only when the poorest among us have money for food, clothing, decent housing. But that does not mean all will be the same. Some will always have more money than others because of hard work or good fortune." She smiled, patting Stephanie's hand. "Do you see what I'm saying? Poverty and injustice must be combatted, but going around in sackcloth and ashes, beating your breast because utopia has not arrived, isn't going to speed it on its way one bit."

"St. Francis did it."

Glenna laughed. "Yes, but he was a saint. I don't think you or I quite qualify."

Stephanie threw her arms around her. "I'm not sure about you, GlennaMa."

"Do you understand? Avarice and injustice are the enemies, not money, and not pretty dresses for a beautiful young woman. Locking up your dresses in a trunk does not—"

"I understand, yes." Stephanie kissed GlennaMa's cheek. "And thank you. I've so much to learn."

"Don't we all." Glenna hugged her a moment longer, patting her back. Then she said, "Say, do you suppose you could endure a slow-footed old woman on your trip to Aurial? I should go while the weather's still nice."

"Oh, yes, GlennaMa, do come." And there was another hug.

Thomas Hodges was surprised at just how quickly he recognized what an utter fool he was. Oh, it did not come at once. The day Stephanie left him, he did his very best to drink himself into a stupor. He couldn't even succeed at that, the brandy bottle providing him not with oblivion, only a massive hangover the next day. His physical deshabille led to a weekend of wallowing in self-pity. Unshaven, unwashed, he wandered around the empty apartment in his nightwear, continuing to drink, berating his ex-fiancée as an unloving, sharp-tongued termagant. He was better off without her. She was stubborn, willful, bent on destroying his future. He'd show her how wrong she was. Yet even as he was berating her, he knew, deep in his sodden brain, that none of it was true and that he was the most miserable of men.

Monday morning Winslow Kincaid appeared in Thomas's office to suggest he leave at once for San Francisco to complete the arrangements for the sale of rolling stock.

"But the strike, sir. I thought I was needed here."

"No. We've lots of people to deal with those bastards. I'm bringing strikebreakers in. I'll show 'em who runs this company." He looked at Thomas. "So you might as well finish the job you started."

"Whatever you say, sir. I'll leave at once."

"Good." Kincaid smiled. "I know you'll miss that little girlfriend of yours, but these things can't be helped."

"She's not here, sir."

Kincaid seemed surprised. "She's not?"

"No. She left, sir." He couldn't tell the truth. "She—she went East—to visit her family. I—I thought it . . . might help her recuperate . . . get over the shock and all."

"Yes, of course. Good idea." He studied Thomas a moment, then turned to leave his office. But, his hand on the doorknob, he hesitated, then turned. "On second thought, Thomas, maybe you'd better hold off on that trip. We might need you here, after all. Legal difficulties can always crop up unexpectedly."

"Whatever you say, sir."

No one had ever accused Thomas of being obtuse. Kincaid's ordering him out of town, then quickly changing his mind when he learned Stephanie was away, was not lost on him. Stevie had said Kincaid tried to rape her. It began to make sense suddenly. The trip out West to "supervise" the sale of freight cars had actually been a waste of time. There really hadn't been much to do. Had Kincaid just wanted to get him out of town? The expensive necklace: No wives or girlfriends of other men had received one. Asking her to wear that sensational gown. It wasn't a seed of doubt planted in Thomas, it was a full-grown forest. If Stevie had been right in this, what else had she been correct about?

In ensuing days he went to the locomotive plant, wondering why he had never once gone there before. The place was shut down because of the strike, but even in silence, the steam turned off, he could sense what Stevie must have seen. He stood in the dark cavern of a building, among the litter, the rats, the machinery, and felt what it must be like to live one's life here. A child of privilege, a lawyer, he had the capacity to visualize himself working here, mentally shriveled, stunted for life. And he saw the workers outside on the picket line, all haunted eyes, bitterness and rage.

The ostensible purpose of his visit was to consult with Rawlings, now back on the job, about strike strategy. Rawlings was full of vindictiveness. "The bastards will pay. I'll break every one of them."

"Will the men we bring in be able to run the plant?"

"Hell, no, but who wants them to? This strike is the best thing that ever happened to Kincaid." He smiled. "Can't make locomotives if there is a strike."

Thomas nodded. It was true. This strike was exactly what Kincaid wanted. He had provoked it. Yet Thomas was appalled.

"When this strike ends, I want the men to be broken. We'll cut the wages, work 'em till they drop. This union talk will end. They'll find out who's boss."

Thomas was shocked at the man's callousness. But he said, "I'm sure they will, Mr. Rawlings."

Perhaps the clincher for Thomas was the arrest of Rose Cook and her son Earl. He went to the jail, ostensibly to "identify" them, which of course he couldn't. Actually he wanted to meet them.

Rose Cook was a lumpy woman in a faded dress and shawl, obviously confused and frightened to be behind bars. There were gaps in her teeth as she smiled at him. "So youse Mr. Hodges." She extended an unclean hand. "An' how is that li'l lady o' yours? She's the sweetest thing."

This was hardly what he expected, yet he managed a smile. "She's fine."

"Jus' the purtiest thing she is. Ya sure is lucky t'have her for a bride, mister."

He could only stare at her, disbelieving. "Yes, thank you."

"I know she won't come down here, but ya tell her for me jus' how glad I is everythin' worked out good for her."

"Yes, thank you. I'll tell her."

He went next to see Earl Cook in his cell. Thomas was visibly surprised at how young he was, not much older than Stevie herself.

"Whatever they do t'me, Mr. Hodges, I got it comin'. She shouldn't ha' been ki'napped. It weren't right."

"You didn't take her, did you?"

"No, but I should ha' let her go, I guess."

Thomas nodded, turned to go.

"Mr. Hodges, she's a nice lady. Tell her. . . ." He seemed distraught, unable to think of what to say. "Tell her I'm sorry for wha' happened. Tell her I—I . . . wish her luck."

"Yes, I will."

He went directly to the office of the prosecuting attorney, meeting with a Melvin Gosling. "Release them."

"Good heavens, why? They're kidnappers."

"No they're not. And even if they are, you have no case. The only one who can identify them is Stephanie Summers, and she won't."

"She'll have to. We'll subpoena her."

"Save your time, Gosling. If you make her testify, she'll make a monkey out of you and your case. Believe me, let them go."

The assistant prosecutor sighed. "Okay, I know you're right."

That night in the lonely apartment Thomas sat down to write a letter. He had in his hand a bank draft. When he had filled in the numbers, he intended to make it for five hundred dollars. At the last moment he had changed it to a thousand. Now he wrote:

Dear Mrs. Cook:

Stephanie and I would like for you to have this. It is not charity. We intend that it be put to good use.

Stephanie has told me of your son Earl's desire for an education. My impression upon meeting him this afternoon is that he is a young person who can, with effort and will, rise above the sort of work he has been doing. Therefore, it is the wish of Stephanie and me that this money be used to procure for Earl the best education possible. I ask only that you not refuse this.

Stephanie has gone to visit her family in the

East. But I know of her great appreciation for the
many kindnesses you extended her. This emolu-
ment is something we both want to do. Please
accept.

> *Yours very truly,*
> *Thomas Hodges*

He read and reread the letter. He was dissatisfied
with the excessively formal tone of the note, its lack of
real warmth. Yet, he sensed he could do no better.

One more time he read it, then thrust it into an
envelope and sealed it. Aloud, anguished, he said,
"Oh, Stevie, does this make it all right now? Will you
come back to me?"

He knew it wasn't enough, not nearly so. The
following day he went to his office at American Western
and extracted certain papers and documents from the
files. Next he sat down and wrote in longhand a letter of
resignation. It was terse, giving no reasons for his
leaving other than "personal." He handed it to his
secretary to type and, bearing a bulging briefcase, he
walked away from Winslow Kincaid forever.

Two days later he entered his father's office in
Washington. He opened his briefcase and laid papers
on the desk of Lawrence Hodges.

"This is all you will need, dad. Here are copies of the
contract with Southern Pacific, Union Pacific and other
western railroads for the acquisition of all rolling stock.
There are minutes of meetings at which Kincaid laid
out his plans for cornering the railroad cars of the
United States. Also, these minutes of the board of the
Railroad Car Trust show their collusion. I have also
given you secret interoffice memoranda showing Kincaid's deliberate provocation of the strike to create an
artificial shortage of rolling stock." He selected a
particular document. "This is one I hadn't seen until
two days ago myself. It shows Kincaid hired goon
squads to derail trains."

Lawrence Hodges looked at none of it, only at his son. "Why are you doing this?"

"Because I have been a fool. I will take the stand whenever you wish, testifying under oath about all I know, including my own involvement. Will this be helpful?"

Father eyed son, full of pride. "Yes, very. We'll stop Kincaid now. If what you say is in these papers, he's finished."

"Good."

"Senator Sherman is starting hearings on his anti-trust legislation next week. This information will be extremely useful."

"I'll testify before Senator Sherman if you want me to."

"Perhaps. I'll let you know." Lawrence Hodges looked at his son. He was happier than he had been in a long time, knowing Thomas had come home, at last. Yet he was not unaware of his son's unhappiness. "I'm proud of you, Thomas."

"I'm not." He looked down, pursing his lips in the characteristic expression. "I can't lose her, dad."

Even though his son wasn't looking at him, Larry Hodges could not repress a smile. "I know. She's at Aurial."

Twenty-four

Danielle Kingston Summers had always had a flare for the theatrical, and upon her homecoming she indulged herself with it. She had wired her mother that Andrew had recovered and *they* were coming home. Thus, when she and Andrew walked into the great house at Aurial, the foyer was filled with family, shouts of joy and innumerable hugs and kisses.

Danielle was particularly overjoyed to have Glenna there, hugging her, whispering against her ear, "I've a surprise."

"What?"

"In a minute."

When she saw Stephanie, so lovely but so obviously unhappy, Danielle's eyes filled with tears. Then, arms outstretched, she beckoned her daughter to her. "Oh, my darling."

"Oh, mother, I'm so glad you're here."

"Yes, and I'll not leave you again."

Danielle's timing was flawless. She let the fuss over Andrew go on for an extended interval, letting him bask in the hugs, the expressions of how good he looked, how he'd grown and such a tan. Once she saw Glenna about to speak, even saw her forming the word "surprise" with her lips. She silenced her with a shake of her head. This was Andrew's time. She didn't want him denied an iota of the attention coming to him.

Finally, just as about all the fuss that could be made had been made and Morgan Kingston was clearly thinking of going back to work, Danielle said, "I have something to show you all. If you'll just wait a moment, I'll be right back." Abruptly she went outside to the carriage.

When she reentered, clutching the arm of Walter Summers, it was to a throng all openmouthed and wide-eyed.

All but Andrew Morgan Summers. "They're gonna be married again."

Ordinarily Stephanie Summers would never have known a comparable joy. To see her mother's happiness, to hug and kiss her father, to know these two unhappy people had at last found themselves and their love would have been the acme of pleasure for her. And it was—in a way. She laughed and squealed with joy, tears streaming down her cheeks, hugging and kissing them both and talking and talking and talking for hours, never quite able to tear herself away from the parents she had never really had. She had to know every detail of their reconciliation and their plans for the future. After marriage at Aurial, a long visit, perhaps a short honeymoon, they were going to live in Colorado. Such a marvelous ranch it was. Andrew left no doubt of that.

"But you'll visit us often, Stevie, won't you?" Danielle said.

"And stay as long as you like," her father said.

"Yes, yes. You won't be able to keep me away."

But her joy was not unrestrained. The dead place where her love for Thomas Hodges had been simply would not heal. It was a black, festering wound, which no amount of happiness about other events would touch.

Danielle saw it. Mother and daughter, father, too, had a long chat about what had transpired in Chicago. Both were sympathetic. Both insisted she had done the right thing. Time would heal the wound. They loved her and would see her through this difficult time. Stephanie was immeasurably grateful for them, for their being together to help her.

Part of what Danielle and Walter had said had by now become a refrain. Everyone was surprised, disappointed in Thomas. The best expression of this came from Stephanie's Aunt Miriam, Thomas's sister. "I just can't believe it. Thomas was never that way."

"I didn't think so either, Aunt Miriam."

Greatly puzzled, Miriam Kingston shook her head, making her blonde curls bounce. "Now, if it had been me . . . I was the one who was grasping, ambitious, determined to rebuild the family fortune, the Prentiss family, that is." She had long since learned to accept the embarrassment of her youthful follies: her girlish hatred for Moira, the stepmother she now loved; her petulant efforts to be like her dead mother, the empty, calculating Priscilla Prentiss, first wife of Lawrence Hodges; her throwing herself into the arms of that wretch Peter Blakeley. Even now she shuddered at the thought of him, how narrow her escape had been, how fortunate she was to earn the love of Morgan Kingston. "But Thomas was always the straight shooter, so honest, so caring and loving." Again she shook her curls. "I just can't believe it. Why, he adored you even as a child, Stevie."

"Please, Aunt Miriam, I don't want to talk about it."

Miriam put her arm around her, kissed her cheek lightly. "All right, darling, I'll say no more. But you better believe that when I see that rascal of a brother, he's going to get a piece of my mind."

Miriam was not long in getting the opportunity, for within the week Thomas appeared at Aurial at the side of their father. Thomas was understandably reluctant to go, but Larry Hodges had said, "They're your family, Tom. You can't hide from them forever. Might as well face up to it now and get it over with." Larry felt, all things considered, he managed to hide his amusement over his son's predicament with at least moderate success.

"Don't say it, Miriam."

"I will if I want to. How did I get such a fool for a brother? Here you have the sweetest, loveliest girl in the world madly in love with you, and you throw it all away."

"I know, I know."

"You lie to her. You practically throw her into the arms of some . . . some thieving brigand of commerce, you discard every principle you were ever taught or believed in, all for a few tainted dollars and a chance to be a big shot. I'm sorry, Thomas, but you don't deserve her. You earned everything that's coming to you."

"Enough, Miriam!" There was a certain amount of sternness in Larry's voice. "He's making amends. There's no point in beating a dead horse."

Thomas sighed. "It's all right, dad. I've said a whole lot worse to myself than sis has."

With the exception of Miriam, everyone else greeted him warmly. His stepmother Moira, whom he had always adored, simply hugged him. "Larry told me what you've done. I'm proud of you, son. It takes a real man to admit he's wrong and try to make amends."

"Thank you, mother." He looked at her, pursing his lips. "Is it too late?"

She hugged him. "I hope not. Lord, I hope not."

Morgan Kingston, his stepbrother, with whom he had always been so close, greeted him like nothing had ever happened. Thomas knew no matter what, he would not lose Morgan's friendship. Danielle and Walter couldn't have been nicer, either. He shared with them his happiness at their reconciliation, promising to visit them in Colorado, too.

"I'll speak to her, Thomas."

He looked at Danielle. "No. That I must do myself."

"She's in the gazebo."

She wore only a simple white blouse and a plain dark skirt, yet the sight of her was nearly unbearable to Thomas: her hair, reddish-gold in the afternoon light, her eyes, the mouth he had kissed, the slender body he had held. He couldn't lose her. No matter what, he couldn't. He had thought a hundred times what to say, but he couldn't remember any of it now.

"May I sit down?"

She looked at him sharply, a hint of annoyance in her eyes. "Don't be absurd, Thomas. We are still family."

She had not really come out here to avoid him. Yet she had seen him arrive with grandfather and left abruptly. She had come to the gazebo, knowing this confrontation was inevitable, trying desperately at the last moment to sort out her conflicting thoughts. She was not very successful.

"I love you, Stevie." His reply was her unblinking stare, as though she were surprised at his statement. "I hoped that might count for something."

A moment longer she looked at him, then down at her hands. "Oh, Thomas, if only it were so simple. If only three little words could wipe away all that has happened."

He was silent for a time. Then he said, "That isn't all that's occurred." He told her, quite matter-of-factly, not at all boastfully, of the documents he'd presented to his father, their likely usefulness, his own offer to testify in court against Kincaid. "I resigned. I'm no longer at American Western."

Without looking at him she said, "I'm glad for that."

He sighed. "Would you like to know what changed my mind?" He saw her nod, although she avoided looking at him. "I got royally drunk after you left—or tried to. It didn't help. You were still all I could think about—you and me, all we had together."

"Please, Thomas. There's no point in—"

"I know. What I really meant to say was that on Monday morning, Kincaid wanted me to finish my trip out West. I said I would. Then he said something about my missing you. I said you had gone . . . to visit your family. Abruptly he changed his mind. I wasn't to go on the trip." He saw her raise her head to look at him, a glint of triumph in her eyes. "I knew at once you had been right. He *had* tried to . . . to take advantage of—"

"The word is rape."

"All right, rape. You were right, and I was wrong to defend him." He gave the smallest of self-deprecatory smiles. "There was nothing else to do but wonder what other things you were right about."

"And?"

"I went to the factory. It was closed because of the strike. Except for pickets, none of the men were there. None of the machines were running. It was nothing like when you visited. Nevertheless, I could see, sense what it must be like to work there. I realized how I would feel if that's all there were in life for me." Again she looked away. "And you were right about that, too, Stevie."

"Is that all?"

"No. Your friend Rosie Cook and her son were arrested. I went to the jail to see them." He saw her raise her head, obviously greatly interested. He sighed. If confession were good for the soul, then why didn't he feel better? "You were right about them, too. She's a fine woman, obviously very fond of you. She asked about you. I'm to give you her best." Another deep sigh. "The boy seems like a good lad. He's very contrite about the kidnapping. Clearly he deserves more in life than working in that factory."

"But you persisted in your charges?"

"No. I went to the prosecutor and told him to drop them." He smiled, couldn't help himself. "They had no case. You wouldn't have testified against them."

"No case. That's all that mattered to you?"

"Aw, c'mon, Stevie, give me a chance. I said you were right. I said they were fine people. I went to the prosecutor to rectify my mistake."

"Yes, you did say that. I'm sorry." Again she studied her thumbs. "I thank you for all you did, Thomas. I'm grateful."

"Thanks, gratitude? Is that all there is, Stevie?"

"I don't know."

Silence stretched between them for an extended interval. He kept studying her face, but she wouldn't look at him. "Stevie, I love you. I can't bear the thought that I may have lost you. Have I?"

Her words, when they finally came, were barely audible. "I think so."

"Why?" When she didn't answer, he said, "Can I ask that? Why?"

She sighed, deeply. "I don't know. Trust, maybe. Yes, trust. Do you remember that first night? I said I didn't know what you were going to do. You said nothing I wouldn't want you to. And I said I trusted you. Do you remember that?"

"How can I ever forget?"

She looked at him now, quite levelly, earnestly. "It wasn't just that night, you and me, in bed, what we did. I trusted you in *everything*. I—I've known you all my life. I thought I really *knew* you. I gave myself to you *completely,* mind as well as body." Again she searched her hands. "I feel betrayed, Thomas. I don't know how to get the trust back. It can never be again—what was."

Her words scalded him. For the first time he had a sense of hopelessness with her. He hadn't realized he'd hurt her so deeply. Agitated, sick with apprehension, he rose and stood in the doorway of the gazebo, looking out, seeing nothing.

Finally he said, "Do you remember when you were talking to the reporters after your release? You said the Cooks were good people, which was true, that they made a mistake in kidnapping you. Everybody makes mistakes, you said. Do you remember how everyone laughed when you said to a reporter, 'except you'?"

"I don't know, I guess so."

"I made a mistake, Stevie."

She looked up at his back for a time. "Turn around, Thomas Hodges." When he had, she said, "Yes, you made a mistake. And if it's my forgiveness you want, you have it. You made amends. And I thank you for that." She could feel her eyes beginning to fill with hated tears. "But I don't know how any of that . . . is going to—to put us back together again."

The sobs were coming now and she couldn't bear it. Abruptly she got up and ran across the lawn to the house. Thomas Hodges watched in the greatest sorrow he had ever known.

Also watching from the same upstairs window as years before was Moira Hodges, joined this time by her daughter, Danielle Summers.

The older woman spoke. "Oh-h, I hoped it wouldn't be that way."

And Danielle said, "Yes, I hoped she was smarter than I."

Twenty-five

It should have been a happy time at Aurial, what with the whole clan gathered and preparations for the remarriage of Danielle and Walter so far advanced. And it was, for all but Stephanie.

She was just plain mystified. She considered herself the injured party, betrayed by the man she had always loved and given herself to. Yet, although she was hardly an outcast, it was Thomas who received all the attention. Moira and Larry acted like the proud parents of a splendid son. Danielle and Walter doted on him, and Morgan acted for all the world like he was his dearest friend, which he was. Even Miriam, who once had scolded him, said no more and offered sisterly affection.

Stephanie was part of the family and made to feel so, yet she hardly felt mountains of sympathy were being heaped on her. She finally said so to her mother.

"Then forgive him."

"I have. I told him so. I thanked him for making amends."

Danielle looked at her coolly. "How very tolerant of you, Stevie."

As her mother walked away, Stephanie could only stare after her, shaking her head in disbelief. She simply didn't understand why she was suddenly on the defensive. After all, it was Thomas who had. . . . Mentally she catalogued his sins. Yes, he had done all that.

There had to be some explanation and she began to seek it. "Am I wrong, daddy?"

Walter Summers put his arm around her and smiled. "Yes, very."

"But how? I don't understand."

"I think you do, honey."

"But I don't."

"Then you shouldn't marry Thomas or anyone until you do."

"Oh, please, daddy, tell me."

He smiled and tightened his grip around her shoulder. "I'm tempted, darlin', believe me I am. But it's better if you figure it out for yourself. And you will, when the time is right."

She could only shake her head. She sought out the woman with whom all this had begun, repeating the same question, "Am I wrong, GlennaMa?"

The answer was the same. "Yes."

"But why?"

"Because you love Thomas and can't forgive him."

"But I have forgiven him, GlennaMa. I just can't—"

"Forget?"

"It's not even that. I just can't feel the same way about him. It's not the way it was before."

Glenna Morgan smiled at her great-granddaughter. "Do you remember when we had our little talk in New York the last time? You had just had your first encounter with poverty, the seamy side of life. Do you remember what I said?"

"No, I guess not."

"I said your reaction was a bit excessive. It still is, Stevie."

Moira Hodges, Stephanie's grandmother, reacted as all the others had.

"Stevie, you are making a terrible mistake." She sighed. "This is all difficult for me to say. I'm hardly proud of it. But I must. I did not marry the first man I gave myself to." Again she sighed. "Or even the second, for that matter. I have regretted it my whole life. Your great-grandmother chose right and found happiness with my father, Daniel Morgan. Your mother did, although she later made a terrible mistake. Happily she is correcting it now by remarrying your father—thank the Lord."

Stephanie looked at her a long moment. "I get the impression there is a conspiracy not to tell little Stevie something she ought to know."

Moira smiled. "It will be better if you come to it by yourself."

Stephanie's defensiveness was not helped by the presence of Thomas Hodges at Aurial. Many times she wished he weren't there, for he was unsettling to her. He never spoke of what had been between them. There was no suggestion of intimacy by word or gesture. Indeed, he didn't even look at her more than necessary. For all the world he acted not like a spurned lover, but like a friend and relative—an older, wiser man. He seemed to have matured and made peace with himself. In contrast, Stephanie felt like a child—a petulant child.

Her defensiveness was immeasurably increased when she received a letter forwarded from the Chicago apartment. Rosie Cook's scrawl was terrible and her spelling atrocious, but she wanted to thank Miss Summers and Mr. Hodges for getting herself and Earl out of jail. The thousand dollars was being used. Earl had quit the factory and was going to school. "Youse a sweethart." She couldn't spell "Stephanie" and ended up crossing it out. "And your man is nice, a real genn'l-man. I know ya'll always be happy."

Stephanie read the letter in dismay. Rereading didn't help her discomfort. He had sent money for Earl to go to school. Oh, why had he done that?

She showed the letter to Thomas. "Why didn't you tell me you sent money?"

He smiled. "I guess I forgot."

"No, you didn't forget." She felt her eyes beginning to smart. It seemed like all she did anymore was cry, or want to. And she hated it. She managed to blurt, "Thank you," just before she ran off.

There was to be a prenuptial ball for Danielle and Walter, one of the grand affairs Aurial was famous for. Friends and neighbors, many of the great and important in Washington and Baltimore, were invited. The great house rang with preparations, not the least of which were the gowns of the Morgan-Kingston women. They had a reputation to uphold, after all.

There was nothing for Stephanie to do but partici-pate, no matter how little she felt like a gala affair. As she dressed for the ball, she felt hopelessly depressed. Somehow the onus was on her. *She* was making a terrible mistake. *She* was to figure out something and was being made to feel like a dummy because she couldn't. All she knew was she had loved Thomas all her life, dreamed about him for years, given herself to him, *trusted* him, and he had betrayed her and that trust, lying, cheating. Why, Earl Cook had done more to rescue her than the man she had thought she loved. Yet, somehow, it was all her fault. Her mind was prey to such thoughts as, woodenly, she went to her closet, selected a gown and donned it. If Thomas was staying at Aurial, she would leave, go somewhere. She had no home here anymore.

When she returned to her mirror, she gasped. Un-willingly, unwittingly, she had put on the reddish-gold Chambeau gown. Why had she done that? It was a symbol of all her unhappiness—Kincaid, her kidnapping, the loss of Thomas, her likeness splashed over front pages in this gown. In something akin to horror she reached behind her back to unfasten it.

At that moment her mother entered the bedroom. Danielle had on the blue gown she had worn to meet Prince Edward and Princess Alexandra. At once she gasped, "Oh, Stevie, how you look!"

Wide-eyed, stupefied, daughter stared at mother. It was Thomas's expression.

"Oh, Stevie, such a *gown*."

"I know. I'm taking it off." Again she reached behind herself.

"You'll do no such thing. Why, you're *lovely*. I can't believe it's really you."

"It's me, all right, mother, too much of me."

"Don't be silly." Danielle went to her, removed her hands from behind the dress, then refastened it. She stepped in front of her, adjusted the straps, the bodice, smoothing and patting at the fabric, her eyes bright with delight. "Do you realize I've never seen you dressed up like this? It's such a thrill—" she smiled, "—I could almost cry."

"Oh, *mother*."

"Such a figure you have, Stevie. You're *glorious*. I'm so proud of you."

Stephanie stared at her. "Proud?"

"Oh, yes, a whole family of beautiful women, and you are the most beautiful of all. You live up to your heritage."

The praise pleased her, but she demurred to modesty. "I do?"

She smiled. "That's a Chambeau gown, isn't it?" Now she laughed. "You must have passed his inspection."

"Yes." Memories of the couturier flashed through her mind. "He raved over me, mother. He said I was. . . ."

"Better than me? Oh, my, yes." She looked at her daughter's nearly uncovered breasts, her tiny waist. "You are simply stunning, Stevie."

"He said he loves you, mother."

Danielle looked at her, giving a wan smile. "Yes, I suppose he does. We were close at one time. I was his first customer. But you must know there was nothing . . . physical between us."

"He said you could have been the greatest woman in the world, but . . . but you are a *hausfrau.*"

Danielle laughed. "Oh, yes, he'd say that. He wanted me to be a courtesan." To herself she added, *I almost was.*

Daughter was not unaware of her mother's reaction. Impulsively she hugged her. "Oh, mother, I wouldn't hurt you for the world."

"I know. And you haven't. Thanks to your father I have learned to forgive myself."

"Oh, mother." Stephanie hugged Danielle tighter. Against her ear she whispered, "I'm like you. When I'm with Thomas, it goes on and on, so wondrously. I can't seem to stop until . . . until—"

"Until he does. I know."

In this most intimate of conversations, the two hadn't looked at each other. Now they did. Stephanie spoke. "Is that my mistake, the one everyone keeps talking about? I won't find a lover as good as Thomas?"

"You may, and he may be as kind and loving as Thomas is, but I guarantee he'll not have read you 'Goldilocks and the Three Bears.' "

"I'm serious, mother."

"I'm sorry. I know you are. No, that is not your mistake. Heavens, one doesn't marry a man because of—of what . . . transpires in bed—because he is a good lover."

"Then what am I doing wrong?"

Danielle smiled indulgently. "Sit down. Let me brush your hair. I won't get to much longer."

Stephanie obliged, but felt far from satisfied with the conversation. "Why is everyone treating me like I'm some kind of—oh, I don't know, dummy?"

"No one thinks you're that. We just want you to—"

"I know. Daddy said it. Figure it out for myself."

"Yes."

Stephanie felt maddened with frustration. "Help me, mother, please. There's no one else."

"All right." Danielle looked at her reflection in the mirror. "Do you remember why you went to Chicago, to live with Thomas instead of marrying him?"

"Yes, I didn't want to—oh, mother, I don't want to—"

"Say it, darling. It's all right."

"I didn't want to make the same mistake you did. I didn't want to happen to Thomas and me what happened to you and daddy."

"Yes. And what happened to your father and me?"

"You found out he was—oh, mother, I can't say it."

"Then don't. It's not the right answer anyway."

"I don't understand."

"You said you didn't want to make my mistake. What was my mistake, Stevie?"

Stephanie's sigh was of pure frustration. "You slept with too many men? I'm sorry, but—"

"It's all right to say. It's the truth. And certainly it was a mistake, but not *the* mistake."

Suddenly, openmouthed, Stephanie was staring at her mother's image in the mirror, seized by instinctive understanding.

Danielle watched her face and felt both relief and delight. "You do understand, don't you, darling? The man I loved came to me, asking forgiveness, asking to start over, patch up our differences. I refused him. That was my mistake." She watched her daughter continue to stare at her, as though seeing a ghost, and knew she needed time to think. She placed the hairbrush on the vanity. "I'll go down now. I think we're all supposed to make an entrance. You come along when you feel like it."

Stephanie watched her mother turn, head for the door. When her hand was on the knob, Stephanie said, "Mother, that wasn't the mistake. I know what it is now, and I know what to do about it."

Stephanie's entrance was surely grand. As she descended the stairs, she felt all eyes upon her and had a sense of pride and heritage. And she knew it was right to wear this gown. It was part of Thomas and her, not a symbol of unhappiness but of something she had learned, something that would make their love stronger. Those at the bottom of the stairs seemed to stare at her a moment. She heard, "Oh, Stevie," "How lovely," then applause broke out. She grinned, then surrendered to greetings and hugs and admiration. Glenna had seen her elegantly attired, but most of the others hadn't. Morgan and Miriam were pure fondness. Andrew Summers was positively awestruck by his big sister.

Young Louise Kingston, her cousin, hugged her. "Oh, Stevie, I want so to be like you."

And Stephanie smiled. "You will be darling. I've an idea you'll be next to exceed us all."

Moira, eyes bright, hugged her, too, whispering, "Danny told me you know. I'm so happy."

"Yes, I am, too."

Larry Hodges said, "You're as lovely as you were in Chicago."

"That's right, I was wearing this gown then. I'd thought no one had seen it."

"Thomas did, too."

"Yes." She felt an impatient heartbeat. "Where is he?"

"Around here someplace."

It took some time to find him. She was just about to panic that he might have left when she saw him in the garden. "Don't hide, Thomas."

"I'm not. I saw you come down the stairs." He hesitated. "For some reason I found it difficult to look at you in that gown." He smiled. "And out here in the moonlight, it doesn't get any easier."

She smiled, loving his strange compliment. "Can I talk to you a minute?"

"You know you can."

"Do you remember long ago when you almost kissed me? We were riding and—"

"I remember everything about us."

"But you didn't. You wanted to wait till I grew up."

"Yes."

"And do you remember in New York when I said I was glad you waited until I was ready?"

"Yes."

"Well, I was wrong. I wasn't ready. It took till now."

He was finding all this difficult—the gown, the moonlight, wanting her so. "I don't understand."

"I went to Chicago to live with you, determined not to repeat my mother's mistake. I wanted to see if there was some flaw in your character."

"And there was. I'm sorry for that."

"No, Tommy. What I really found was the flaw in my own. I know that now."

"Don't be silly, Stevie. I was the one who—"

"Just listen to me, Tommy. I was a young, silly girl, in love with love. And I didn't love *you*, the real Thomas Hodges. I loved a dream, an idealized you, a perfect person. And when you turned out to be—"

"I'm sorry for that. I only wanted to be perfect for you."

"No. You weren't, you aren't, you can never be. And I'm not, either. That's what I've learned."

"What are you saying, Stevie?"

"I'm saying I've finally grown up. I see my own mistake now, Thomas. I told you that first night I trusted you, but I didn't really. I trusted Prince Charming, my own fantasy of perfection. And when you didn't measure up to that fantasy, I blamed you. It took me too long to question *my* fantasy, *my* idealizations and expectations, but thank God I finally did. And I don't want a fairy-tale hero anymore, Thomas. I want you. I love you just as you are—and however you may be the rest of our lives." She moved closer to him, turning up her lips. "Now, will you kiss this grown-up woman—you less-than-perfect man, you?"

"Oh, God, yes, Stevie." And he did—for a long, lustrous time. Then, as they walked back toward the house, arms around each other, Thomas Hodges said, "Do you suppose they could marry mother and daughter at the same time?"

An ecstatic Stephanie Summers answered, "I don't see why not. It's happened before. There's a heritage for everything in this family."

About the Author

Elizabeth Bright, creator of this romantic saga that began with *Reap the Wild Harvest* and continued in *Passion's Heirs* and *Desire's Legacy,* has, in her own words, "been earning a living at a typewriter for . . . years." She is also the author of *A Lasting Splendor,* as well as numerous other works of both fiction and nonfiction.

A former newspaper and magazine writer, Liz has an avid interest in the history of social reform in America —particularly abolitionism, women's suffrage, and trust-busting—as is evident in nearly all her novels.

Curiously shy about her popularity as a romance novelist, Liz keeps a low profile in a small Ohio town.